YOUNG KNIGHTS

MERLIN

Books by Julia Golding

The Young Knights Trilogy
Young Knights of the Round Table
Pendragon
Merlin

*

The Companions Quartet
Secret of the Sirens
The Gorgon's Gaze
Mines of the Minotaur
The Chimera's Curse

*

The Ship Between the Worlds
Dragonfly
The Glass Swallow
Wolf Cry

YOUNG KNIGHTS

MERLIN

Julia Golding

OXFORD
UNIVERSITY PRESS

OXFORD
UNIVERSITY PRESS

Great Clarendon Street, Oxford OX2 6DP

Oxford University Press is a department of the University of Oxford.
It furthers the University's objective of excellence in research, scholarship,
and education by publishing worldwide. Oxford is a registered trade mark of
Oxford University Press in the UK and in certain other countries

Copyright © Julia Golding 2014

The moral rights of the author have been asserted

Database right Oxford University Press (maker)

First published 2014

British Library Cataloguing in Publication Data

Data available

ISBN: 978-0-19-273224-8

1 3 5 7 9 10 8 6 4 2
Printed in Great Britain

Paper used in the production of this book is a natural,
recyclable product made from wood grown in sustainable forests.
The manufacturing process conforms to the environmental
regulations of the country of origin.

For Heidi and James Golding

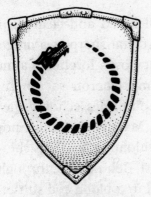

Prologue

Stonehenge, Salisbury Plain, England

IN the shadow of Stonehenge, Roxy and Rick crouched over Merlin's scrying glass. Remembering her few successful attempts to work the spell, Roxy breathed on the surface. A lock of copper hair flopped forward to brush the mirror. Rick reached out and tucked it behind her ear.

'Can you see them?' asked Rick.

'Wait: it's not that simple.' Roxy shut her eyes, hiding their familiar green sparkle, freckled nose wrinkled in concentration. She held the mood she wanted to match with their enemies. Vigilance. Intense dislike. She had to bring her own internal magic to sync with the enchanted mirror.

The glass flickered and cleared, pearly surface becoming as crystal-sharp as a dragon's tear. Rick and Roxy bent closer, foreheads almost touching.

'Report.' King Oberon sat on his ice throne, carved white pinnacles echoing the points of his silver crown. Massive in build, powerful like a mountain dominating foothills, he ruled Avalon with an iron fist. Behind him, through the window, the sky blazed in a blood-red sunset; dark bars of clouds gathered.

'Your majesty, the rebels have fled.' Morgan La Faye knelt at his feet, long black hair curtaining her pale, battle-stained face. A sword-cut on her arm dripped on the stone floor. A wolfish hobgoblin pup lapped up the blood.

'How could you let this happen?' Oberon's voice crackled with fury; his blue eyes burned with cold fire.

'Sire, I have failed you.' Morgan swallowed, bowing her head even lower as she waited for him to strike.

Lightning flashed, throwing the master and his most loyal servant into stark relief. Thunder boomed. Rain fell with the suddenness of a monsoon shower, droplets driven inside the audience chamber by the stiff breeze. An armoured troll guard hurried to wrestle the window closed.

Oberon dropped his head on his hand, weary, almost sympathetic for a brief second. 'Get up, commander. I am not going to execute you—not today.'

The window blew open and banged against the wall. A pane shattered.

'See, Morgan, my hold over the weather in Avalon is already weakening. The supply of magical energy from Earth is failing—our enchantments are breaking. I have no time to punish those that remain loyal, no matter how much they deserve it.'

His brief weakness passing, Oberon leapt to his feet and strode to the maps strewn on his council table. He cracked his knuckles.

'The changelings have recruited Arthur, you say?'

Morgan rose warily. 'Yes, sir.'

Oberon picked up a dagger from the table and tapped his mouth with the hilt.

'I have made a mistake. I should have killed him when I had the chance.' He flipped the blade so that the jewelled handle rested in his palm. 'Still, he can do little without the magic of the Round Table behind him, and for that, he needs Merlin.' Quick as a cobra's strike, he threw the dagger. The point buried itself in the hob pup close by Morgan's feet. The creature gave a little yelp, a shudder, then keeled over. 'We must eliminate

Merlin, crush the rebels, then take over the source of magic. Earth will be returned to its natural state—without humans. Its sole purpose is to feed Avalon, not rear these parasites.'

'I'll see to it at once, my lord,' said Morgan, backing away to carry out his orders.

'Oh no, commander. Not you.' At those few words, she flinched, her standing in the court instantly plummeting. 'I cannot afford another failure. I will see to this myself.' Oberon strode past her. 'Bring me my sword, troll!'

The mirror clouded as Roxy's grip on its magic slid away.

'Something wicked this way comes,' she muttered, wrapping the mirror in its red satin cloth. 'Merlin's in big trouble. Linette and Tiago too.'

Rick stood up. 'Let's tell Arthur. We've got to hurry.'

They ran for the king's tent.

Chapter 1

San Francisco, USA, One Year Earlier

'ARE you sure it's him?' Linette handed the binoculars back to Tiago.

The two teenagers had got as near as they could for their spying mission, lurking in the shrubbery across the road from the building that held their target.

Tiago focused through the archway on the slender, long-haired man sitting cross-legged under a magnolia tree in the courtyard, face tilted to the sky, sunglasses protecting his eyes. He compared the suspect's appearance to the photo they had printed out from the Pip Enterprises home page. It was a match—down to the black ponytail and the scattering of white at his temples.

'Yeah, that's him: Mr Ambrosius, founder of the company.'

Linette wrinkled her nose with disdain. 'But, Tiago, he is wearing socks with sandals! Not to mention jeans and a horrible old T-shirt.'

Tiago smiled to himself. His friend was half-French and could not forgive such blatant fashion sins. 'At least the shirt looks well-washed.'

Linette puffed out a breath. 'Charity-shop reject. *Mon Dieu*, someone should tell him that is so not a good look.'

'From here I think it says: "Every Little Thing I do is Magic".' Tiago passed her the glasses so she could check it out. He stroked his little black and white terrier, Bob, under his chin.

Bob yipped.

'I was expecting . . . well . . . more.' Linette shrugged.

'So was I. At least some magical defences.' They had been able to get off the subway in Cupertino and walk right up to the shiny new company headquarters. Nestled between other technology firms, it looked like a slice of black-glass cheese, solar panels harvesting the bright light of the San Francisco Bay. It was such a new urban area with no roots in myths or legends that it was impossible to believe they were in the right place.

'So maybe it's not him.'

'Only one way to find out.' Mr Ambrosius had seemed too obvious, hogging the business pages with his ingenious inventions. 'Even if it's not him, you have to hand it to Mr Ambrosius, *amiga*: he's built the most powerful company on the planet. No digital device could function without a Pip chip. They say his is the seed from which Apple, Microsoft and the others grew.'

'But we're not here for an upgrade; we need a warrior magician. He doesn't look as though he could battle his way out of a paper bag.' Tucking the binoculars down the side of her wheelchair, Linette put her baseball cap on and pulled her dark hair through the back. 'So what do we do now? Go up to him and ask if he's a sixteen-hundred-year-old magician?'

'Maybe not so blunt, no?'

'And you're sure about needing him?' Linette scratched at the hole in her jeans, making it fray a little more around her knee. After months of searching, her confidence in the plan had disintegrated.

'Surely you realize by now that setting up a Round Table is the only way we can fight magical armies? We have to use it to tap into the Fey power so we stand a chance against Oberon.'

'Not much of a chance, is it?'

'Better than nothing.' Tiago rubbed Bob under the chin. 'Let's go test the water.' He slipped his shades back on to hide his silvery eyes. 'You ready?'

Linette released the brake on her wheelchair. '*Oui.*'

They crossed the road and took the ramp up to the main doors of the building.

'I'm-meeting-my-dad-for-lunch excuse?' whispered Linette.

Tiago nodded. Linette stopped at the low section of the reception desk; Tiago hung back with Bob. Two white robots whizzed past, delivering coffees to the workstations, making happy little beeping noises.

The well-groomed man in a blue Pip T-shirt and purple chinos smiled down at her. 'Can I help you?'

'I am meeting, 'ow you say?, *mon père* for eating, yes?' She gave him a charmingly innocent smile. She was dead good at those.

'Your father?'

'Yes, yes, *exactement*!'

'Who is he? I can ring up and tell him you are waiting.' The man picked up his phone, hand hovering over the keyboard.

''E 'as ze meetings. Always meetings. We are waiting here.' Linette gestured to the sunny courtyard.

The receptionist gave Bob a doubtful look.

''E is very good dog. No misbehaving.'

Bob cocked his head in his most winning expression.

The receptionist put the phone down. 'OK, sure. You can wait over there. Let me know if I can call him for you.'

'*Pardon*? I not understand.'

The receptionist sighed, deciding that letting her do what she wanted was the quickest way to deal with them. 'Please wait there.'

'Of course. I do zat.'

Linette led Tiago and Bob to the bench at the edge of the courtyard. They were over the first hurdle.

'Zat and ze?' teased Tiago. 'Linette, you speak at least three languages fluently.'

'I know, but that was fun!' She beamed at him. 'OK, you listen in.'

Thanks to his Fey blood, Tiago had better ears than an ordinary human. He could hear what was going on across the courtyard without anyone suspecting he was eavesdropping. There were a few people gathering at the cafe tables in the far corner. Mr Ambrosius had been joined by a number of young office workers, all dressed in very casual clothes. They were seated on the grass in a circle, chatting to their neighbours, making friendship bands or daisy chains, as if this was a picnic, not a meeting. Streamers in primary colours hung from the roofs of the buildings surrounding the courtyard. A breeze picked up and they rippled in the wind, adding to the festive scene.

Mr Ambrosius clapped his hands. 'Gather round, people: time for a thought sprinkle!' He flicked his fingers over their heads. Tiny silver sparks rained down on them.

'Did you see that?' Linette nudged Tiago, trying not to look as if she was looking.

'Yeah, magic. It's got to be Merlin.'

Mr Ambrosius stretched out on the grass, eyes closed; anyone would think he was about to nap rather than drive his business forward. 'Let's brainstorm, people. What's hot in R and D?'

'Research and Development,' Tiago whispered for Bob's benefit. The dog jumped on his lap and sniffed the air with interest.

A young woman began speaking but Tiago didn't understand half of what she was saying as she used lots of initials and terms he had not come across.

Mr Ambrosius sighed. 'Ah, Gemma, Gemma—I thought I told you: we've exhausted solar for the moment. I want you to look into lunar power.'

The poor woman looked to her colleagues for support. 'I know, Mr A, but we don't get what you want from us.'

'We can't see how we can turn moonlight into energy, boss,' added another of the circle.

'Not moonlight, people—moon energy!'

Bob leapt off Tiago's lap and trotted over to the outdoor meeting. Too late to call the dog back, Tiago let Bob go see what he could do. What Bob did was thrust his muzzle into Mr Ambrosius' right hand, which lay relaxed at his side.

'Ah, what's this? Hey, dude, how's it going?' Mr Ambrosius sat up and pulled Bob onto his lap, stroking him with absent-minded affection. 'Gemma, tell me: other than light, what does the moon give us?'

Tidal power. Tiago saw it instantly. Gemma took far too long, a whole minute of um-ing and ah-ing before she reached the same conclusion.

'That's right. It isn't just the seas that feel the pull of the moon's presence. All materials do. What I want you to do is find a way of harnessing those tiny fluctuations to power our microchips. The drawback of solar is that we have to expose the surface to daylight; with the moon, the power is available at all times, even buried deep in a machine. Devices without the complications of mains electricity or batteries—that's what I want you to invent for me.'

'That's inspired, Mr A!' said Gemma, coming to her knees to applaud. 'But is it possible?'

'I think so.' He coughed modestly and rubbed his nails on his shirt.

'Boss, you're awesome! Why didn't we think of this?' asked a second woman.

Mr Ambrosius' tanned face wrinkled into a grin. 'Because you're not as old as me, guys. I've been around the technology block a few times; I know this will be the next big leap forwards for nanotechnology. Pip must be the front-runner.'

'Like always,' said Gemma proudly.

'And that's why you all work for me. Go forth and multiply these ideas, people!'

Laughing, the young designers got up and hurried back to their offices, voices chattering excitedly. Mr Ambrosius watched them leave with a slightly anxious expression. Then opting for some time out, Mr Ambrosius stripped off his socks, lay on his back and wiggled his bare toes in the soft grass. Bob licked his face.

'Where have you come from, buddy? Should you be here?'

'I hope my dog isn't bothering you?' Tiago crossed the grass, Linette following on behind.

'No problem. I love animals, especially intelligent ones like this.' The inventor's face clouded as he looked more closely at Bob. 'Very intelligent. Who are you?'

'Santiago Dulac, sir. This is my friend, Linette Kwan. That's Bob.'

Mr Ambrosius sat up and pushed Bob gently back in Tiago's direction. 'Cool. But I have to run—conference call with Japan at twelve. Enjoy your visit.' He was rabbiting on them, running back into his warren. Maybe he smelled the magic on Bob?

'Excuse me, sir.' Linette manoeuvred to put herself between Mr Ambrosius and the way out of the courtyard. 'We were wondering if you could spare us a minute. We need to talk to you. It's urgent.'

The inventor cast a glance around him, checking for the nearest security guard. 'I'm a busy guy, honey. If you want to ask about internships, contact the Human Resources department.'

'It isn't about your company, sir.' She reached out to catch his sleeve before he disappeared. 'We need your help. It's about saving the Earth from the Fey.'

His dark eyebrows winged up. 'I dunno what game you are playing, but—' All friendliness had dropped away.

'No game, Mr Ambrosius, sir,' said Tiago firmly. 'We need your help really, really desperately.'

'Security!' squawked the inventor.

A dark-suited heavy appeared from behind a

smoked glass door. He looked like he ate kittens for breakfast and spent the rest of the day picking the fluff from between his teeth. 'Sir?'

'These kids are trespassing!'

Tiago tried to interrupt. 'But Merlin—'

He span round, fists clenched. 'My name is Mr Ambrosius, understood?'

Tiago glared at him.

Mr Ambrosius swung back to the guard. 'Why were they let inside?'

'Sorry, sir. I'll look into that.'

'Search them. I suspect that they are industrial spies, sent by our competitors. I want to see everything they brought into the building, no matter how innocent-looking.'

Kitten-Eater clicked his fingers. Six others of his gorilla-build appeared from every quarter—perhaps the security had not been so lax after all. A guard rapidly frog-marched Tiago into a room that was made of mirror glass—he could see out but no one could see in. Linette was taken by a female colleague to a cubicle next door. Even Bob was scooped up and placed in a third, despite his whining protests.

'You'd better not hurt my dog!' Tiago struggled to free himself but the grip on his neck did not falter.

The man said nothing as he patted Tiago down with professional disinterest. He removed Tiago's wallet, keys and the spelled seashell he used to communicate with Rick and Roxy.

'Hey, they're mine! You can't take them.' He couldn't lose the shell—it was the only way he had to get in touch with his friends.

The guy raised a mocking brow and bared his teeth. 'Tough luck.'

The security guard passed the objects to the man on the door. Tiago watched as the minder carried the tray to Mr Ambrosius. He disregarded the money and the keys but his hand paused over the shell before he pocketed it. Face white with rage— or was it fear?—he gestured abruptly to the guard. Tiago didn't need to hear to know that meant 'get rid of them'.

The guard returned and handed the keys and wallet to the Kitten-Eater who in turn gave them back to Tiago.

'Now get lost. If I see you around here again, I'll—' Kitten-Eater paused to think of a plausible threat to use on a teenager.

'What? Grind my bones to make your bread?' Tiago mocked. He knew trolls who would actually do that so this guy's threats did not bother him.

'No.' He leant forward, getting right into Tiago's personal space. 'I'll take your dog to the pound.'

'Beast,' muttered Tiago, knowing he was defeated. For now.

When Tiago emerged from the room, Mr Ambrosius had already disappeared. Linette and Bob were waiting for him, flanked by their minders. The security guard gave them no chance to talk or plead their case. He took over Linette's chair and pushed her out of the front door. Tiago and Bob had to follow.

'If I see you here again—' growled the guard.

'You won't,' said Tiago, adding under his breath, 'see us.'

They walked slowly away on the pavement in front of the building, glancing up at the sheer black cliff of wall separating them from the person who could help save the world, if only he'd listen. Tiago would lay money that Mr Ambrosius was watching them from somewhere inside.

'It was him—I'm sure of it,' said Tiago.

'OK, so now we know: he's an ostrich,' said Linette, rubbing her arms. She sounded brave but she was shaking. 'He's burying his head in the sand.' She glared at the harsh reflections bouncing off the building. 'He'll have to listen to us eventually.'

'Maybe.' Tiago whistled to Bob. 'Let's hope he doesn't come to his senses too late.'

Chapter 2

TIAGO let himself into the house on Spruce Street that his guardian, Natalia Ventikos, was renting across the road from the University of California campus. He had left Linette at her home two doors away; her parents were just starting up the barbecue and had invited him to come back later.

'Hey, I'm back!'

Natalia, a half-Fey whom they had befriended in Oxford, came out of the study stroking a piece of ochre and dark grey pottery to her arms as another person would a pet cat. Beautiful, with keen grey eyes and long chestnut hair, she had the elegance of a queen even when wearing a lab coat and flip-flops, as she was now.

'Where's Bob, Tiago?'

'At Linette's. They've invited us for supper. Bob's stayed to "help" with the food preparation.'

'We'll be lucky if there's anything left. So how did it go?'

Tiago shook his head. He was gutted: after such a long search they had failed miserably.

'It wasn't him?'

'No. I'm sure it was.'

Natalia knew exactly what that meant to them all. 'At last! That's great news.'

'It isn't. He threw us out on the first mention of the Fey, before we could explain about setting up the Round Table or fetching King Arthur.'

She put the pot down with a thump. For a moment, she looked as if she might give him a comforting hug, but then thought better of it. The Fey found displays of affection as awkward as giraffes found scratching their necks.

Tiago wrinkled his nose, disgusted with himself. 'And now he knows we are here. We made a complete mess of it.'

'Oh dear.'

'Yeah, "oh dear" with knobs on. Our mission is stuffed and put in the oven to roast.'

'Did he find out that you're part Fey?'

'We didn't get that far.' Tiago went through to the kitchen and pulled open the huge American fridge to get some juice. 'But he guessed we had magic—he confiscated my shell.'

Natalia followed him, getting out a glass so he wouldn't drink straight from the carton as he would have preferred. He didn't mind her fussing though; it felt good to have someone grouching at him like a parent. 'Manners, Tiago. But does he know you are Mage?'

'Half Mage,' Tiago corrected, sloshing apple juice into the glass.

'Half then. But he could be prejudiced against your kind. Unfortunately, many of the Fey are.'

Tiago felt the familiar sense of injustice as she reminded him of his second-class status as far as the Dark Folk of Avalon were concerned. Mage Fey were a minority species, famed for their technical brilliance. Tiago had found out only last year that his father had been the Mage king, Malduc of Misty Lake, one of the most hated figures in that world. Dethroned and exiled to Earth, Malduc had met Tiago's Aztec mother and Tiago was the result. Spotted by a Fey informer, Tiago had been taken to Avalon and locked up in Dark Lore training camp with the human changelings. He only escaped when he had helped Rick and Roxy defeat Malduc's attempt to regain the throne. As a hundred years in the human world passed for one year in the Fey realm, Tiago returned to Earth aged eleven, but his date of birth was now some six hundred years in the past.

Like the changelings he was out of his time, but unlike them, he had no real place to call home. Earth was no more ready to accept a half-Mage Fey than Avalon.

'No, Mr Ambrosius didn't see my Mage eyes so I don't think that was part of it. He just doesn't want any contact with his past.'

Nodding, Natalia beckoned him to follow her into her study. 'Come, Tiago, I want to show you something I've been working on.'

Tiago was always happy to be invited into her room. Natalia was an expert on the ancient world and had an unmatched collection of her own pots and jewellery. When they first met, Natalia had worked for a museum in Oxford. After Tiago and Linette returned from Avalon fired up to organize the hunt for Merlin, she was the first person they had contacted. It had been a bit of a gamble, but as a rejected niece of the Fey King, Natalia had been happy to help them. She had thrown in her lot with their cause, applied for guardianship of Tiago, and organized, with the little help of a persuasive spell, a lecture tour for herself and Linette's academic parents at a series of American universities so that they could search for the wizard where rumour last reported him to be living. Linette's parents had not suspected a thing; they just thought American academia was being very, very generous.

'What do you want to show me?' Tiago let his fingers walk over the objects on her shelves—a shield boss, a fragment of glass, a bead—tiny traces of a once-complex culture that ruled the Mediterranean.

'This.' She put a wristband on his open palm. It was gold, engraved with a scene from Greek mythology—the Minotaur in the middle of his labyrinth.

Tiago ran his nail lightly over the etching. It vibrated with a hint of magical energy. 'You've spelled it?'

'Yes. It's original—dug up from the maze itself. I've added a little twist. If you run your finger through the maze to the Minotaur, it will spring a defensive shield spell—one you don't have to use your magic to sustain as the thread connects to my power. Wherever I am, my strength will keep the shield up.'

'That's really clever. I didn't know you knew how to do that.'

She smiled. 'I may not be a technical genius like you but I have my little ways. I've got another for Linette.' She showed him a thinner bracelet decorated with owls.

'It's great.' Tiago slid the band on, feeling the comfortable weight of it sit on his forearm. 'I wish I could tell Roxy and Rick about this.'

Natalia shook her head. 'You really mustn't expect them back so soon. Only four days have passed for them in Avalon.'

'Yeah, I know.' He turned the wristband around so the Minotaur faced outwards. 'Why are you giving this to me now, Natalia?'

She paused before putting the owl bracelet in a little gift box. 'Can't you feel it?'

'Feel what?'

'Things just don't feel right. Humans are getting less inventive—society cracking up.'

Tiago thought of the Pip employees struggling to come up with ideas. 'Yeah, you're right.'

'If we're running short of power here, Avalon must be hitting magical rock-bottom. I worry about you and Linette doing all this on your own. I thought you'd need a little extra protection.'

'We explained: we thought we as kids would pass unnoticed—be safer all round.'

'And you have. Until today.'

'Yeah, we blew it.' Tiago's grim mood darkened.

'No, you didn't. It's a setback—not the end of the story. It's time I helped out directly.' She bunched her hair, twisted and fixed it on the top of her head with a lethal-looking pin. 'Merlin may know about you, but he doesn't yet know about me, does he?'

Tiago smiled for the first time since leaving Pip Enterprises. 'No, he doesn't.'

'Well, then. He won't see me coming, will he?'

Linette carried a bowl of salad on her lap to the terrace by the little swimming pool in their back garden. The water shimmered invitingly in the late-afternoon sunshine, very like the David Hockney print on the living-room wall, a net of white reflections fracturing a transparent turquoise pool.

'Put that on the table, *cherie*, and I think we're ready,' called her mother from the barbecue pit where she and Linette's dad were grilling kebabs.

Two dogs sat attentively at their feet, waiting for something to drop. They made a comic pair: the tiny Bob with his tail swishing to and fro, Gordon the huge chocolate-coloured Gabriel hound beside him, droopy-skinned and with a matching droopy expression. Gordon was no ordinary creature: Gabriel hounds usually travelled in packs as harbingers of doom, flying over the roofs of houses where death was soon to visit. Against type, Gordon had a sunny, affectionate disposition that made him most unsuited for this task, like someone tone-deaf born into the Mozart family.

He was much happier being a slipper-fetching pet that did nothing more challenging than go for walks and eat up scraps. Linette had to admit that he did not lack bravery as he and Bob had been insistent on coming with Tiago and Linette to America, gazing mournfully at their humans until they gave in.

The garden gate clicked.

'Hi, everyone,' called Tiago. Natalia waved a greeting and added a Greek salad to the spread.

Mr Kwan broke away from the grill to fix drinks. 'How's the lecture series going, Natalia?' He handed her a tall glass filled with ice.

'Fine, thank you.'

'It's amazing how we are being invited to the same universities. The odds must be very small. Students aren't as bright as I expected, but there you are.' He shrugged.

Linette exchanged a worried glance with Tiago.

Natalia gave him a relaxed smile. 'I agree, but we have to do our best with the students we have. As for odds, I must admit I've been looking for the opportunities so that we can follow you. It's been good for Tiago and Linette to be together, hasn't it?'

Mr Kwan nodded. 'True. I think that's why she's settled so well into school here.'

'It would be a shame to move them, wouldn't

it? They're used to the American system now. I've heard your name mentioned for the opening here as a visiting professor at the economics faculty.'

Opening? Linette would bet that Natalia had been busy behind the scenes doing more of her extraordinary fixing.

'Really?' Mr Kwan shot a pleased look at his wife.

'Yes,' continued Natalia. 'And I know that you would be a shoe-in for the physics chair if you wanted it, Veronique.'

Tiago nudged Linette. 'Natalia's decided we are sticking around for a bit.'

'You told her—about Mr Ambrosius?'

He moved them further away from the table so they would not be overheard. 'She's going to help, but I'm guessing she thinks we need more time. Are you OK with that?'

'As long as my parents don't suffer for it.'

Veronique Kwan clapped her hands. 'Let's eat. Dogs, please get out of the way.' Gordon and Bob graciously scooted back as she carried the platter to the table. Linette moved to her place. *Bon appetit.* Ah, this is the life. Lovely though Oxford is, it can't compare to the weather here. I could get used to dining outside most days, couldn't you, Nathaniel?'

Mr Kwan handed her a drink. 'Maybe. Let's not

count our chickens, my dear. Help yourselves, everyone.'

Linette looked round for Tiago. He hadn't come to the table but was kneeling at Bob's side. Unusually, both had forgotten the plate of sizzling kebabs and were having one of their silent intense conversations through eye-contact. She manoeuvred her chair nearer them.

'Aren't you hungry?'

Tiago stroked Bob. 'He caught a whiff of something odd.' He pointed to the far side of the pool where a tangle of spiky bushes and bamboo defended the boundary fence.

She couldn't see anything out of place. 'Probably just the neighbour's cat. It's got very bold recently. Not the slightest bit scared of Gordon.'

Tiago shook his head at the Gabriel hound, who was successfully begging titbits from Linette's father. 'No one with any sense is afraid of him. He has to be the world's worst guard dog. If someone did break in, he'd probably greet them with a woof and show them where the valuables are.'

Linette patted Bob's head. 'Was it a cat, Bob?'

The terrier tensed, one paw lifted, nose quivering. He then began yapping furiously, each bark lifting him from the ground.

'Tiago, please tell your dog to stop making so much noise,' called Veronique. 'We don't want our neighbours complaining.'

Tiago caught Bob around the muzzle. 'Hush, we get the message. There's something there but not a cat.'

Bob strained to go and look.

'No, stay here. We don't know yet what we are dealing with.' Tiago glanced over at Linette. 'It could be that Merlin's sent people after us. Back at Pip, one of them threatened to take Bob to the dog pound. I can't risk him.'

Linette's gaze searched the bushes: was there something moving or was it just the breeze? 'You think he'll come after us?'

'I would, if I were him. He'd want to find out how much we know and we did tell him our names. We wouldn't be hard to find.'

Linette put her hands to the rim of her wheels to go closer. Tiago held her back. 'Don't.'

'But it's my garden.'

'And his city. I think he's kept himself safe by having the place pretty much sewn up for decades. No one would want to cross the inventor of the digital age.'

Linette wasn't sure if she shared his fear. Why would Merlin—if he was Merlin—want to harm two teenagers who had only asked for help? He was supposed to be a good guy, wasn't he? If he was having them followed, that could be a positive sign. He might have changed his mind. She tried to move again. Tiago did not release his grip.

'I'm serious, Linette. You don't understand the Fey world. Merlin knows if he is caught he's likely to be executed by Oberon. After this morning, now he's had a chance to think, he may see getting rid of us as a small price to pay for keeping safe.'

Linette didn't want to ask him to define 'getting rid of'—she'd seen a Fey battle with dragons and understood the utter ruthlessness of Avalon. 'So he's an enemy now?'

Tiago shrugged. 'He's not acting like a friend, that's for sure.'

The bush rippled then went still. Bob whined.

'Gone?' asked Tiago.

Bob yipped.

Tiago relaxed his ready-for-anything stance. 'OK, let's go eat then. We must all be very, very careful.' He touched the gold wristband on his arm. 'Natalia was right: we need to take our protection more seriously. She's got one for you too. They come fitted with a shield spell she's devised. Make sure you wear it, OK?'

'Yes, of course.' Linette followed him to the table even though she no longer felt the slightest bit hungry. It was bad enough having a Fey king as an enemy, but adding a legendary wizard just sucked big-time.

Chapter 3

LINETTE wasn't sure what woke her. She rubbed her eyes—they still felt heavy with sleep, dry and gritty. The room was very dark, her wardrobe and dressing table thicker shadows in the blackness, so it must be the middle of the night. Far too early to get up. Her bedside clock ticked with soft insistence. Ordinarily she never noticed the noise but it sounded urgent in the stillness.

She propped herself up on her elbow and took a gulp of water. Her new bracelet lay beside her water glass, the tiniest glow coming from the surface like moonshine. She was thrilled to have her first magical possession—if you didn't count Gordon. She had been so proud when Natalia entrusted it to her after supper and showed her how to spring the shield. It made her feel safer knowing it was there. Natalia was a hard person to get to know but the gift proved that she cared about them, the human instinct for affection winning over her Fey coolness.

Two o'clock. Time to turn over and go back to sleep.

Then she heard it: a scratch at the windowpane. Linette's pulse jumped. Her ground-floor window was clear of plants; nothing should be touching it, let alone scratching at the glass.

What to do? Should she turn on the light? Call for help?

Calm down. You're fifteen, not a baby. It could just be a wild animal. She waited, wanting confirmation before she broke the night's peace.

The curtain billowed in a draught. She always left the window closed during the summer as the house had air-conditioning. Someone must have eased it ajar.

Linette opened her mouth to scream but no sound came out. It wasn't terror drying up her words. She had felt this choking sensation before: the intruder had cast a muffling spell on her.

She threw aside the sheet and groped under the bed for a weapon. Her hand came up with a shoe. She chucked it at the curtain. The shoe hit something with a soft thud, momentarily out-lining a shape. There was a body between the floor-length curtain and the window. She threw a second shoe then the novel she had been reading, her heart racing. She drummed on the wooden bed frame with her fists. *Come on someone, hear me!*

Her bedroom door pushed open and Gordon bounded into the room. He made straight for the window, barking his deep bell-like booms. When his nose hit the curtain it went flat against the wall. The muffling spell broke. Whoever had been behind it had fled.

The light went on. Linette's father stood in the doorway, black hair going every which way.

'Dad!' croaked Linette, holding out her arms.

He rushed to her side and gave her a hug. 'What's up, Linny? Why's Gordon barking?'

'There was something at the window. They got inside.'

Nathaniel hurried over and shoved back the drapes. The window was closed. Gordon was quivering, giving the occasional bark to make his point. 'But, darling, the window lock is still engaged. How can there have been something there? Are you sure it wasn't a nightmare?'

Magic could undo locks. 'There was a . . . a person, Dad. I know it. Look, I threw stuff at them.'

Her father eyed the collection that had gathered

around the window. Suddenly he knelt and patted the floor.

'My word, you're right. The carpet's wet.' He sniffed his fingers gingerly. 'And it smells of chlorine.' He stood up. 'I'm going outside. Veronique, someone got in the house!'

Linette's mother bustled into the room. '*Mon Dieu!* How can they?'

'Not sure but I'm going to check they've gone. Come, Gordon!' Nathaniel clicked his fingers and the dog trotted after him.

Linette had gathered some of her scattered wits. 'Please, Dad: it might be dangerous!'

'Don't worry: I've got this fearsome beast with me.' He patted Gordon's head. 'One look at him and any thief will run for his life.' Her dad left the room. A moment later the outside lights came on.

Veronique went to the window. 'I can't see anything. But how did they get in?' She checked the lock—the frame didn't even rattle when she tried.

After some barking and moving about outside, Nathaniel and Gordon came back. 'No sign of our intruder but the poolside is wet. They must have fallen in.'

'A tramp?' suggested Veronique. 'A drunk?'

'Something like that—or even a student playing some kind of prank. I doubt they'll try getting in again now they know someone is sleeping on this level. They probably expected us all to be upstairs.'

Linette shivered. She had to sleep downstairs and it was no joke being reminded that hers was the first bedroom an intruder would enter. Without her having to say anything, her parents came over to hug her. Gordon joined the huddle, thrusting his nose between them.

'Thanks, Gordon,' whispered Linette.

'Why doesn't he stay in here tonight? I'll feel happier if I know he's with you.' Veronique scratched Gordon between his serious brown eyes.

'So would I. Gordon, stay?' Linette asked.

Gordon padded over to the rug between her and the window. He turned twice and lay down to sleep with a sigh.

Nathaniel shook his head, a bemused smile on his face. 'I didn't think he'd prove any use but I'm pleased I'm wrong. When the chips were down, he found his inner guard dog.'

Gordon twitched, already fast asleep. Linette's tension drained away, leaving her feeling exhausted. If he wasn't worried, then she knew she need not be.

'I'm OK now. Thanks.'

'Goodnight, love. Goodnight, you magnificent dog.' Her mum turned off the light.

'I'll make sure it doesn't happen again,' her dad promised. 'Perhaps a metal grille over the window, hmm?'

'Yes, good idea.' Linette doubted bars would keep out a trespasser who knew spells. She was determined to consult Tiago first thing. It was past time she learned how to defend her family against magical attack.

Tiago's Pluto alarm clock barked and wagged its tail. Swatting it on the head to kill the noise, Tiago leapt up, throwing back the duvet with an enthusiasm that saw it sailing off the end of the bed and over a startled Bob, who was snoozing in his basket. The dog burrowed out and gave a reproving nip in the direction of Tiago's bare toes, which he easily avoided by jumping over him. Bob was not a morning dog. Tiago gave him a scratch between the ears and under his chin. He was surprised they had not been disturbed; after the disaster of the meeting with Merlin and the feeling of being followed, he had expected a few nightmares for them both.

Teeth brushed, face scrubbed, clothes pulled on, Tiago jogged to the kitchen. He poured dog biscuits into Bob's bowl and moistened them with some warm water. It took ten seconds for the terrier to wolf it down. 'Ready to rock and roll, Bob?'

Bob trotted to the door.

Tiago made a honey sandwich and grabbed a banana from the Mexican pottery fruit bowl on the kitchen counter. He was planning to get a drink at the coffee outlet at the metro station. He had a passion for the bizarre combinations you could order—whole or skinny, soy, misto, macchiato, mocha, chai, latte, chai-latte, flat white, with an extra shot, wet or dry, with a squirt of syrup, with cream, with cream and marshmallows and a chocolate stirring stick—every day was a challenge to come up with a new one. The assistants waited for his arrival with comic dread.

'I'm going out!' he called to Natalia. The American school holidays were almost at an end but Linette and Tiago still had a few days to enjoy their freedom. Project Merlin temporarily suspended, they had arranged to go together to take a look at the carousel, an old-fashioned amusement ride preserved like a gilt and white butterfly in a glass cocoon right in the heart of the skyscraper district in downtown San Francisco.

'Be careful.' Natalia's voice came from the bathroom where she was taking her morning shower.

'We will.'

Tiago pressed the bell on Linette's door. After a few moments, it opened a crack.

'Thank goodness, it's you.' His friend opened the door fully, her hand resting on Gordon's collar.

Something was wrong. She never normally answered the door so cautiously.

'What's up?'

She backed out of the way so he could come in. 'Sun, clouds, stars.' She gave him a warning look as her father came out of his study.

'Morning, Tiago. We had intruders last night so I want you to be extra careful today.'

Tiago glanced at Gordon, who dolefully confirmed this with a nod of his saggy head.

'Yes, we'll be on our guard.'

'I'm sure they won't dare come back, Linette, but if we are out, don't come into the house alone. Get the dogs to check it out for you. Better safe than sorry.'

'Yes, Dad.'

Mr Kwan bent down and kissed the top of her head, pushing some dollar bills in her hand at the same time. 'Here, treat yourself to lunch somewhere. After last night, you deserve a nice day.'

Tiago waited until they were on their way to the metro before he asked for a report.

'They got right into your bedroom? *Maldito*, Linette, that's really bad. I didn't think Merlin would go that far so soon. I'm sorry.'

'It's not your fault, Tiago.' Linette went to press

the button for the traffic lights but Gordon's nose was there before her. The two dogs loved the countdown that controlled the pedestrian crossings, telling you how long you had to cross. 'But it was definitely a magical visitor, not a burglar as Dad thinks. He used a muffling spell so I couldn't call out.'

'Why didn't you use the shield spell?'

Linette touched her owl bracelet. 'How would that help?'

'It blocks magic. If you'd surrounded yourself with it, the muffling spell would've been cut off.'

'Oh, I didn't know.'

'Our fault. Natalia and I should've explained. What I don't understand is, if Merlin sent someone after you, why they didn't, well, *do* something.'

'You don't think it was Merlin himself?'

Tiago shook his head. 'No, he's too powerful. The break-in seems clumsy. He could have spirited you away from your bedroom without you knowing anything about it. I doubt he would do anything to risk exposing his magic to normal people like your parents.'

'You're not comforting me here.'

'I wasn't trying to.'

They took the ramp down into the metro.

'We've got to do something. My parents might get hurt if they get in again.'

And so might Linette, Tiago added to himself. As a non-magical teenager, she didn't have the same recourse to defensive spells as he did. In that way, she was the weak link in their team—one Merlin would try to exploit.

'I'll think of something,' he promised.

'Can't I learn some magic?'

'That's not how it works. You have to have lived in Avalon or been part of the Round Table to develop a store of magic—a bit like charging a battery. I could teach you the shapes and the feel of each spell but without the power it wouldn't do anything.'

'OK that's a dead end for now, but isn't there some talisman, some protection my parents can use—you know, like garlic?'

'That's vampires and, if they exist, I doubt a funny smell would put them off.'

'You know what I mean. Stories are full of them: a four-leaf clover, a rabbit's foot, a lucky charm. One of them must work.'

'Not getting you a rabbit's foot—that's just cruel. But I'll ask Natalia—she might know what would help. I was thinking of leaving Bob at yours. Gordon's a good dog but he lacks . . . .'

Gordon gave him a look dripping with disappointment.

'What I meant to say is that Gordon, who is

obviously fully capable of guarding you himself, could do with a second pair of ears to help him in that vital task.'

Bob barked his agreement.

Gordon gave the smaller dog a dignified sniff.

'There, that's settled. I'll feel better if you have both of them with you.'

They all enjoyed the ride on the carousel. Linette sat in one of the golden carriages with the dogs facing her, while Tiago rode a painted horse. The other people on the ride had applauded as Gordon howled along to the old-fashioned fairground music, managing a tuneful counterpoint. Next, they decided to have lunch picnic-style in the nearby Yerba Buena Gardens, mainly because Bob liked the fifty-foot-high granite waterfall—a memorial to the great American Martin Luther King, one of Tiago's heroes. There was a shady passageway behind it, a relief from the midday sun if they needed it. Skyscrapers bristled around the park like concrete trees in a forest clearing. Keeping to that scale, it made Tiago and Linette feel the size of beetles.

Linette propelled her chair along the concrete tunnel cooled by tumbling water. Opposite the fall, the wall was covered with Luther's words in many languages. She translated the Chinese characters for Tiago's benefit. He did the same with the Spanish for her. Bob and Gordon played chicken, dipping their noses into the falling water to see who could stay there the longest.

At the end of the passage there was a bundle of clothes slumped in a dark corner. When it moved, Tiago realized it was a homeless person. He dug in his jeans pocket for some spare change.

'Here, *amigo*, get yourself something to eat.' He dropped the coins where he judged the man's arm to be hidden.

A blue webbed hand snaked out and grabbed Tiago's ankle.

'Don't leave me!' The bundle of rags fell back from a matted head of rubbery black hair and a nix warrior gazed up at Tiago. Linette yelped.

'Troll spit! What are you still doing here?' exclaimed Tiago. It was the nix warrior that Malduc had carelessly sent over to the human world when he was demonstrating his invention to maintain the balance between Avalon and Earth. But that was over a year ago—Tiago had assumed the soldier had found his way back through a Fey portal many months back.

'Please, please, don't leave me here.' The soldier was very young—just a teenager in nix terms, even though he would probably top six feet when he stood. The sea-turtle armour he had worn for the battle had gone and he was wearing a weird collection of human clothes—beach towel and Hawaiian shirt covered by an oily coat. The worst thing was that he looked really sick. Nixen in their natural state in the seas of Avalon had shining blue-scaled skin and fresh dark green hair rippling down their backs like seaweed. His kelp-locks were dry and black, his skin tinged grey and covered with sore pink scabs. Even his double row of pointed teeth looked stained. He smelt like rotting fish.

'Oh, Tiago, the poor creature!' exclaimed Linette, glancing around in case someone else came into the passageway. 'We've got to hide him.'

Tiago quickly cast a shimmer spell to shield the nix from prying eyes. 'What can we do for you?' He knelt beside the boy.

'I hate it here. Please, please, send me home.' Tears pooled in the nix's black eyes.

'Send you back?' Tiago rested on his heels. He knew that theoretically he, as a half-Fey, should be able to cast that spell, but he had never done so. Besides, sending back a nix was a sure way of betraying their location to Oberon. 'I'm not sure I know how.'

The grip on his ankle tightened; the nix was afraid Tiago would run off and leave him. 'You must—or I'll die here.'

'How did you find us?' Linette asked, handing him a bottle of mineral water.

The nix looked at it suspiciously.

'Go on: it's just water.'

'Salt?' He licked his cracked lips. His shark mouth was much wider than a human one, disconcerting as it opened.

'No, fresh.'

He pushed it away. 'I only drink salt water.'

Tiago reached in his pocket and pulled out a packet of crisps. He had brought the sort where they provide a little sachet inside. He ripped off the top and tipped it in the water. 'There you are.'

The nix took a sip—then smiled in surprise. 'Perfect.' He frowned, searching for an unfamiliar word. 'Thank . . . you.'

'What's your name?'

'Litor. My father is Prince Litu, leader of the nixen.'

'I remember him!' exclaimed Linette. 'He carried me out of the sea when I went swimming, Tiago, near the battle that had destroyed the Wild Ride.' She turned back to the nix. 'We met before, when you went in to the Fey reactor even though Gordon warned you not to.'

'Yes. Malduc sent me here.' Litor's gaze turned vicious for a second. 'I follow you—my changeling.' He pointed at Linette.

'Me?' She touched her chest.

'Of course!' Tiago snapped his fingers, understanding now how the nix had found them. 'Malduc swapped Litor for you, Linette, creating a magical bond between you. You can sense each other's presence.'

'But you go far, far away,' grumbled Litor. 'I had to swim.'

'What—you swam here from . . . from England?' Linette's face mirrored Tiago's astonishment.

Litor nodded. 'I cannot survive far from the sea so I had to go round to reach you here—through a thin water link.'

'You swam the Panama Canal? Wow.' Tiago couldn't imagine what that journey had been like. Litor had swum thousands of miles to get to San Francisco.

'But I get sick. Out there is much, much stuff.' He pointed to a scrap of plastic, which he had tied round his webbed toes to hide them. 'Your oceans are ill. I get ill.' He showed the worst of his scabs on his forearm. It seeped horrid yellow pus. 'I cough blood now and have pain in my head. I die if I do not go back at once to heal in my ocean.'

'Oh, Tiago, we have to help him.' Linette looked quite sick herself.

Yes, they did have to help, but it would be a terrible risk. The nix's father was in league with Oberon. If the Fey King found out where they were, he'd come after them.

'How long have you been following us here?' Tiago asked, worried the alarm bells would already be ringing in Avalon.

'I arrived yesterday. I go in her house,' Litor pointed to Linette, 'but the Gabriel hound scared me away.'

'So it was you, not Mer—'

'Let's see what we can do for you.' Tiago interrupted Linette before she blurted out Merlin's name. 'But you'll have to come back with us. I don't know how to make a portal spell.'

The nix clicked deep in his throat.

'Not yet,' Tiago added hastily. 'I expect I can learn but there're too many people here to experiment.'

The nix finally released his grip on Tiago's ankle. 'Yes, I come with you.'

Tiago stood up and rubbed his foot to get the blood flowing again. 'Cast a quick glamour over yourself to disguise your appearance and we'll go back by metro.'

Litor pulled his coat hood back over his head. 'I don't know that kind of spell. I only know how to fight.'

'Hold my hand and I'll do it for you.'

With some reluctance, the nix put his cool flipper-like hand in Tiago's. It held on to his fingers with tensile strength.

'Ouch—I'm not going anywhere, *amigo*.'

The pinch eased a tiny amount.

What disguise to use? Tiago opted to work with the nix's height rather than disguise that. He hid the soldier under a glamour of Linette's dad.

Linette shook her head, unnerved to see her father standing passively beside Tiago. 'That's just bizarre. I thought I was used to magic by now.'

Tiago whistled to the dogs. They had been so busy with their game in the waterfall neither had taken much notice of the nix. Now they caught a whiff of him, they barked excitedly.

'Hush now!' said Tiago. 'He's a friend.' Sort of.

Gordon obligingly fell silent but Bob was not so gullible. Protective instincts on full alert now, the terrier insisted on walking between Tiago and Litor all the way home.

Chapter 4

'SO where can we hide a six-foot-tall blue sea creature?' Linette asked the question as they sat on the metro watching the stations flick by. She knew she was close to an outburst of hysterical laughter. Her life since meeting the changelings was one bizarre thing after another.

Tiago scratched the back of his head and stretched. He had grown over the last year, and gave the impression he wasn't sure what to do with his lanky limbs when sitting still. Roxy and Rick were going to be in for a surprise when they returned from their few days away in Avalon. He still kept one hand firmly clasped round the nix's fingers. It would not do the citizens of San

Francisco any good if a magical creature suddenly appeared in their midst. It was wackier than most North American cities but even the Bay area had limits.

'I was thinking we could park him in your pool for the moment.' Tiago gestured to the drying skin of the nix. Litor was slumped asleep, exhausted by his struggle to survive in a hostile world.

'You don't think my parents would notice?' she said in a choked voice.

'I'll sort it out—make a fixed glamour spell with a pentangle. That should keep the illusion of an empty pool when I'm not there.'

'But if they decide to go for a swim?'

A mischievous twinkle appeared in his eyes. 'Then Litor better evacuate pretty quickly. Besides, it would only be for a day or two while I research the portal spell.'

'We're sending him back?'

'I don't know. It's dangerous to do but impossible to keep him. Can we risk our mission?'

Litor stirred. His pebble-black eyes flicked open and fixed on Tiago. 'You will do this for me?'

Tiago shrugged awkwardly. 'I don't like to see you suffer.'

The nix sighed, a hiss like air escaping a puncture. 'Thank you, thank you. I will be in your debt.'

'But you have to promise to say nothing about

47

us. We just want to live quiet lives here, not have Oberon breathing down our necks.'

The nix nodded solemnly. 'Yes, quiet lives. I understand.'

The nix found the pool very acceptable as a haven. He said the chlorine burned his skin but in a good way, cleansing the pollution he had had to swim through on his marathon journey. He found all the pool toys fascinating and soon developed his own games with them. War games, Tiago explained, as the beach ball hit the inflatable crocodile right between the eyes with deadly accuracy, but Linette enjoyed watching the nix play—it was like having her own sea-lion show. After having seen him reduced to a pile of rags, it felt good to watch him laugh and have fun. He slipped through the water so elegantly, putting Olympic divers to shame.

Tiago was busy setting up the pentagon of power. He asked for five objects of the same type so she had found him a set of flowerpots. When the last one was in place, he sketched a shape in the air and a ripple like a heat haze fell over the pool. The nix disappeared, leaving only the undulating water behind.

'Amazing. He's still there, right?' asked Linette.

'Yeah, of course. Litor, you OK?'

'Yes, mage-boy.' He was close but invisible.

'Name's Tiago. I'd appreciate it if you'd remember.'

'Yes, mage-boy Tiago.'

'Are you being deliberately annoying?'

'Yes, mage-boy Tiago.' A splash of water came out of nowhere and sprayed them both.

Tiago grinned. 'Great. I think he's feeling better. You stay on guard; I'll go find out what I can about the portal spell.'

Linette took a book and sat under a sunshade, listening to the sounds of the nix enjoying the invisible pool. Bob and Gordon kept watch by the gate to give warning of visitors. Late afternoon she made a round of tuna sandwiches and put them by the steps. When she looked up ten minutes later, they were gone.

She must have drifted off to sleep for the next thing she knew was a paw on her knee, closely followed by a 'Hello, darling!' from the house. Her parents had returned.

'Hi, I'm out here!' she called, before adding in a lower voice, 'Litor, you've got to be quiet now!'

The splashing in the pool stopped.

Her mother came out into the garden carrying a huge bunch of flowers. 'Oh *cherie*, I've got such good news! The coincidence is amazing. I've been invited to stay another year as a visiting professor and your father has landed an exceptional position in the economics faculty. Oxford has given us their blessing to remain for the year. So you can continue at school here—won't that be nice?'

'That's great, Maman.' Linette detected the hand of Natalia behind these arrangements. 'Well done.'

'We're *tout etonné* how it all worked out—it is like a fairy godmother granted us our secret wishes.' Veronique chattered away, her excitement making her fizz and pop, a little human firework display. 'So we've decided to throw a party for our colleagues tonight. Your father is cooking so steer clear of the kitchen. I'll need your help getting the garden ready. Such a lovely evening. I've told everyone to bring their swimming costumes.'

'You have?' Linette squeaked as the rocket of that announcement streaked across her thoughts.

Her mother surveyed the lawn and the patio around the pool. Strategically positioned pink flowers nodded in their planters, holding the illusion in place. 'What are they doing there? People will trip over them.'

'You mean the flowerpots? I put them there. Don't you think they look nice?'

'I like geraniums but they are too close to the edge. Here, I'll just move them back a bit.' Bent over, Veronique did not notice the collapse of the spell, like a shimmery gauze curtain rippling to the ground. 'There, that's better. What's the matter, *cherie*, you look quite terrified. Not still thinking about last night?'

'No . . . I mean, yes.' Linette couldn't see the nix. Litor had managed to hide but where had he gone?

Veronique patted Linette's cheek. 'Enjoy the party and forget about it. We'll make sure the house is properly burglar-proof, especially as we're planning to stay now. Would you like something to drink?'

'Er, yes please. Juice. With ice and . . . lemon.' Anything to keep her away.

'When did we become the Hilton, *cherie*?' laughed her mother. 'I'll be back in a minute.'

As soon as Veronique went inside, Linette manoeuvred to the edge of the pool. She searched for Litor but only spotted him in the deep end when Bob barked at the inflatable crocodile. A blue arm kept it tethered in place, hiding the nix underneath. He had to have been under for a few minutes.

'Litor?'

No response. She only had seconds to get him out of the pool and into the tool shed—the only possible hiding place.

'Bob, fetch!'

The terrier looked at her with surprise.

'What? You don't swim?'

He hung his head.

Gordon bounded by and leapt in the pool with an almighty splashing, soaking Linette and Bob. Graceful as a seal, the Gabriel hound dived down to the nix and nudged him to the surface. Litor slipped onto the poolside.

'Quick, in there!' Linette pointed to the shed. 'Please, stay hidden.'

Litor dripped his way to the shed and disappeared inside. There was a telltale trail of webbed footprints but Bob trotted over and shook himself on the spot, confusing the marks.

'What is that dog doing in the pool?' exclaimed her mother, hurrying over with a tray of drinks.

'He fell in. You know how soppy he is.' Poor Gordon was swimming in circles. He could fly out as he was a magical dog, but Tiago had impressed on him that he shouldn't use this power in front of humans. That left him stranded.

Veronique dashed back to the house. 'Nathaniel, Nathaniel! I need your help. Gordon's drowning!'

With the aid of two adults, Gordon was hauled ashore. He rewarded his rescuers with a vigorous shake.

'Aargh!' Veronique held her sopping-wet shirt away from her chest. 'You infuriating hound!'

Gordon licked her hand.

'You'd better go change, darling. Our guests will be arriving soon.' Linette's dad patted

Gordon on the head. 'No more pool, Gordon. Understood?'

Gordon gave him one of his devastatingly sad gazes.

'Oh, you foolish animal: you make it so hard to tell you off! Just stay out of trouble, OK?'

That wasn't very likely, thought Linette, not with a nix hidden in the shed and a party about to start. She'd better warn Tiago.

'Bob?'

He looked up at her.

'You know what to do.'

He trotted off, slid under the gate and went to break the news to his master that their plan had gone badly wrong already.

Her parents' party carried on far into the night. When Nathaniel and Veronique decided to celebrate, they really went overboard, setting up an impromptu dance floor by the pool, coloured lights and amplified music, spreading the table with enough food and drink to feed a small army. Linette stationed herself strategically between the dancers and the shed. Would the guests never leave? Time seemed to be stretching, each minute crawling by.

Her father jived past, doing an embarrassing dad-dance that proved he had reached the point of the night where he no longer thought of himself as a serious head of an Oxford college on a lecture tour but a carefree teenager. Hits of the eighties blared out and from the movement of his lips he knew every word.

Tiago sidled up. 'How's our visitor doing?' He jerked his head at the shed.

'Bob's been ferrying in food and drink. I think he's OK. How's the spell coming on?'

'Natalia hasn't done it either but she says she thinks she knows how it works. We can have a go together when it quietens down. We're still not sure if we can risk sending Litor back though. It may be better to hide him somewhere here for the moment.' A gaggle of guests chose that moment to let off a barrage of poppers, releasing streamers into the air. 'I didn't realize your parents were such party animals.'

Veronique let out a husky bellow of laughter at a guest's joke. She went to lean against the table, misjudged it, and stumbled a few paces, laughing even harder. Nathaniel jigged back into view, dancing with a wig of paper streamers draped over his head. He began to do the moonwalk.

'Just kill me now,' muttered Linette. 'They are so uncool.'

'They're enjoying themselves,' corrected Tiago. Linette knew that human standards of coolness did not really interest him.

'I wish they'd just go to bed.'

'I thought they were supposed to say that about you as their teenage daughter, not the other way round.'

In the small hours, only a few of the most persistent guests remained and the mood mellowed.

'I know: let's get some more loungers out of the shed and watch the sunrise!' declared Veronique.

Let's not. 'Um, *Maman*, don't you think it's time we went to bed?' suggested Linette desperately.

'You go, *cherie*. Us old ones get a thrill from staying up all night—reliving our youth, aren't we?'

The remaining guests began on a new round of reminiscences of their wild pasts.

'Think of the neighbours,' Linette tried.

Veronique laughed. 'I have. They are all still here.' Mr and Mrs Fallon from next door waved at Linette from the other side of the pool.

Tiago hastily whispered something to Natalia. She put down her drink and crossed to the shed.

'Let me get the loungers, Veronique. Tiago can help.'

Veronique pulled her away. 'No, no, Nathaniel will do it. It's a bit cobwebby in there.'

Tiago bounded to the door. 'But I love spiders.'

Linette's dad held him back. 'Seriously, Tiago, they may not be friendly ones—not like the harmless sort in England. Let me go in first.'

Short of shoving her chair forward and knocking her dad over, there was nothing Linette could do. She had to hope it was too dark for him to see their visitor. He dipped his head into the shed and passed out a red striped chair to Tiago.

So far so good.

'I'm sure there's a matching one in here somewhere.' Her dad's voice floated out, a little muffled.

Linette bit her lip, praying for a miracle.

'Out! Get out!' Scuffling noises emerged from the open door. Something big clattered to the ground. Bob joined in with sharp barks.

'What is it, Nathaniel?' Her mother pushed past Tiago. The guests clustered around the door. Linette's dad emerged dragging a coat sleeve containing one very startled-looking nix.

'I've found an intruder.'

The pool lights fell on Litor's face, sharp teeth glinting, black eyes set wide in his rugby-ball-shaped head.

'Oh my goodness, what is it?' shrieked Mrs Fallon.

'He's my friend,' Tiago said quickly. 'He's just back from a fancy-dress party.'

'But it can't be a costume—look at his mouth!' cried Mr Fallon. He grabbed the pool rake. 'Get back, everyone. We've been invaded by aliens.'

Linette's dad dragged on the coat with one

56

hand and pushed Tiago out of harm's way with the other, moving him too far for him to cast his glamour spell.

'Call the police!' cried Mrs Fallon. A guest pulled his phone out of his pocket but before he could put in 911, he found himself nudged by Gordon towards the pool. He lost his balance, losing hold of his mobile as he began to fall.

Then he stopped, body at an acute angle over the water, arms flung wide. His phone was poised at the apex of its arc above the water.

'What's happening?' Linette could feel the drag on her, as if time had slowed to a sludge. With great difficulty, she threw it off. She looked round to see that her parents and guests were stationary; only a few people were moving. Natalia was checking Mr Fallon's pulse as he was arrested halfway through swiping the air with the rake, mouth open in a yell. Mrs Fallon had her hands over her eyes, a silent scream of terror. Litor had slipped out of the coat, leaving it suspended. Her dad stood in a matador's stance, shaking the empty garment like a red cloak at a bull. Her mother had frozen, hands warding off the creature. Tiago was trying to pull the man back from his fall into the pool but couldn't shift him. It was as if everyone and everything was freeze-framed. San Francisco was still: no sound of vehicles or a hint of breeze.

Even the stars no longer twinkled, their light a steady gleam.

Litor ducked under the rake that had been aimed at his head and spat at the feet of his attacker. He dived into the pool and came up with a spout of water that hit the phone man suspended overhead.

'Time must've stopped,' Tiago announced. He put his hands in his jeans pockets, taking in the eerily silent night. 'And as we are the only ones still moving, I'm guessing it has something to do with the balance. We were warned about taking too many people across from one world to the other as it would mess up time.'

Linette tried not to panic. She had been through some weird stuff with her friends already and they usually found a way out. Natalia came to their side. 'I guess someone could have brought a lot of Fey Folk across and destabilized Earth.'

'Oberon's invasion?' Linette suggested shakily. 'It's started?'

'Maybe. Or it might be Roxy and Rick doing something. They might be back with Arthur already.'

'But would just three people upset time like this?'

Tiago shrugged. 'I really don't know. The point is, how do we get time started again? If we don't, the freeze will deepen, Earth will go into a Time Ice Age, and it will be harder to get things back to normal.'

'The water is moving where Litor is touching it but not elsewhere,' Natalia observed.

'Yeah, our contact with Avalon seems to have protected us from the effects. Linette, how are you feeling?'

'Really heavy—like I'm half-asleep.'

'That figures—you were only in Avalon for a couple of hours so your protection won't be as complete as ours.'

Linette felt her eyelids drop. 'Tiago, I can't stay awake!'

Bob nipped her fingers where they drooped over the armrest of her chair. She jolted awake again.

'Bob, don't let her slip into the freeze with everyone else,' warned Tiago. 'This makes the decision for us. Whatever the risk to us, we have to send Litor home and start restoring the balance or we'll lose the Earth anyway.'

'Oberon will come after us,' warned Natalia.

'I know.' Tiago's expression was bleak. 'But I can't see another way; can you?'

Linette's eyes drifted closed.

'Quick: before we lose Linette too!'

Tiago's shout woke her up. She didn't want to drop out of existence like this without a struggle.

'Hurry, please,' she croaked. The chill was creeping back over her. 'I can't hold out much longer.'

'Hang on, Linette. We'll make a portal and send the nix back. Hey, Litor, are you ready?'

Litor leapt from the water. 'Yes!'

Natalia eyed the swimming pool. 'He'll want to go back to the oceans so let's make the water our doorway.'

'Good thinking.' Tiago moved to the other side. 'I make the shape here, yes?'

'Think of it like weaving—take a thread of our world and send a shuttle to catch the warp of Avalon.'

Tiago closed his eyes, then opened them again. 'Where will this door open to?'

'Earth maps onto Avalon—it is layered like seeing one through the tracing paper of the other. You'll be opening a doorway in the western ocean.'

'You OK with that, nix?'

Litor whistled his agreement.

'You'll find your folks?'

'I can sing like your whales and find my way home through many, many miles.'

'And you won't betray us?'

Litor clicked his teeth in annoyance.

No guarantees, but there wasn't time for second thoughts. Face furrowed, Tiago began to move his hands fluidly through the air. Linette struggled to watch as he pulled on something in his chest, gossamer strands of magic, and cast them over the water. The edges of the pool began to shimmer and blur as though encased in a rainbow. The strength of the magic made the hair prickle on the back of Linette's neck.

'I think that's it!' Tiago declared. 'But it's not very stable. Litor, do you want to risk it?'

The nix's answer was a perfect swallow dive into the water. The splash fountained on the rippling surface. Linette craned over the edge but Litor was gone.

'You did it!'

'I hope I did.' Tiago began unweaving the door spell, his hands shaking with the pressure of maintaining a disciplined retreat from a powerful but unfamiliar use of magic. 'Any change?'

Linette took her mother's hand. It wasn't cold, just not alive—caught in a moment of nothingness. She shook her head.

'I can't keep awake. Perhaps you should let me sleep with them. I don't want to go on if everyone else is like this.'

Natalia put her arm around Linette. 'Have a little faith. You won't have to wait a hundred years for a prince to kiss you awake. We'll reverse the damage sooner than that.'

And then, just as suddenly as it had stopped, time started again. The man fell in the pool, the coat billowed to the ground, Mrs Fallon screamed and the rake clattered on the spot where Litor had stood.

'Where's he gone?' Mr Kwan kicked the empty coat discarded by the poolside.

'Who?' asked Natalia innocently.

'That blue creature.'

'Nathaniel, I think someone must have put something odd in the drinks. You've all been acting most oddly since you found that old coat in the shed—claiming we had been invaded by aliens.'

'But we were!' shouted Mr Fallon.

The man crawled out of the pool. 'My cell phone—it's ruined.'

'*Maman*, Dad, I think this party's over,' said Linette, folding her arms across her chest and giving her parents a reproving stare.

It wasn't until much later the next morning that they discovered Mr Ambrosius had disappeared. Linette's parents were sleeping off the excitement, so she and Tiago had the living room to themselves.

'He can't have gone—I don't believe this!' Linette switched off the television and threw the remote on the sofa. The twenty-four-hour news channel was reporting the mysterious absence of America's top businessman from outside the Pip Enterprises HQ. The flippy-haired broad-caster seemed to think it was all one big joke and

Linette could not bear another moment of her drawling voice.

Tiago sagged back in his armchair. 'Yeah, apparently he has these phases where he goes on a walkabout. He says he needs to get in touch with his creative soul. To spot him on one of his retreats from the world has become a more popular sport in the US than phantom sightings of Elvis.'

'I knew he was cracked.'

'The thing is, *amiga*, has he gone willingly or was that time-freeze yesterday something to do with it?'

Linette threw up her hands in despair. 'How would I know?'

Tiago smiled sourly at her response. 'I was kinda putting it out there as a whatyoumacallit—a rhetorical question.' He got up and walked to the window. 'I wish we could talk to Rick and Roxy—compare notes—but Merlin took my only link with them.'

Linette thumped her thigh in frustration. 'And my old UK phone number doesn't work here. I've got a new SIM. We should've thought to set something up before we left Oxford, not just rely on your magical connection through the shells.'

Tiago rubbed the hanging frond of a spider plant, removing a light coating of dust. 'Merlin's been on the wanted list, like, forever. I'm wondering if

Oberon staged a quick snatch—sent over a team that disrupted the time flow, grabbed Merlin and then went back. I doubt us sending one nix over was what made the difference.'

Linette experienced a familiar sensation of being out of her depth with Fey matters. She guessed it was frustration mixed with fear of the unknown but much more of this and she'd end up a nervous wreck. *Keep calm, Linette*, she told herself, *keep it together for Tiago's sake*. He was relying on her as his partner in this mission. 'So what do we do now?'

Tiago sat cross-legged on the windowsill. 'See if we can find out where he's gone—and wait.'

'With our future—Earth's future—in the balance?'

'Not much else we can do. Natalia said at least it would give her an opportunity to embed herself in his organization in case he is free to come back.'

'And if he's not?'

Tiago bumped his head gently against the window. 'I guess we'll have to work something else out. We'll give it a few days—Avalonian days.'

Chapter 5

Ten months later

THE phone vibrated.

'Finally!' Tiago did a somersault on his bed. The news feed to his mobile had flashed up at seven a.m. with the news that Merlin—or Mr Ambrosius as he was known to the world— was back. More than back. With his gift for showmanship, he was announcing his return by displaying the fruits of his creative retreat at the California Academy of Sciences in Golden Gate Park at midday.

They had been preparing for this. Natalia had talked herself into a job as a consultant to a Pip design team working on an Ancient World app, which gave her access to the company's headquarters. She had been working at Pip for months, earning the company's trust. For all her snooping she had found no hint of the boss's whereabouts. In addition to the under-cover stuff of going to school and pretending to be ordinary, Tiago hadn't been idle: he had been train-ing Linette in ways of combatting magical attacks, preparing her for the day when she would be able to use magic as a member of the Round Table. He judged that she was ready. Only problem was that they were missing the key link in the chain. Merlin. He wasn't going to slip away again. Earth had run out of time. As humans lost the Fey power to invent and imagine, they were increasingly unable to cope with their own world. Piles of unwanted technology appeared outside houses: DVD players, computers, TVs, washing machines, all discarded as too compli-cated to understand. When things broke down, few knew how to fix them, leading to long delays at air-ports, hospitals and in shops. They had begun the slow slide that would take human civilization back to cave-dwelling.

Tiago rang Linette.

'Hey, *amiga*, Thunderbirds are go!'

'What?' She sounded sleepy, fumbling her phone.

'Didn't you watch that programme? That was one of the ones we were allowed in Dark Lore training camp. For a while I thought humans really did have strings.'

'Tiago, what are you going on about?'

'Merlin's back.'

That woke her up. 'When—where?'

'Today. Get dressed. I'll tell Natalia. He must have kept his return very quiet if even she didn't know.'

Tiago hopped his way into some fresh clothes, booting Bob out of his basket. Tiago and Linette had been waiting so long for something to break—either Merlin's return or news of the quest for Arthur—that Tiago had begun to wonder if he would be an old man by the time Rick and Roxy came back from their mission in Avalon. He had calculated that only a week had passed there since they split up into separate teams but that meant two years for him on Earth. He was now more or less the same age as Rick was when he left and much older than Roxy. Bizarre. More than once he had been tempted to recreate the doorway to Avalon to go look for them but only the knowledge that, first, he would end up in the western ocean, and secondly, that he was expected to be on the spot to catch Merlin, had stopped him.

'Natalia—Merlin's returned!' Tiago's shouts were echoed by Bob's barking.

'He has?' She hurried from her bedroom wrapping a black silk kimono around her waist.

'Yep. Golden Gate Park this lunchtime.'

'So he wasn't a prisoner.' Natalia ran her fingers through her hair, combing out the night-time tangles.

'Seems not. He's got some super-duper new invention to announce. He says it's so simple and clever everyone will be able to use the technology—not like the stuff they've been throwing out. The press are going bananas—seems this is his pattern: disappear and pop up with some great new idea.'

She pulled open the curtains to let the light stream in. 'Come on, we need a plan to capture him.'

Tiago did a little tap dance in the kitchen, juggling the lemons from the fruit bowl.

'I said we need a plan.' Natalia shook her head as she put on the coffee-maker.

'This is me thinking.' Movement always helped him puzzle his way through problems and had the side benefit of working off some of his nervous energy. He didn't know what it was like for humans to think, but for him it felt like he was in the middle of a snowstorm of ideas, each one crystal-perfect and individual, waiting to be noticed under the microscope of his attention. 'OK, we have to make him listen. So how?'

'We just need to make Merlin stick in one spot for a few minutes so we can lay out the facts without him calling in his bodyguards to run us off.'

Tiago's brain cleared; one flake chosen. He snapped his fingers. 'Stick, did you say?'

'Yes. He's like a cloud—try to keep him in one place and he drifts off through your fingers.' Natalia poured a cup of tar-thick espresso.

'I've got just the spell. You can be the bait and Linette and I can be the net.' He quickly thought through what he knew of the Academy of Sciences building. Apart from some really cool animal habitats for real penguins, rainforest creatures and sea life, it also had a less-visited green roof with hobbit-like domes. Merlin wouldn't be able to disappear from there before Tiago had had a chance to use his favourite glue charm. But then again, Merlin was a top wizard and Tiago not even an apprentice. He was gifted at trickster charms but this was playing way out of his league. Tiago frowned down at Bob. 'This had better work, *amigo*. I guess if we lose him again, we'll have lost our chance for good.'

Mr Ambrosius' big announcement took place in the planetarium in the Academy of Sciences, a sky-at-night film replaced by some of the wizard's pyrotechnics to impress the reporters. Natalia was able to sneak in the back by showing her Pip employee badge while Tiago and Linette set up their ambush on the roof. They had left Bob and

Gordon at the far end of the museum, happily admiring the penguins in their special glass pool.

'What do you think he's doing down there?' asked Linette. They had found a corner of the roof out of sight of the main entrance. Tiago was busy spreading his glue charm while Linette gazed at the view across the parklands with its Chinese pagoda, bandstand and monuments peeping out over the tops of the mature trees. There were some sour notes: broken-down cars had been left to rust in the car park, no one able to fix them; the museum had a pile of defunct aquariums stacked out back for the same reason. Otherwise, it was a peaceful view: people clustered around the stage where a free concert was in progress; a large group practised ballroom dancing under the pines, inviting novices to have a go; kids cycled; dads threw footballs; mums practised yoga. It looked like a tourist poster for all the reasons why you should find time to visit the city.

'I think the choice of venue was the hint—planets and all that stuff. Maybe he's worked out how to harness the lunar power.'

'I'd get more excited if I knew what that meant,' Linette said wryly. 'Mr Ambrosius is not very heroic. I mean, running at the first hint that we needed his help?'

The charm pattern was completed and disguised. Tiago checked it over—he couldn't afford to mess up with even a wisp of stray magic. 'I don't remember any of the legends saying he was a hero. Wily, cunning and clever—yes; brave, selfless and ready to take on all comers, no.' Tiago cocked his head, straining his ears. 'I think I can hear them. Let's get out of sight.'

They ducked behind the cube housing of an air vent.

'Mr Ambrosius, your ideas are revolutionary.' Natalia was laying it on a bit too thick but Merlin didn't seem to mind. 'I'm speechless. It's a big day for you—thanks for sparing the time.' Their footsteps came closer.

'No need to thank me. I've heard very good things about your work—a game based on the inventor Daedalus, inspired! You are bucking the trend: all my other workers are short of ideas these days.'

Tiago wanted to peep round the corner but he daren't risk it. He could hear the slap-slap of flip-flops. Mr Ambrosius had observed his usual dress code for his announcement.

'I love this view,' Natalia said airily, moving to the roof edge. That was the signal. Tiago activated the charm. 'So, here's my design for the second part of the game.'

'Thank you, Natalia.' Pause. 'What's this? Am I reading this right? *Please, we need your help. Oberon will wipe out humanity if you do not help us SET UP A ROUND TABLE!'*

Tiago and Linette emerged from their hiding place. Natalia had her hand on Merlin's elbow. The wizard had changed little in his time away; he was even wearing the same T-shirt that Linette so disliked.

The wizard shook Natalia off. 'Not you lot! You're insane—all of you. Just leave me alone!' Merlin slipped out of his flip-flops when he realized they were stuck, only to get his bare feet trapped—even better than Tiago had imagined. Ten toes wriggled in the magical glue.

'Please, Mr Ambrosius, please listen,' begged Linette. 'We've waited almost a year for you to spare us five minutes—surely you can do that?'

'No way, José! Fey matters are poison—touch them and you die. What kind of charm is this?' He tried a severing spell but the magic got stuck to Tiago's extra-strength adhesive. Tiago couldn't help feeling a little pleased to have outwitted a world-famous magician—if only briefly. Merlin would soon work out a dissolving charm was the one he needed.

Natalia was not to be cowed. 'But you can't pretend the storm isn't coming by hiding under the flimsy pretence that all is well and normal. Look at the technology being thrown out, the dumbing down of the human brain! Avalon is suffering too.

Earth is about to get invaded—you have to help these young warriors defend it from the Fey.'

Merlin had cottoned on to the correct spell and had his left foot free. He was now pulling on his right, his sunglasses knocked askew in his effort. A hint of light grey scared eyes peeked over the rim.

'What d'ya take me for? A sucker? Helping you is a death sentence. Nimue taught me my lesson. Fool me once—shame on you; fool me twice—shame on me.'

'Just because one Fey trapped you in the roots of a hawthorn tree for decades does not mean that we're going to do the same!' exclaimed Natalia.

On the other hand, thought Tiago quickly, a knock-out sleep spell like the Fey enchantress had used might just be the ticket to buying them more time.

'I'm sure your arguments are all very strong, blah-blah-blah. Everyone always thinks they know best, but I'm outta here.' Merlin's right foot was free. 'Don't approach me again or I will turn my magic against you—and it won't be as harmless as these childish spells you've used on me.'

Tiago loaded his palm with the sleep spell. He stepped forward to take the heat from Natalia. 'OK, Mr Ambrosius, sir. You've convinced me.'

'What?' Merlin had the wind taken from his sails by Tiago's easy admission of defeat.

'We'll forget about you and go try save Earth ourselves.'

'Tiago, we can't!' protested Linette. She had placed her chair between the rail and the door to the stairs to make Merlin's exit more difficult.

Tiago couldn't risk tipping her a wink. 'Yeah, you've been more than reasonable not blasting us to annihilation for our cheek. I mean, you—the greatest inventor the Earth has ever seen; us—mere lowly soldiers trying to save the world in which you make your fortune.'

Merlin's brow wrinkled. He hesitated. 'I'm glad you see it that way.'

'So long, Mr Ambrosius. Nice knowing you.' He offered his palm for a shake. One touch and the wizard crumpled like a felled tree, falling face forward, his sunglasses skittering over the edge of the roof and tumbling out of sight.

'Oops, should've done a cushioning charm,' said Tiago, not feeling the least bit sorry that Merlin now had a bruised forehead and nosebleed. The coward deserved them for refusing to help.

Linette passed Natalia a tissue to mop up the blood. 'Now what do we do with him?'

'Take him somewhere where he has to listen to us. I still think he's in "run" mode and not seeing the full picture. *Amiga*, do you mind an extra passenger on your chair?

'No problem.'

It was fortunate that Merlin was a small man. Natalia and Tiago picked him up and put him on Linette's lap.

'Is that OK?' asked Tiago.

'He's a bit heavy, but I can cope until we get out. Are you going to disguise us somehow?'

'Uh-huh. I'll make you look like an old lady wrapped in a blanket. Keep his dangly limbs in the spell zone; don't want a pair of disembodied feet peeking out of the glamour and giving the humans a shock.'

Natalia took over pushing Linette's chair. 'Did you notice his eyes? He's part Mage.'

'Malduc once told Rick and me that he thought Merlin was half Fey so I guess that makes sense. Merlin's brain works in the same way: tricks, inventions, cunning. It also explains why he's lived so long.' Tiago blew his dog-whistle to summon Bob and Gordon. 'Any idea where we can take one very angry wizard so he has to listen to us?' Tiago was beginning to wonder if his impulse to knock out Merlin had been a good one. It was like taking a beehive prisoner and then not knowing what to do with it.

Linette shifted Merlin's head so his neck was supported. He looked ridiculous, like an enormous baby lying across her lap. 'We need a place that he can't escape.' Merlin let out a loud snore. 'And I've just had a totally fabulous idea!'

Tiago saw it the same moment she did. 'Do you mean "Where can we find a prison that managed to keep hold of the most dangerous men in America with few or no breakouts?"' He grinned. 'Alcatraz Island. San Francisco Bay.'

Alcatraz had been built on an isolated island in the fast tidal waters of the bay, tantalizingly in sight of the city and the Golden Gate Bridge, but it was a place where escape meant drowning. The ultimate prison, the buildings occupied almost the entire surface, a modern take on the medieval castle keep. The shuttle boat that had brought them over to the island earlier in the day departed, taking the Alcatraz guides with them as the museum closed for the night. The prison fell silent, the thud of feet on the metal walkways stilled after hours of tour parties passing through. The birds were almost the only occupants of the rocky promontories: seagulls dining on the scraps left behind by visitors, bickering like rioting inmates; cormorants with a flash of police blue on their throats patrolling the bay.

Tiago, Linette, Natalia and the dogs emerged from their hiding place in the old prison mortuary, a tiny, half-collapsed building that visitors were not allowed to enter, unless they had magic, of course. They'd left a sleeping Merlin stretched out on the mortician's table among the rubble, a fact that Tiago feared might just go on the list of 'Things I'm going to punish Tiago for' being compiled by their dreamer.

'OK, where shall we wake him up?' he asked.

'I'm expecting him to behave badly to start with,' said Natalia, 'so my vote is for a cell.'

Linette pushed her chair up the slope to a fire exit. 'I think this goes into the main cellblock.'

A tendril of mist curled round the lighthouse at the city-facing end of the small island. Tiago shivered. The temperature was dropping rapidly as the Pacific sent another bank of fog their way. It billowed in, eating up the lights on the Golden Gate Bridge. 'I'll float him there on the table. Natalia, can you break in?'

She nodded and opened her mouth to make a comment.

'Don't say it,' said Tiago with a quick grin.

Linette said it for her instead. 'You don't want us to say that "I bet we're the first people to try breaking in to Alcatraz?"'

'Don't you just love life's little ironies?' said Natalia, forming a key out of shimmering magic and slotting it in the lock.

Tiago conducted the floating table so it moved like a magic carpet—a charm he'd picked up from Rick. It looked well past odd to see Merlin surfing along with his hands on his chest like a tomb effigy.

Linette rubbed her arms. 'This place gives me the creeps.' She bumped her chair over the doorsill and into the long corridor between the two-storey row of cellblocks. It looked like everyone's image of a prison: small rooms, three sides solid walls, one of bars, arranged like stacked boxes. It was impossible to see out of the high windows.

Bob whined.

'Yeah, barbaric isn't it?' murmured Tiago. 'They're basically cages for humans judged too dangerous to mix with each other.' He floated Merlin into the nearest cell while Natalia closed the bars. 'I promise we won't trap him for long.'

Bob hid his head under his paws, rump in the air. Gordon had disappeared, anticipating wizardly fireworks.

'OK, everyone ready for me to wake him up?' asked Tiago.

Natalia and Linette ducked behind the end of the row of cells, like demolition experts getting out of range of their own dynamite.

'Go for it,' said Linette, giving him a thumbs up.

Tiago planned his escape: he had to touch Merlin to remove the spell. Then he would roll out of range and into the cell next door. There he'd be close enough to talk to him but a brick wall would separate them.

Unless Merlin knew how to curve elf-shot spells.

Tiago had a sneaking suspicion that was the very least of the wizard's retaliatory magic.

'OK. One—two—three!' He removed the sleep charm.

Chapter 6

COLD fury was Merlin's response. With a white flash of power, he simply melted the bars and walked out.

'No!' Tiago rushed to his own cell door and found it had been locked. He shot magic at the catch but he couldn't counteract it. Tiago realized that he had been lulled into underestimating Merlin because of the jeans-and-flip-flops image, but this wizard had once been the mentor of the most famous warriors in human history. Just because he had taken a different route in the twenty-first century it did not mean he had forgotten how to use his power.

Merlin stood at the bars and looked in, a satisfied smile tugging the corners of his mouth. Tiago had

nowhere to hide as the cell was barely furnished—
just a concrete bed. 'Not very funny being on the
other end of that kind of spell, is it? Thanks for the
lesson in not letting down my guard. I learnt that
first sixteen hundred years ago but, hey, it's always
useful to have a refresher course.' He turned his
back and walked away, like a cowboy coming out
on top in a shoot-out.

'Wait! You can't leave me here!' called Tiago. He
gripped the bars, straining to see the corner where
he had left his friends.

'Oh but I can. Have fun explaining your presence to the authorities when they arrest you
tomorrow for trespass. *Hasta la vista.*'

'Don't you touch the others!' Tiago felt his voice
choke: their one chance to survive was just striding off.

'I don't go to war with women, children and
dogs. You're lucky.' Merlin had reached the fire
exit. He opened it with a wave of a finger. How
had Tiago thought even for a second he could
outwit him? Fog rippled in, lapping at Merlin's
ankles. A faint howl reached Tiago's ears. It
sounded like . . . like wolves. Tiago sniffed the air;
there was a taint on the breeze, a smell of stagnant
water and rotting flesh. Goosebumps stippled his
skin. He had caught a whiff of something like that
before, when he strayed into the tunnels below

Dark Lore training camp. His curiosity had almost ended with him being supper for Oberon's pack of hobgoblins.

Merlin slammed the doors closed, sketching a sign that produced a magical shield charm over the entrance. It hung across the double doors like a golden net. 'You fools! What have you done?' His voice crackled with anger.

Tiago's cell sprang open. He ran to his friends and found them curled up asleep together in a heap like a litter of mismatched puppies. Merlin clicked his fingers and they woke up. Bob backed away, growling.

The wizard pointed at Natalia. 'Explain: why has Oberon sent a pack of hobs to San Francisco? How does he know we are here?'

Natalia rose elegantly to her feet, managing to look unruffled despite being on the losing end of his spellwork. 'I don't know, but maybe now you'll listen to us?'

'If you tipped him off to where I'm living just to get my attention, then, sister, as they say these days: you've screwed up big-time.' The logo on Merlin's T-shirt began to glow, his fury making the words spark: *Everything I do is magic.* 'I live in San Francisco because there is no land connection on the other side—just sea. It's supposed to be safe. How does Oberon know I am here?' He turned his glare on Linette, who shrank back in her chair.

Tiago wasn't having him bullying her. 'Hey, dude, it was my fault, OK? We had a stray nix and sent him back—we had no choice. Oberon must have joined the dots—he's not stupid. But don't you see that he would have found you eventually?'

'No, I don't see that, *dude*,' Merlin replied sarcastically, ignoring Gordon who was butting him in the back to get his attention. The Gabriel hound wanted someone to do something about the approaching hobs and had decided Merlin was his best bet. 'No one has hassled me for centuries.'

'Yeah, but now magic's running out in Avalon. My money is on Oberon opting to invade Earth to get his hands on the green energy supply.'

Merlin's eyes glinted. He was listening despite himself.

'If he wins, it's no more digital age; no more human civilization; no more Pip Enterprises,' Tiago concluded. 'Already your market is shrinking as humans lose their ability to work technology.'

Linette moved her chair to Merlin's side. 'Our friends have gone to Avalon to fetch Arthur but we need you too. We need a Round Table to stand any chance in a battle with Oberon's forces. I have no magic and my friends say theirs isn't strong enough as it is.'

Merlin rubbed the back of his neck. All of them could feel the tingle of tainted magic like the taste of blood in the mouth. The hobs were coming closer.

Natalia hushed Bob, who was growling and worrying Tiago's trouser bottoms. 'I'm sorry to rush everyone but I think we need to deal with the hobs before we do anything else. What defences can we use against them?'

'OK, people, face facts: I'm no hero.' A howl cut through Merlin's words, scraping on the nerves like the squeal of metal on metal. 'Let's just get off this island alive and leave it there, agreed?'

Not OK, thought Tiago fiercely.

Merlin hastily shook out a plan of the island from the stack of tourist brochures, his finger tracing a perimeter. A glow appeared on the map, which disappeared and reappeared outside. 'There—that should slow the hobs.' Beckoning everyone to follow him, he headed through the prison to the warden's house at the end of the island facing the city, near the lighthouse.

'But you can turn them away with magic?' Linette asked.

'It ain't that easy, girlfriend,' Merlin drawled. 'They have their own magic. Even though I've set up a magical barrier, they'll be able to burrow through with time. You may take out a dozen but there are always more who follow on. We need hundreds of us to mount a resistance and we would have to be prepared to make a few sacrifices even so.'

'He means some of us will die,' glossed Tiago.

'Yeah.' Merlin turned in the direction of the city. 'So I vote we give up on the idea of making a stand here, where we are so easily cornered.'

'Then what do you suggest?' asked Linette.

'We run.'

Linette wheeled herself to the foot of the lighthouse near the derelict warden's house. The lights of San Francisco were lost in the mist; the beam of the lantern above strafed the darkness but it was absorbed by the fog, rather than illuminating it. They were alone—a tiny island surrounded by hobs.

'How will they get here?' she asked.

'By water. They don't fly.' Merlin seemed to be considering something, leaning back and surveying the top of the tower.

'Gordon flies.' Linette scratched the back of the Gabriel hound's neck. 'We should let him go. No need for him to stay for this.'

Tiago was leaning over the parapet on the eastern side. It overlooked the little harbour, the only landing to the island. 'I can see some boats approaching. A lot of boats.'

Linette moved to join him. Her human eyes weren't able to make much out in the fog—just some faint lights. 'Maybe it's one of those Alcatraz-by-night tours?' She didn't really hold much hope that her guess was correct.

'Not unless the tour guides are ogres. I can hear them from here. They must have hijacked all the shuttle boats.'

Linette turned back to see Merlin leaning over Gordon and whispering something in his ear.

'Got that?'

Gordon woofed.

'What's going on?' Linette asked.

'We're escaping from Alcatraz—always wanted to have a crack at it. I've a plan but it depends on our friend here. With this fog I can't see my way to the shore, but he can fly there. Go on, off you go. Quick as you can.' He gave Gordon a seagull feather to hold.

Gordon licked Linette's hand in farewell, took a shambling run, then strode off into the air, ears flapping, tongue lolling from the side of his mouth. His movements were as ungainly in the sky as on land until he picked up enough speed to soar.

'Way to go, Gordon!' whispered Linette. Her heart leapt with pride: she had never seen him fly properly before.

'The boats have moored!' called Tiago. 'They're coming!'

'Don't worry, my perimeter will hold for a while yet. Dr Ventikos, check no one is landing on the western side.'

'Yes, boss.' Natalia went to keep watch on the steep cliffs on the other shore of the island.

'But what's Gordon doing?' Linette hated feeling like a passenger in the crisis. She wanted to do something to help but the three half-Fey had everything covered between them.

'We can't escape them by water so we are going by air. Gordon has taken my beacon and will fix it to the tower on Telegraph Hill. That will show me where to send us all when we slide out of here.'

'Slide?'

Merlin cracked his knuckles. 'A magical connection like a zip wire.'

Linette gaped. 'Are you mad? I don't know if you've noticed, but I'm in a wheelchair.'

'And when has that ever stopped you?' He really wasn't giving her his full attention, too busy setting up the spell needed to make the link to the land. 'All that's required is a few adjustments to the harness and you'll be fine.'

A flash from the magical barrier warned them that the hobs were attacking the perimeter defences. Their cries carried on the wind, chilling her blood.

'Couldn't you just fly us there? Tiago does a spell like that.'

He frowned. 'How much magic do you think I have? I'm keeping the barrier up, making a cable link and you want me to fly all of you across? I could do it, of course, but it would be slower and, besides, where's the fun in doing something so predictable? And I imagine the ogres have archers posted. We need to move fast. No, the zip wire is better. Ah, that's the signal. Your dog has landed.'

Linette had no idea what he'd heard or sensed but somehow he knew his beacon was fixed in place.

'You, boy, you go first.'

'The name's Tiago.' Tiago rushed past them both.

'Yes, yes, get up there and go! I'm counting on you to catch this girl at the other end if she can't stop.'

'This girl is called Linette,' she muttered.

Tiago used his glue charm to scale the side of the tower. 'Carry Bob for me, Linette?' he called.

'Of course!'

Bob jumped on her lap. He was shivering, sensing the approach of a predator who would think nothing of chewing on his bones. The next thing she heard was a whistling sound and she knew Tiago was gone.

'You next.' Merlin tapped the seat and back of

her chair. 'You won't have much control—in fact it's best not to interfere. Your friend will get you down at the other side.'

'Merlin, we've got visitors on the western approach!' called Natalia.

'Running out of time here, peeps. Go!'

This last order was aimed at Linette. Her chair wobbled into the air, swinging on its magical hoist. She and Bob were lifted to the top of the tower and then changed direction. With a push from behind, they began to scud across the gap between island and shore. The two points were on more or less the same height so it was a level journey, magic giving the high-speed propulsion. Linette shrieked—she couldn't stop herself: no seatbelt and she was roaring across the waters of the bay surrounded by fog. It didn't help that Bob had his nose buried in her armpit. He wasn't convinced Merlin knew what he was doing either.

A white tower loomed out of the fog directly ahead: the top of Telegraph Hill.

'Ti-a-go!' screamed Linette.

At the last moment, she spotted him clinging to the side. He screwed up his face in concentration. Her chair slowed and hit the wall with a soft bounce. She managed—just—to keep hold of Bob.

'Now, that's a cushioning charm,' Tiago said with a grin when he saw she was safe.

'Oh lord.' She hugged the terrier, both of them shaking.

'Hang on: I'll just get you down.' Tiago waved his hand at the harness of magical strands Merlin had woven. They stretched and gently let her down to the ground.

'Never again,' vowed Linette.

Gordon sniffed her apologetically.

Tiago leapt down beside her. 'Stick with us and I fear it's very likely.'

Natalia landed, then Merlin. The wizard reeled in the threads he had used to span the gap between island and shore, an undoing spell summoning his magic back to him.

'That's such an awesome spell.' Tiago watched the wizard closely. 'I've always had to transform objects to make connections like that; he just does it with power. I wonder how that works?'

'No time to teach you today.' Merlin took over Linette's chair and began jogging down the hill, pushing her in front of him. 'The hobs know we've gone and they'll be after us. We need to get out of the city.'

'And go where?' Linette twisted in her seat to check if the others were following.

'We'll go across the Golden Gate Bridge and into Marin County. It's right on the San Andreas Fault, which is one of the hottest green power spots in

America. We'll recharge our magic there and work out what to do next.'

Tiago caught up with Linette. Their eyes met. Merlin was still thinking this was just about evading Oberon temporarily. Now they had to persuade their reluctant recruit to come fully over to their side.

Chapter 7

AT the bottom of Telegraph Hill, among the close-packed, expensive town houses and tiny driveways occupied by huge American automobiles and defunct machinery, Merlin stopped Linette's chair. Tiago and Natalia halted either side. The chilly fog had driven most people inside but there were still streams of cars driving the roller-coaster roads. San Francisco looked like a city riding on a frozen tsunami.

In the distance a pack of hobs howled.

'Blast him to Jupiter—it seems that Oberon has sent another division. We need transport.' Merlin tried flagging down a taxi but it revved away when it saw the two dogs.

'Where have they all come from?' asked Linette.

Merlin touched the bump on his head, gained when Tiago had sent him to sleep. He frowned, clearly remembering how much he held against them.

'I think Oberon must have sent them cross-country,' said Tiago quickly before the thought became action. 'I guess from out of the nearest land connection to Avalon.'

'We need to get over the bridge before the hobs work out which way we have gone,' said Natalia. She tried opening a parked car by magic but only succeeded in setting off the alarm.

The fog shifted, a theatre gauze curtain rising on the next act. The Fey King was doing his utmost to make it difficult for his quarry to hide from his hunting packs.

'How about one of them?' Linette pointed at a green cable car as it trundled by on its track. It looked to Tiago like a shoebox running on tram-lines—and about as fast as a snail.

'That'll do.' Merlin set off in pursuit of the cable car as it rattled its way along the street. The wizard sprinted at quite a rate, considering he was sixteen centuries old. Tiago and the dogs only just beat him to the stop. Tiago got in at the front and slapped a sleep charm on the driver. Fortunately the cable car was near its terminus so the driver was the only person they had to abandon on the pavement.

Natalia and Linette caught up with them.

'I drove something like this during the war,' Natalia announced. 'In London during the Blitz. That was a tram but the principle is the same.'

'OK, you be the gripman.' Merlin threw her the cap he'd stolen off the sleeping driver. 'I'll be the brakeman. These things work on cables towing them along underground. You'll need me to slow you down on the steep parts. All aboard.'

Tiago and Merlin lifted Linette into the cabin as the dogs jumped onto the open seats at the rear. These faced sideways so the dogs took up position barking warnings at anyone who tried to board. Natalia settled in the driving seat.

'Mind the doors!' she called, pulling a lever to set them off down Mason Street.

'We're going the wrong way!' called Linette. 'I thought we were heading for the bridge.'

'Look west,' Natalia said tersely, her concentration on the controls. The illuminated curving run of Lombard Street some ten blocks away came into sight at the far end of an avenue. Normally the view was of cars making their way slowly down the chicane in single file between the thickly planted flowerbeds, but now all that could be seen was a stream of grey backs bobbing up and down like swarming rats. These had to be the hobs following their scent and heading right for them.

'Just how many of them are there?' asked Linette. Her voice shook but Tiago could hear she was trying to keep her head, even though San Francisco had gone Fey-crazy.

'Hundreds—thousands maybe.' Merlin tapped the brake stem, sending a flash of magic down to the cable buried in the road. The car picked up speed—a lot of speed. The shops and houses now whisked by, the breeze making Gordon's ears flutter. 'I did say that the problem with them was numbers, not the individuals. Oberon will be trying to overwhelm us. Ring the bell, Dr Ventikos.'

The cable car was disobeying all rules of the road going at this furious pace. As it rattled through the junctions, vehicles were driven up onto the pavement or into each other to avoid colliding with it. A delivery van ran up against a fire hydrant, releasing a fountain of water into the air. Police sirens joined the howls.

'Won't that cause another time collapse?' Linette clung on as the cable car bounced over a set of points.

'If they stay for any length of time, yes. He's playing a high-stakes game.' Merlin sent a propulsion spell to knock out of their path a couple of Chinese students who had stopped to take photos, unaware of the danger they were in. He zapped the students through the doors of the nearest house and sealed the entrance. 'Get undercover everyone!' he yelled, magically magnifying his voice.

Tiago hung off the back, keeping a watch on the eastern approaches. 'I see more coming from the waterside. The hobs from Alcatraz must've landed.'

Natalia wiped a bead of sweat from her brow; it was unusual to see the elegant doctor ruffled by anything. Not a good sign.

'A pincer attack, funnelling us north to the water's edge,' she concluded. 'They know we have to stop when we reach Fisherman's Wharf. Get out of the way!' she shouted at a bus that was too slow across the track. Linette shrieked, Bob yelped, but they missed it by a whisker.

'Where now?' asked Tiago.

'We need to get somewhere they can't reach us or smell us.' Merlin pulled on the brake, bringing the cable car to a halt at the bottom of the hill among the white-painted wharves and restaurants. They all got out. A steel sculpture of a crab danced with blue banner fluttering, greeting visitors to the waterfront. That welcome was about to turn very ugly indeed.

The wonderful odour of baking bread hit them: homely and sweet, so out of place with the sick horror of being hounded across the city like this. They had abandoned the cable car right on the doorstep of the famous Boudin's bakery, whose ovens kept going all night. Maybe the yeasty scent would confuse the trackers?

'Can we hide in there?' Tiago asked urgently.

Merlin understood what he meant. 'The smell wouldn't fool them for long. They have amazing tracking abilities.'

'Where can we go where they won't find us?'

Merlin pivoted on the spot, seeking inspiration. 'I've got it!' He jogged towards the docks.

Linette was the first to start after the wizard; her back and hands had to be hurting with all this pushing her wheels along at high speed. Tiago came to help her.

'I wish he would just stop . . . and explain sometimes,' she complained to Tiago. 'This following him blind is getting old.'

'Everyone, inside!' boomed Merlin, firing spells to force anyone he saw off the street. People scattered, diving for the nearest cover.

Merlin led his party to the USS Pampanito, a World War Two submarine now moored as a tourist attraction on the quayside. Like a huge grey metal boot the length of a basketball court, it bobbed on the bay, going nowhere in its retirement. That didn't deter Merlin: he blasted through the mesh fence blocking the gangway and hurried aboard.

'Come on, people!' he called.

They had no choice. From the screams and cries coming from behind them, the first wave of hobs had arrived. Tiago prayed Oberon had ordered that they hunt only their quarry but there was no time to stop and help anyone.

'Get in!' Merlin ordered, taking guard position at the top of the gangway.

Tiago used his magic to float Linette's chair in through the heavy watertight hatch and down into the equally grey cylindrical corridor beneath. He parked her chair in a corner of the control room, a chamber not much bigger than a jumbo jet cockpit, and immediately began to study the dials. His brain was good with engineering problems and he quickly gained a sense of the pattern behind them.

'There are loads of buttons.' Linette put her hand on a vital switch that would be a disaster to flick on prematurely.

'Linette, don't!'

She withdrew her hand quickly. 'How can you work out which one to turn? To me, the handles and gauges all look equally important.'

'You deal with that one.' Tiago drew her attention to a lever that had only three commands on it: 'start', 'run' and 'stop'.

'OK, I understand that.'

Bob and Gordon came to sit at her side. Tiago

gave Bob a wink, instructing him to stop Linette touching anything she shouldn't. Bob was also very technically minded. He jumped on her knee, alert to the danger. Merlin and Natalia came in, slamming the hatch closed. The two adults made a strangely harmonious team, Tiago noticed.

'We've cut free,' announced Merlin. 'I've boosted the engines with some of my power. I don't have much to spare—just enough to run this submarine out into the bay and dive. We'll sit there and wait for the hobs to give up once they realize they've lost our scent.' Merlin unfolded the periscope. 'Start her up.'

Tiago span two wheels on his side of the control room; at Bob's nudge, Linette moved her lever to the start position. The engines rumbled into life. Vibrations rattled through the hull.

'Ease her out; nice and smoothly does it. Mind the end of the pier.'

A crunching sound suggested that manoeuvre had not been successful.

Merlin winced.

'Who's steering this thing?' Linette asked.

No one answered.

'That explains it. Where's the wheel?' Merlin now noticed the white steering column near his periscope. 'Oops, my bad. Full speed ahead, me hearties.'

Able to relax now they were relatively safe, Tiago chuckled. 'Aye, aye, captain.'

'We're safe now?' asked Linette. Looking at her in the lights of the control room, Tiago noticed that his human friend was looking pale and close to exhaustion.

'Yes, for now,' he told her. 'We've made a brilliant get-away.'

'Don't tell me you two are enjoying this?' Linette asked. 'You can't be.'

'Mage blood,' Merlin and Tiago said together, then looked at each other in surprise that they had been thinking the same thing. Merlin glanced away first; Tiago hoped he was embarrassed now that he had been all too happy to abandon his fellow half-mage to his doom without a hearing.

'Yeah, insane risks are part of our inheritance,' Tiago continued, filling the awkward silence.

Merlin swung the periscope and checked their wake. 'I wish I could film the hobs sniffing for us on the quayside only to find we've vanished.'

'I'm sure someone is uploading it to YouTube as we speak,' muttered Linette darkly.

'Oh no, they won't. Magical creatures like hobs don't register on human digital cameras—I made sure of that when I invented the Pip chip.'

'But the witnesses? Your spells?'

'No one will believe them. I think they'll blame

it on mass hallucinations brought on by pollution of the water supply, or a huge hoax by Berkeley students. I'll get my guys onto spreading rumours tomorrow—if we survive that long. Tiago, take us down. We'll wait at the bottom of the bay under the Golden Gate Bridge. I'll do the first watch with you; ladies, you take the second.'

As simple as that, they were nominated part of Merlin's crew of submariners.

Chapter 8

KNOWING that they were unlikely to have any peace in the next few days and should snatch the opportunity to rest, Linette and Natalia went in search of some berths further down the thin cigar-shaped hull. The cabin they chose was little more than a shelf bunk-bed with lockers underneath. There was no food or water but the crew quarters were fully supplied with mattresses and sheets, part of the exhibition about life as a World War Two sailor. Natalia hefted out the manikin of a sailor and dumped it in the corner.

'Our need is greater than his,' she said firmly.

The oily smell and the vibration of the engines had a numbing effect on Linette's senses. She tried not to think about the weight of water overhead and the fact that the submarine had been pensioned off many years ago.

Once she had transferred from her chair to lie down on the bunk, Linette patted the wall. It sounded pretty sturdy.

'Do you think she's still seaworthy?'

'I hope so.' Natalia climbed in the bunk above.

She couldn't do anything about it if the submarine wasn't—other than trust her magical companions to get her out. 'My parents will be going nuts about my disappearance.' She sipped from her bottle of water, which she kept in her backpack attached to her chair. She offered it up to Natalia, who waved it away.

'I texted your mother back at Alcatraz while we were waiting for it to close. I thought we might be caught up for a while.'

'Caught up' was one way of describing the madness of the last few hours. 'What did you say? *Hey, trapped ourselves a wizard and won't be back for dinner?*'

'Funnily enough, no. I told her we were going on an educational trip with my students and that I'd look after you.' The bunk creaked as Natalia turned over. 'I will make sure you come out of this OK, I promise.'

'Yes, I know—if it's possible, you will.' Linette fiddled with the owl bracelet, wondering if Natalia could defend her from all the perils Oberon was throwing in their path. 'I can't think how this is going to end though, can you?'

Tiago realized this was the first quiet moment he had had with Merlin since they'd met. They weren't running for their lives, Merlin wasn't running from them, and there were no big security guards to frogmarch Tiago away. He stole glances across the control room. Granted, Merlin's parentage did not include Aztec as Tiago's did, but still it was freaky to think that in sixteen hundred years he would still be fairly fit and healthy thanks to his Mage blood.

'What's wrong?' Merlin rubbed his cheek. 'Don't tell me I've got dirt on my face?'

'No. I was just thinking. You're the first person like me that I've met. You aren't as old as I expected.'

Merlin snorted as he adjusted the steering. 'I'm not as old as you think.'

'You, King Arthur and the Round Table were around in the fifth century. That makes you sixteen hundred at least.'

'No, I'm not. I sat out a few of the most horrible centuries in Avalon—Viking invasions, bubonic plague, religious persecutions, large parts of the eighteenth century when the fashions were just

104

too vile for men, and both world wars. I am about seven hundred years old. I spent the time tinkering in my private laboratory in an isolated part of Avalon. In fact the last fifty years are the most extended period of time I've spent here without any long breaks.'

That made sense; Tiago didn't think he would have liked to be around for Hitler and Hiroshima if he could have avoided them. 'Did you ever meet the old Mage king, Malduc? He was here in exile. Went by the name of Professor Marmaduke.'

'I knew about him. Steered well clear. I heard how he ran Avalon when he was in charge and I didn't think he would be sympathetic to part-humans like me.' Merlin checked the periscope. 'Bring her to full stop.'

Tiago moved the lever to cut the engines. 'He's my father.'

Merlin raised an eyebrow. 'You have my commiserations.'

'Yeah, well, I didn't know till a couple of years ago when we crossed paths in Oxford. Do you know who your father was?'

Merlin polished the brass work on the dial nearest him with the bottom of his T-shirt. 'My mother was the Mage Fey. She met my father, a druid priest, on a visit to this world and I was the result.'

Tiago's stomach rumbled, reminding him they'd missed quite a few meals. He dug out a tube of mints from his pocket. 'Is she still alive?' He offered Merlin a sweet. The wizard refused but both dogs accepted.

'My mother? No. She was killed defending me from my father's people.'

'They turned on you? That's really harsh.' Tiago so far had been lucky with the humans he had met.

'Those were dark days, Tiago. They thought I was evil—it didn't help that I gave off magic sparks as a baby—so they tried to kill me; my mother sacrificed herself in my place to give my father time to run away with me.' He lifted his sleeve to reveal a tattoo on his upper arm—a warrior woman with long black hair stood armed against all comers. 'I had this done in her memory in the South Seas a few centuries ago. She was a great person; I'm only sorry I was too young to help her fight them off.'

'I'm sorry you lost her.' Tiago couldn't imagine ever having a tattoo done of his own Mage parent. Malduc was very short on paternal loyalty, having once threatened to kill Bob. It was heartening to hear that one Mage had made a good parent.

'She taught me to make a stand even when it's difficult and dangerous. That's why I've kept going all these years, trying to lead humans into a less self-destructive path.'

'So why won't you help us?'

Merlin scowled. 'I have a mission—I can't abandon it or humans will struggle to see out this century with anything approaching civilization.'

'Yeah, I get that it's really important: they've got to change. Hopefully you can get back to that as soon as we've dealt with Oberon—but we do have to face him first.'

'That's a big thing to deal with, Tiago. Round Tables are no guarantee of success; you need the right people to sit around it. I'm not refusing to help because I am scared but because I think you are on the wrong track.'

Merlin switched the cabin to low-power mode so they were bathed in red light.

It must have been a lonely life, thought Tiago, hiding and dodging Fey attention for so long. Tiago had learned recently how important it was to be in a team with Rick, Roxy and Linette; once he would have understood Merlin but now he couldn't imagine making the same choice to go it alone. Merlin had once had allies. 'Even so, why did you never go and rescue Arthur? I thought you were friends.'

Merlin slumped forward, head hanging between his arms as they rested on the steering wheel. 'You don't understand. Arthur is safer where he is.'

'What do you mean?'

'There are two reasons. First, he doesn't know how much time has passed. He's lost his kingdom, his friends, his wife—what was there for me to bring him back to?' Merlin rubbed his chest as if his heart was hurting. 'Second, legend says he'll be needed one day. I know better than to mess with that kind of magical prediction. He's human, with a human life span: if I brought him back early just to keep me company, what if he died before the hour of need came? And how do I know when that moment has arrived? No, he was best left alone.'

Tiago hoped that Merlin was wrong, otherwise Rick and Roxy were heading into trouble for nothing. 'We think the moment's arrived. My friends have gone to get him.'

'So Linette said. I think it's a mistake. A big mistake.'

'You only don't want to have to explain why you left him in exile so long when you could've taken the risk and freed him.'

Merlin smiled wryly. 'Maybe you're right. He's not going to be happy when he sees me again.' He tapped a dial. 'Bit low on magical juice and we need to keep the engines ticking over for lights and air filtration. You got any to spare?'

Tiago pressed his fingers against his chest. His magic lodged there like a huge diamond ready to shoot a laser beam. 'Sure, but I don't know how to transfer it. What do I do?'

Merlin frowned. 'Don't you know what magic is?'

'Yeah, it's the product of Fey power mixed with the Earth's green energy.'

'Yes, that's how it is made but what it *is* . . . now that is a different question. How does it feel to you?'

'It's like . . . ' How did magic feel? It was limited. You drew on it, shaped it, spread it, but it was lighter than air, thinner than any substance he knew from Kemystery. 'I guess it's like electricity but electricity with body.'

Merlin nodded. 'Not bad. It's the fifth element—what the ancients called the quintessence—"quin" being the word for five. You can pour it from one vessel to another just as you can shape spells out of it. Fine filaments connect to your brain in a kind of elemental consciousness so it belongs to you and does what you want it to as long as there is enough of it to sustain the charm—that's why you can't just make up a spell to, say, disappear Everest: you don't have enough of the quintessence to do that.'

'OK, so I can fill up the tanks of the submarine if I concentrate and tell it to go?'

'Don't fill them up—we want you to save enough to fight off attacks. Just give the tanks a little extra. Here—this is the fuel indicator: run it through that.'

Tiago spread his hand over the dial and imagined his magic running down his arm and into the submarine fuel tanks—a bit like filling up a car at a petrol station.

Merlin tapped his shoulder. 'That should be enough, Tiago.'

He disengaged and saw that he had managed to lift the needle off the red. 'Cool. Thanks for the lesson. We weren't taught that at Dark Lore.'

'No, you wouldn't have been because ignorance keeps you prisoner better than walls.'

Taking their turn later, Linette and Natalia had a quiet watch. The biggest problem, after the little detail of being hounded by hobgoblins, was that they were all hungry and thirsty after a day spent at the bottom of the bay. Natalia had stocked up on some supplies at the cafe on Alcatraz but these were soon eaten and there had been nothing appropriate for Gordon and Bob. Merlin insisted they wait for nightfall.

'We can't bring her up during the daylight hours. The humans have noticed she's missing—'

'Ya think?' murmured Tiago, making Linette smile.

Merlin resettled the captain's cap he had stolen from the exhibition on his dark hair. The brass buttons on the jacket he had taken off a manikin gleamed in the red light. He made a very slovenly sailor.

'They believe she came adrift in some freak accident which, with the chaos on the waterfront last night, seems plausible. They've found her by sonar and are now planning how to retrieve her. They're just waiting for heavy-lifting equipment.'

'How do you know all this?' asked Linette. 'Magic?'

Merlin smiled. 'Actually, radio. That was one of my suggestions in the nineteenth century. Like it?'

Linette folded her arms. 'Is there anything you didn't invent—or suggest someone invented?'

Merlin wrinkled his brow in thought. 'I didn't invent the combustion engine—knew that would be a disaster. I do hold my hand up to the steam engine though, which started the whole mechanical power ball rolling. I should say, however, that I only ever nudged; the clever work was done by the humans.' He winked at Tiago. 'Mostly.'

He rubbed his hands then checked his wristwatch. 'OK, let's bring her to the surface. I'm planning to come up by the northern stanchion of the bridge. We'll climb—or float—up to the road from there. The hobs will catch our scent again as soon as we get into the open but I'm counting on

III

them being too far away to stop us escaping into the countryside.'

'Why can't you land us on the far side?' asked Natalia.

'No suitable harbour—it gets too shallow for us. And before you ask, I don't want to go back to Fisherman's Wharf—that'll be watched by Fey and humans. No, we should benefit from the element of surprise. We'll get on the bridge, borrow a vehicle and head for the fault so Tiago, Dr Ventikos and I can recharge.'

Tiago exchanged a glance with Linette. They wanted something more than just a pit stop; they needed a plan. 'Then what?'

'Then we'll try to lose Oberon again, I suppose.' Merlin scratched his nose.

'We're going to have to fight him,' said Tiago.

'So you say. I believe in hiding. It's worked for centuries.'

'Not this time.'

'We'll see.'

Yeah, Tiago thought, Merlin and humanity would see very soon that Oberon wasn't just going to look away.

The top of the submarine conning tower was concealed from the salvage vessels by a little glamour spell that made it look like another boat. After it broke the surface, Tiago cracked open the hatch. Water dripped down his arms but the air smelt good after hours of breathing the stale, processed stuff inside. He emerged to stand on the small deck area. The salvage team had floodlit an area of the bay more or less over where they had spent the day hiding. No one was paying attention to the two tide-washed supports of the Golden Gate Bridge. Tiago gave a soft whistle—the sign for all clear.

Natalia lifted Bob up, then floated Gordon and Linette through the gap. As captain, Merlin was last to leave the vessel. He closed the hatch with a fond pat.

'No hint of hobs?' the wizard asked the dogs.

Bob sniffed and went still.

'He can smell them but they aren't nearby,' explained Tiago.

'Then we'll make a run for it now.' Merlin shaded his eyes and gazed upwards. 'Magnificent, isn't it?'

And it was: a complex puzzle of sturdy red beams and delicate suspension wires linking the city to Marin County on the northern side of the bay, huge in scale now they were so close to the structure.

'I'll go up first,' offered Tiago, 'so I can be there to help Linette and the dogs land.'

'Be careful!' called Linette as he leapt to reach the first bar.

He swung up and gained his balance; he grinned back down at her. 'When am I not?'

'Do you really want me to answer that?'

He gave her a cheery wave and set off to the next level. He enjoyed scaling the beams after being inactive all day. Fully rested, it was just what he needed to shake off the fidgets. He was more cautious as he climbed over the rail onto the road. Even at night the bridge saw a steady stream of vehicles and it wouldn't do for a concerned driver to stop and see what he was doing. The skin on the back of his neck prickled but he rubbed it away, intent on getting the others up and off this bridge quickly.

Next up was Natalia. She managed with an experienced rock-climber's ease. Then came Linette and the dogs, lifted up on a neat spell of Merlin's that moved them as smoothly as an elevator. Finally the wizard clambered up, using a mixture of muscle and magical power.

Tiago began to relax: they'd done it—escaped the city and the hobs.

Linette was the first to notice that something was wrong. 'Where are the cars?'

'I dunno.' Tiago scratched his head. His hair was tingling, rising up like it had become charged with static electricity. She was right: the bridge was unnaturally quiet. 'There were plenty earlier—people fleeing the hob packs.'

Fog rolled towards them from the sea, a slow rubbing out of land and water. Stars winked out, one by one. Bob whined, yipping and snapping at nothing. Gordon dashed into the middle of the carriageway and barked at the empty road back to the city. Bob joined him, facing the other way, growling. Fog hid the shore so they were stranded in one little clear pocket in the middle of the bridge. The air smelt sour. All the sea birds had gone.

'Merlin!' The announcement cracked in the air like thunder. Tiago's heart thudded as if he had just missed his footing on a tightrope. 'Give yourself up or I will kill everyone with you.'

'Tiago!' gasped Linette, clutching the arms of her chair with white knuckles.

'It's Oberon,' said Tiago. He glanced at Merlin. The wizard looked distinctly unthreatening in his bare feet, unbuttoned jacket and T-shirt; how would he stand up to the most powerful Fey?

'Merlin, will you surrender?' Oberon emerged from the fog at the head of a squad of his ogres. Behind him were the ranks of hobs: yellow eyes shining like dull lightbulbs in the dark, white foam flecking grey muzzles. To the north, their retreat was cut off by yet more hob packs held on straining leashes. They were trapped.

Oberon strode closer—and closer. Silky robes billowed behind him like a cloud of mustard gas. Tiago had last seen him in Avalon where he was rightly famed as the most handsome of the Fey, more than seven feet tall with the body of a sculpted Greek god. Seeing him here dressed in golden robes, against the grey road, stark red beams of the bridge and dark skies, he was like a tiger out of his cage and prowling, beautiful but incredibly dangerous. You could sense the merciless bones, skull and teeth beneath the smooth bronze skin, the bitter spirit behind the blue glittering eyes. His aura hurt Tiago's nerves like touching an electric fence. Brought up on fairy tales of handsome princes, a human might expect him to be gallant and kind; Tiago knew this king was ruthless and completely selfish. He had a renewed appreciation of Merlin's grey streaked ponytail, flip-flops and rumpled T-shirts.

'Merlin, you should give up now before I hurt your companions,' Oberon continued. His tone sounded so reasonable.

Merlin muttered something under his breath. The bridge began to twist and shake in his simulated earthquake.

Oberon smiled and flicked his hand. The tremor stopped.

'I won't fall for that bluff. You won't risk your friends—that was always your weakness. You should've continued to work alone. You were always much stronger that way.'

Merlin folded his arms and stood square on to the Fey King. 'They aren't my friends. They kidnapped me. Take them if you want—just leave me alone.'

'Weasel,' whispered Linette.

Tiago, however, guessed it was another ruse; Mage bloods would try any trick to buy time and get them off the hook.

'If you don't care for them, then you won't mind if I do this then?' Oberon sent a snake of magic, hissing silver sparks, across the gap separating them. It seized on Linette's chair, lifted it and whipped it over the railing. She screamed and clung on. Bob and Gordon barked in terror. Tiago and Natalia tried to lasso her back but Oberon's magic frazzled theirs on the merest touch.

Merlin's face paled. 'Leave her out of this, Oberon. She's no threat to you.'

Oberon jiggled the chair up and down, not watching his victim but intent on the face of his old adversary. 'I know that, fool. Are you ready to give up? I'd prefer not to have to take you in a fight but I'm more than ready for one if you insist.'

From behind Oberon, the hobs began to bark. His gaze flickered in that direction once and a hint of a frown marred his smooth forehead.

'Uncle, leave her be.' Natalia moved forward, placing herself between Merlin and Oberon. 'Even you can't be so cruel as to pick on a defenceless child.'

His blue eyes skimmed over Natalia, his sister's half-human daughter and family disgrace. 'I don't recognize mongrels. Don't presume on our blood relationship, woman.' He glanced behind again, attention snagged from his quarry. 'What's this?'

Tiago heard the growl of a large vehicle approaching—no, he could now see that there were several of them. He couldn't believe it: three rubbish collection vehicles, headlights dazzling, were mowing down the hobs. The ogre handlers had turned to make battle with the metal sides but made little impact on the already dented lorries.

'Who has broken through?' Oberon bellowed at his chief guard. The guard cringed. 'Imbecile!'

Just then the whop-whop-whop of a helicopter bore down on them, wind from the blades whipping Tiago's hair in his eyes. He began to have a ridiculous hope—the tiniest belief that they had allies coming to their rescue. But who?

'Humans, your majesty,' reported an ogre.

'Then we'll just have to get rid of them.' Oberon's focus flicked away from the little group he had trapped as he turned to give battle to the trucks.

Tiago was too slow to realize what would happen next. Oberon's concentration broke, the spell holding Linette aloft failed, snake vanishing in a glitter of sparks. She plummeted towards the water two hundred feet below.

Chapter 9

'LINETTE!'

Tiago dashed to the side, kicking off his trainers in preparation to jump, but Gordon was there before him. The dog leapt and dived, using his flying power to accelerate his speed. He caught the belt on Linette's jeans in his teeth a moment before she hit the water. Her chair smashed into the hull of the submarine and fragmented with a dull boom. Able only to carry her as far as clear water, Gordon splashed down in the bay, the tide sweeping him and Linette under the bridge and out the other side.

Tiago didn't see what became of them because at that moment a helicopter searchlight blinded him. A rope unfurled and hit him on the head.

Shading his eyes, he looked up into the deafening clatter above and saw a boy, uncannily like a younger version of Oberon, manning the controls.

'Fey attack overhead!' yelled Tiago.

Bob barked, jumping at the rope.

'Tiago, get up here!'

Tiago's Mage hearing allowed him to hear the voice amidst the racket. 'Roxy?' His friend stood in the open rear door of the helicopter. He had never been so pleased to see anyone in his life.

'Quick, get on board before they shoot us down!'

The ogres had woken up to the new threat and were hurling kerbstones at the low-flying helicopter. The pilot was dodging them as best he could, Roxy repelling the rocks by magic, but soon one would take out something vital—or a kerbstone would fall back and kill one of them on the bridge.

Tiago passed the rope to Natalia. 'You go first. Make sure they know they have to save Linette. Gordon has her.'

'I'll tell them.' Natalia glided up and was pulled aboard by Roxy.

'You next, Merlin. Take Bob.' Not giving the wizard a chance to argue, he bundled the dog in Merlin's arms.

Oberon slashed his hand through the air. One of the rubbish trucks exploded. The driver dived out and jumped from the bridge, using a traffic cone to fly. From this distance, the driver looked very much like Rick. The king drew his arm back—the cabin door to the middle truck opened and a man leapfrogged the nearest ogre and went over the rail. The lorry blew up, scattering burning litter over the heads of the hysterical hobs. The last truck standing trundled forward, a white-faced driver sitting bravely at the controls, steaming towards Oberon.

The king hesitated, seeing his rebel daughter at the wheel. 'Cobweb?' He took a breath and roared: 'COBWEB!'

An ogre ripped off the door and the girl driving kicked him in the face. Stepping on the ogre's head, she bounded up on the roof, ran the length of the truck, jumped off the back and vanished.

Having seen Oberon explode three rubbish trucks without breaking a sweat, Tiago knew that the king would take out the helicopter next. His heart pounded horribly with the knowledge of what he had to do.

'Go!' He thumped Merlin on the back, and attached a glamour of himself to the wizard at the same moment as he assumed Merlin's appearance. He ran towards Oberon, arms up.

'OK, I surrender! I, Merlin Ambrosius, surrender!'

Bob squirmed free of the real Merlin and tumbled to the road as the wizard was whisked away, hanging from the rope. The dog snapped his deep displeasure at Tiago's heels as he followed him towards Oberon.

Oberon turned from having exploded the last truck. Glancing up, he gathered a fireball in his palms. The helicopter wheeled away, flying quickly out of range. Tiago collided with Oberon, knocking the missile from his grasp. The fireball span like a bowling ball, knocking over three ogres and taking out the southern abutment with a huge crack. Steel cables whipped to the ground, lashing holes in the tarmac; the bridge creaked and groaned, road buckling. The structure began to tip.

'Retreat!' ordered Oberon.

The ogres conjured Fey portals and herded their hobs back into Avalon. Oberon seized Tiago's neck and chucked him through the nearest one, Bob holding on to Tiago's trousers by his teeth. Remembering that the western ocean lay on the other side, Tiago took a deep breath and fell . . .

On dry ground.

Lifting his head, Tiago saw that he was lying on the main deck of the king's battle cruiser. Oberon had brought his fleet to launch his army across to San Francisco—and now Tiago and Bob were in the middle of it, having to explain to a furious king why Tiago was not Merlin after all.

*

Linette clung to Gordon's neck. He was the only thing stopping her going under in the strong tide whipping them out to sea. His paws kept scooping the water in a determined doggy paddle but he wasn't sure which way to head and Linette couldn't help, as she was concentrating on keeping her head above the waves.

'Hey, Linette!' The voice was much closer than seemed possible. She snatched a glance behind.

'Rick!' Her friend was skimming along, hanging on to a bright orange cone, his toes tapping the water. Blond hair blowing in the wind, arms taut as they clung to his odd flying machine, he looked completely, wonderfully unchanged from when she had last seen him two years ago.

'Just hang on to Gordon; Roxy will be here in a moment,' he called.

Then when Linette thought things could not get any weirder, a man joined them, swimming strongly with accomplished crawl strokes. His grey-shot brown hair lay sleek against his skull like an otter, his whisker-like beard bristling with droplets. He had dark slashing eyebrows, which added to the grim determination in his eyes. He overtook her.

'With your permission?' He reached towards her.
'Please!'

He put an arm round her waist to help Gordon support her weight.

'She's freezing,' the man told Rick.

'I'll go up a bit and signal to the helicopter where we are.' Rick rose smoothly with the cone like he was taking an invisible lift. He shot a beam of magical light like a stream of fireflies into the sky.

'W . . . who . . . ?' Linette's teeth were chattering.

'King Arthur, at your service. Hold on to my arm maiden; the mechanical bird will soon be here.'

His next words were lost as there was an ear-splitting creaking behind them and then a crash. The central span of the Golden Gate Bridge had just collapsed.

'Take a breath!' warned Arthur.

A great shockwave of water bore down on them. Gordon had no hope of paddling fast enough to out-swim it, though he gave it his best shot. Linette tightened her grip. She was a good swimmer in pool conditions but in an estuary like this she would be lost if they got separated. The wave broke over them, forcing her apart from her rescuers. She went under—black water in her mouth, nose and eyes—tumbling like a sock on spin cycle. Trying not to panic, she waited for the wash to pass then pulled for the surface, breaking into the air with a gasp. Salt stung her eyes. Her shoulders were exhausted as her arms took the strain of keeping her afloat.

'Got you!' Arthur grabbed her hand.

Gordon surfaced at Linette's side, nudging her cold hand with his nose.

'I'm . . . OK.'

A helicopter circled and a cable dropped from the cabin, Rick steering it to reach them. The waves combed out in concentric circles in the downdraft. Arthur trod water as he secured a harness around her. He yanked it twice when she was ready. Linette was smoothly lifted from the bay, Rick accompanying her as she rose.

'It's good to see you,' he shouted. 'News later, OK?'

He flew back down to give assistance to the two still in the water. Roxy and Merlin tugged Linette inside the open door of the air-sea rescue helicopter. The harness was detached and sent straight back down. Roxy and Merlin supported her to a seat and handed her a blanket.

Linette searched the cabin for her friends. Natalia was up with the pilot shouting directions so he remained hovering over the right spot, but where was Tiago? The boy at the controls was too tall for him, his hair a shocking creamy white against his skin, a darker, younger version of Oberon.

Gordon arrived next in the cabin and immediately shook himself over everyone. Linette was too wet and tired to care. The last aboard were Arthur and Rick. As soon as the door was slid shut, Rick dropped the cone, removing whatever spell he had been using to make it fly.

'That everyone?' he asked, looking round the cabin. 'Cobweb wasn't in the water, was she? I hope she got off the bridge in time.'

The Fey boy at the controls gave a thumbs-up and started heading out to sea, away from the commotion around the bridge.

'Where's Tiago?' Linette rubbed her face with the edge of the blanket.

'He didn't make it aboard,' said Roxy.

'He's not here?' Rick dashed to the door, ready to jump out again.

'What!' gasped Linette.

Roxy pulled Rick back. 'It was awful: he stayed behind—he was so brave—you should've seen him. He stayed to distract Oberon. We would've been blown out of the air if he hadn't.'

'He was on the bridge when it fell?' asked Linette in horror.

Roxy wiped her eyes and shook her head again.

Merlin cleared his throat. He had been staring at Arthur like a man gazing at his mirror reflection after recovering from amnesia, reacquainting himself with his features. 'I saw Tiago taken through a Fey portal. He pretended to be me. Oberon has him—Bob too.'

Gordon howled.

Linette felt as though, after thinking she was on firm ground, she had just stepped off a cliff. 'They're prisoners?'

'That's the best we can hope for,' said Merlin soberly. 'He did it to save me. He's a brave kid.'

The helicopter circled down to land at the headland in the Golden Gate Park. The door slid open again and a slim Fey girl who appeared to be about Linette's own age got aboard. She rubbed her hands.

'Hi, everyone. Wasn't that brilliant?' She looked round the gloomy faces. 'What did I miss?'

'We lost two, Cobweb. Your dad has them,' Rick explained.

Her chocolate-brown hair was straggled over her face, her blue eyes bright with intelligence. 'Who?'

'Our friend Tiago. And his dog familiar, Bob.'

Cobweb sat down cross-legged on the floor. 'Hobspit. That's not good.'

The pilot called over his shoulder. 'Hey, humans, shall we get out of here? I think this fuel thing that keeps the heli-bird up is not very full.'

Rick clambered forwards to the Fey boy at the controls. 'Your sister's aboard. Let's take this back to the airbase and get as far away as we can before we are arrested for blowing up the bridge.'

The passengers strapped in for flight. Roxy took a seat beside Linette and wrapped her arms around her shoulders. 'You OK?'

Linette nodded, though she wasn't—not really. 'I lost my chair.'

'Yeah, I saw.'

'Will Tiago and Bob be all right?'

Roxy squeezed her tighter to her side. 'I don't know—I really don't know.'

Chapter 10

TIAGO got to his feet and gathered Bob into his arms. Getting upright didn't make their position any better, though he could now see the grey-blue horizon surrounding their vessel like the rim of a vast platter. The sea-disc wobbled precariously, a plate whose spinner had not reached it in time to keep it even.

At least thirty other ships formed Oberon's fleet but theirs was by far and away the largest. The king's white pennant snapped overhead with the sound of a giant laundress shaking out a sheet. Tiago knew he could do with a couple of giants on his side right now.

'Sorry, Bob,' Tiago muttered.

The dog licked his cheek. Oberon's ogre guard

penned them but made no move towards their prisoners, content to know there was no place for them to go. If Tiago tried to conjure a portal spell they would crush him like a bug.

Oberon was busy firing off orders to his sailors and had yet to deal with them. 'Send word to Mountain Division that they're to send the cattle back to restore the balance.'

'Aye, aye, sir.' A Fey colonel saluted, which in Avalon consisted of a hand thumped on the heart. He then took out a razor shell and began issuing his own commands.

'Take us back to the mainland, full speed.' Oberon's smooth voice was overlaid with invisible barbs when you listened closely. It rubbed Tiago's senses the wrong way like the fleshy pink of a tiger's tongue that would take the meat off your bones.

The captain of the king's flagship, a nix warrior dressed in a suit of woven yellow-gold seaweed and too many shell embellishments, clicked his teeth three times. This appeared to be the signal for the seamen to weigh anchor as they jumped to their positions. Even in his dire position, Tiago couldn't help but admire the vessel. The blade-prowed ship had three masts; the sailors pulled on the lines to release billows of silver sails. The cloth was made from a weave of sylph hair, brilliant at catching every breath of wind. Metalwork, crystal windows, and gilded decoration sliced and diced the sunlight. It was a fantasy of a ship but had magical technology that added speed to its beauty.

'Power supplies?' Oberon had turned his attention to Tiago but not yet touched him. That would come, Tiago had no doubt.

'We've twenty prisoners, sir,' the captain replied. 'It should be enough.'

'Send them to the galley. Don't spare their strength. I must be home by midday.'

'Yes, sir.'

Oberon tapped his long fingers on his thigh. Tiago noticed with a nerve-driven urge to laugh that he had a piece of smouldering newspaper stuck to his boot. It had to have come from the rubbish trucks. Perhaps, if he were really lucky, the king's poisonous robes would catch light and solve his problem of what to say.

'You are not Merlin.'

Tiago gulped. 'Not last time I looked, no.'

'Yet the last time I looked, you were him. Think it amusing, do you, to make sport of me?'

There wasn't a safe answer to that question. Tiago looked down at his feet, at the grubby toes of his unlaced trainers.

'So, nothing to say for yourself?' Oberon squeezed Tiago's cheek between finger and thumb, letting the nails dig in. 'I saw you only a few days ago on the beach when we defeated Malduc, did I not, but you have grown. You've been on Earth all that time?'

This he could answer. 'Yes, sir.'

'So you are nothing to do with the rebellion your friends have stirred up here—Dark Lore ransacked and my castle defences breached, not to mention the release of the dragons and the torching of Deepdene Hunting Lodge?'

Roxy and Rick had managed all this in a few days—respect! 'No sir. I don't know anything about that.'

'No, you've just been conspiring with Merlin, one of the most wanted people in my kingdom. How did you find him when my spies failed?'

'It . . . um . . . wasn't that difficult in the end.'

Oberon looked over his shoulder to his second-in-command. 'Execute the head of intelligence.'

The soldier saluted. 'At once, sir.'

'No, wait!' Tiago didn't want to be the cause of anyone's death. 'What I mean is . . . he was in plain sight, sort of, but disguised . . . '

'No one who holds a position in my court can afford to make mistakes.'

Bob shuddered. Tiago hugged him closer.

Oberon removed his nails from Tiago's skin, the dents taking a while to disappear. 'So what shall I do with you?'

It wasn't a question the king expected Tiago to answer. Oberon had a plan in mind and was just toying with him, cat with mouse. 'Your friends will come for you. Morgan told me that the eldest one—Elfric—was absurdly gallant. She has used this against him many times. Arthur had that same weakness so it is safe to assume they are hatching some troll-minded plot to save you.'

Another remark to which there was no safe reply.

'I don't need you alive. They will come for you no matter what, not knowing you are already dead. I could throw you to the sharks.' With his stark-boned face and predatory manner, right then Oberon reminded Tiago very much of a Great White. Yet digging deeper in his impressions, Tiago sensed there was something off about the king said to be the most handsome of the Fey. Tiago recalled the human Queen Elizabeth I, smothering her face with white lead paste to hide the loss of youth, demanding all her courtiers pretend she was still ravishing. In Oberon's case the change was subtler; the repulsiveness lay just under, not on the skin.

At that moment, the ship surged forwards and up, the hull parting company with the waves as it now travelled on a cushion of magic like a soap bubble. The sailors staggered a pace and regained balance; Oberon hadn't moved a jot.

Tiago licked his lips, wondering if any plea would work. His brain spun through the options like a slot machine unable to come up with the combination for the jackpot. But he didn't have to speak; someone else got there first. A young nix stepped out of the crowd and knelt before the king. It was Litor, looking far healthier now he was back in his native seas.

'Sire, I crave a boon.'

Prince Litu, leader of the nixen, a magnificently dressed warrior in turtle shell armour who stood at the head of his marine troops, tried to pull his son back. Litor shook him off.

'Well?' Oberon arched a brow.

'I beg you spare this boy's life. He showed me mercy. He saved me by sending me back.'

Oberon tapped his chin with his forefinger. 'True. Your song of return exposed their hiding place. It was foolish of the boy to give himself away like that.'

Litor shot Tiago a guilty look. 'I thought only of the joy of my return when I sang. But sire, he knew that might happen when he sent me. His kindness was greater than his concern for himself.'

'A human characteristic. Mage half-breeds are weak that way, easy to eliminate. But I am grateful to you, Litor, for the information and so I won't throw him to the sharks. No, we can use him to help bring us home quickly.'

'Thank you, sire.' Litor smiled brightly at Tiago, considering his debt paid. 'You will not regret it as he is not evil, not like his father, Malduc.'

Maldito. Tiago really wished Litor hadn't said that.

'What?'

The ship fell eerily silent. Only the creak of the timbers and the hum of rushing wind broke the quiet.

Litor's black eyes rested on Tiago. 'You did not know about his parentage, your majesty?'

'Another thing Intelligence had forgotten to tell me. Interesting.' Long fingers tapped on a gold sleeve, his mouth curved in a grim smile.

Not interesting: terrifying.

'But it answers the question how to use him. Captain, I will deplete his strength and then you can lock him in the brig. Both the boy and his father shall entertain us at the Fey Games. I look forward to it.'

The captain beckoned two sailors. 'You know what to do.'

The seamen had the green-hued skin of mermen but the long legs of a Fey rather than fins—two more examples of a mixture of Fey species but a new one to Tiago. Their touch on his wrists was cold and tight, manacles of ice. They pulled his arms apart, forcing him to drop Bob. Tiago floundered like a netted fish, flipping hopelessly in their grasp.

'Come,' one said in a scrape of a voice, full of sand and grit.

Litor stood up, his eyes sorrowful. 'I'm sorry.'

Tiago hung his head. He tried for a silver lining. The nix had done his best and bought him a little time. A day or two attached to the galley oars to wear him out was not as bad as sharks, surely?

'Put the dog below deck,' ordered Oberon. 'See the familiar gets food and water.'

At least the king intended no harm to Bob. The Fey were unusually soft-hearted when it came to familiars, following an unwritten code that exempted them from the hatred directed at their masters.

'I'll be fine,' Tiago reassured Bob as the dog whined a protest.

Litor picked him up. 'I will attend the little hound. It is the least I can do.'

'Thanks.' Tiago took a last look at his best friend before the sailors led him away.

The mer-Fey marched Tiago down two ladders below the level of the decks where the soldiers were lodged. Tiago caught a glimpse of a seagull flying level with a porthole before they entered cloud. The flagship was now soaring rapidly through the sky, dipping on turbulence, not waves. The next layer down held the stores and smelt pleasantly of spices—nutmeg and cinnamon mingled with rare oils. The very bottom level was where the ballast and cargo was stowed, as well as the hob kennels. The hobs were baying, scratching at their cages. He hoped they would stop before they reached those. To his mechanical mind he could see no point having the oars below water level and he was yet to see how they worked in the air.

'Far enough yet?' he asked, pausing at the last ladder. He had a strange sense of foreboding that if he took a step down he was going further into the gut of some beast waiting to digest him.

No luck: he was shoved between the shoulder blades and forced to the lowest, windowless deck below.

The galley was a dark hole in the middle of the ship: no benches, no oars sticking out on port and starboard. He peered down through the hatch. 'Where are the oars?'

'Oars—what oars?'

'But I thought . . . ' He let his voice trail away. Better not to offer any thoughts. He would find out soon enough what they intended.

The mer-Fey gave a whistle. 'Another for you, sir.'

A bush of silver-green hair appeared in the gap. 'Yes, send him down.'

Tiago's heart lifted. 'Dr Purl-E!' The pixie owner of the startling fuzz ball of hair was his old Feysyks teacher from Dark Lore. Nothing too awful could happen if he was in charge, surely?

'Oh, it's you, is it, Tiago?' The pixie's tone was flat as he glanced down between the curled toes of his boots balanced on the rung. 'I suppose this is on his orders?'

'Yes, sir. King's command,' said the mer-Fey.

'We'd better get on with it then.'

'Get on with what?' Tiago didn't like the pixie's body language. He wasn't meeting his old pupil's eyes. 'Dr Purl-E, what's going on?'

'Can't talk now, Santiago, too busy. Got a ship to get home at the double.' The tips of his silver-green hair were disappearing back into the hole like a fox dragging home its kill of bright-feathered hen.

'Go on.' The mer-Fey enforced his words with the prick of a polished shell knife.

Tiago could see no way out for himself. He had to trust in the pixie. 'OK, OK, I'm going.' He swung round to climb down the ladder.

At the bottom a faint light cast everything into greyscale. Two ogres passed him carrying a body on a stretcher. One arm—a Fey arm from the looks of the long-fingered hand—dangled, knocking against beams and crates with no care for injury.

'Is she dead?' Tiago asked hoarsely.

The mer-Fey hooted softly. 'No, just used up.'

Tiago's quick brain was piecing together the evidence: Oberon had spoken of prisoners, using them for power. He hadn't meant muscle power but magical energy. Tiago should have guessed. 'Is it permanent?'

The mer-Fey shrugged. 'No idea. Not my problem, is it?'

'It will be if you fall out of favour with Oberon—and from what I've seen, that's not hard.'

His cheek was repaid with a clip round the ear. 'Where do you want him, Dr Purl-E?'

'Take off his jacket and strap him to the table there.' The doctor still wasn't looking at him, busy checking dials and monitors. A heavy wooden plank served as the table. It pivoted at the centre like a seesaw so anyone strapped to it, even a troll, could be raised or dropped by a pixie with the push of a finger.

Tiago started to shake. No way was he going on that table. Bad things happened to people who got strapped to that kind of contraption. 'Please . . . !' Where was Bob? He wanted Bob. Bob would bite someone for him—do something.

'Don't start, Santiago. You brought this on yourself.' The troll-fart of a teacher was talking to him as if he had failed to get his homework in on time.

The mer-Fey grabbed Tiago from behind, lifted and swung him onto the plank. Bumped sharply down, he lay stunned for a second—enough time for them to fix his wrists and ankles with the leather ties. It had happened so quickly he'd not had a chance to struggle.

Dr Purl-E dabbed a little cold liquid on Tiago's chest and stuck a sucker over his heart. 'Monitors your pulse,' he explained, acting as if it were all very reasonable to torture a past pupil.

'I feel sick.'

'That's within normal parameters. Understandable reaction. If you feel the urge, say "Feysyks" and I'll spin the table so you can use the bucket.'

That was when Tiago knew he was lost. If Purl-E had systems in place to deal with terrified Fey victims, he was hardly going to change his ways for a part-human, even one he knew.

'If you'd just relax, Santiago, you'd see how interesting this is. Now magic is running out, we have to find new ways of extracting energy. Humans have driven us to this extreme.'

'So you are taking it from Dark Folk—turning cannibal. How can you live with yourself?' Tiago whispered.

Dr Purl-E fluttered his hands in the air. 'Such drama! We must do what we must. No need to be shocked. Your human side is showing, Santiago.'

'And your monstrous side is looking right back at me.'

The pixie frowned and clamped a thick five-pronged cord to each of the fingers of Tiago's right hand. The wires led to an ornate padded chair in the centre of the room under the only skylight.

'I thought pixies had loyalty and . . . and understood family—Roxy always swore that you did. Nicest of the Dark Folk, she said. You were like a father to me at Dark Lore. Told me I was your brightest pupil.'

Purl-E winced then straightened his posture. 'You were—but you went wrong when you stayed on Earth.'

'That's when I began to go right.'

'I think we can afford to give you the fast upload. That'll quieten that tongue of yours.' Purl-E put another five-tenacled tube on Tiago's trapped left hand.

'Troll-brain.' The Fey didn't have the words strong enough so went for a human one. 'Jerk.' Purl-E attached another lead to his foot. 'Malduc told me you didn't have the intelligence and I didn't believe him. You're just the tool of a tyrant.'

His assistant, an earnest-looking Fey with long fair hair whom Tiago only just now noticed, cleared her throat. 'Is that wise, Dr Purl-E? The process is known to be quite stressful.'

'He's half-human—he doesn't feel stress like us,' said Purl-E dispassionately.

Tiago was shaking. 'I hate you—no, worse: you don't deserve hatred. I despise you!'

Purl-E clamped a final cord on Tiago's other foot. 'Tell the king we're ready,' he barked to his technician.

She opened her mouth to make another protest.

'Can't you take orders, Amythene? Would you prefer it to be you lying here?'

That settled it. The Fey assistant spoke into a communication shell. 'Your majesty, we're ready for you.'

A few long minutes later, Oberon joined them in the galley. He took his seat on the throne-like chair and grasped the other end of the leads attached to Tiago—a monstrous baby latching on to an umbilical cord. He swept Tiago briefly with his blue gaze, cruel smile dancing on his lips, then ignored him.

Oh fey bells, he shouldn't have lost his temper like that. Tiago closed his eyes. At first it felt like a gentle tug on his power. The tug became a suck. He could feel the power running out at all four extremities. It hurt—his body couldn't compensate for what was being taken. As he diminished, Oberon bloated like a tick swelling with blood. The gap in Tiago's chest grew until he felt he was splitting apart.

He began to scream.

Chapter 11

THANKS to Merlin's ability to commandeer a private jet at any time of day or night, they touched down at Southampton airport, England, only twenty-four hours after the events on the Golden Gate Bridge. Linette was now equipped with a lightweight wheelchair—with 'hidden extras' according to Merlin. What they were, she and the wizard were keeping very quiet about but everyone had noted that the two of them spent a good half hour at Pip Enterprises in a closed conference room running through the chair's capabilities. After that it had been straight to the airport and a trip across the Atlantic. A couple of company limousines met them. The chauffeurs were too well-trained to object when Merlin demanded his party and the luggage be dropped off in the middle of Salisbury Plain with no shelter in sight. The CEO of Pip Enterprises had fostered an image of being reliably eccentric so anything went as far as they were concerned.

Once the cars had driven off, Arthur took charge and led the way back to the camp. He offered his arm to Natalia in an old-fashioned gesture of a knight escorting a lady. She did not quite know how to react but, on a nudge from Linette, rested her hand on his. They'd recruited a man from the fifth century so a few archaic manners were to be expected.

Rick, Linette and Roxy dropped back behind the others to talk. Rick noticed that Archer and Cobweb were in close conference; he'd had the impression the twins were planning something. Only semi-attached to the resistance, they couldn't be expected to stay much longer. Their mother, Queen Titania, leader of the Fey rebellion, would expect them to return home soon.

They reached the gently rising ground that led to Stonehenge. Dusk was falling across the plain; swifts performed an aerial ballet over the stones; the clouds drifted in ragged flocks on the pale pink sky-field. It all looked so rural, so peaceful, that it only needed some orchestral music by Elgar to complete the English scene.

'It looks normal,' Linette remarked. 'Are you sure the changeling camp is still here?'

Rick rolled back a gap in the wire fence for her to go through. 'Oh yes, they're still here.'

He enjoyed the expression on her face once she had crossed over the spell's boundary. The busloads of tourists saw only the empty grass around the henge; in reality, the changelings had set up an elaborate camp, decorated with flags, sparkling strings of CDs and plastic bottles, multi-coloured tents made from the material they had appropriated: stolen picnic blankets, tarpaulins and coats. Tepees, yurts, bell tents, two-storey wigwams—the changelings had gone to town with their innovations, occupying every inch of space within the circle of stones. Everything looked flimsy—a child's play camp—until you saw the spells reinforcing the boundaries and making the tents weatherproof. With so many feeding the defensive charms with their magic, it would take a powerful wizard to break in.

'Yo, guys, we're back!' called Roxy.

Edgar and Simon, two of the oldest boys, advanced from behind a slab, both holding swords, covering their bodies with shields. Ahmed and Tabitha trained arrows on them from the shelter of one of the upright stones.

'Stay where you are and speak the password!' demanded Simon. He was valiantly ignoring

Gordon, who had taken no notice of his order to keep back and was sniffing around his shoes.

Rick saw Arthur nod in approval. 'Pen Draig,' the king said.

Edgar was about to drop his shield when Simon nudged him and whispered something.

'Oh yes. Show us Aethel!' Edgar demanded.

Rick hadn't expected this new elaboration on their security protocols but it made sense. No Fey interloper in disguise could manufacture something as unique as his snake torc which turned into a living dragonet. He brushed her awake. 'Reassure our boys, will you?'

Aethel unwound, blinking sleepily at him. Her tongue kissed his ear with a flicker.

'Go to them.' They had to see her close up to check she wasn't an illusion.

Aethel slipped down his arm, over the wheel of Linette's chair and across the grass. She circled Edgar's ankle and let her tongue lick the back of his knee in the ticklish place she knew he had. A broad grin broke across the homely face of the medieval peasant boy.

'It's OK everyone—it's really her,' Edgar announced.

The rest of the changelings and other camp dwellers emerged from hiding. Roxy's pixie family cartwheeled over to her. She rubbed noses with the wild purple-haired father, Frost-E, and the bronze-topped matriarch, Miz-Begotten. She then exchanged hugs with Trix-E, a pixie girl who was short even for her species and always wore her white-blond hair in two plaits. Arthur was busy greeting Peter, his Fey puffin with a rainbow beak who had been his only companion during his imprisonment on Dragon Island in Avalon. As for Merlin, he was surrounded by a wary but fascinated group of changelings. Edgar and Simon had taken his luggage and were stowing it in the guest tent.

Tabitha, the leader of the changelings in their absence, came forward, lifting her long skirt above the stubby grass. She exchanged smiles with Rick before holding out a hand to Linette. He was pleased Tabitha had thought to make his friend welcome. As a quiet Quaker child from the early days of American settlement by Europeans, Tabitha had a peacefulness about her that re-assured even the most suspicious people.

'Hello, you must be Linette. Is that your dog, Gordon?'

Linette accepted Tabitha's hand. The Quaker girl bent down and kissed her cheek in welcome, then ruffled Gordon's ears.

Linette smiled up at her when she moved back. 'Yes, but I'm not sure I'd exactly call him mine. I might be his; I haven't worked it out yet.'

Tabitha laughed. 'It's always like that with our familiars. Welcome to Stonehenge, heart of the Earth resistance against Oberon.' She looked past Linette down the track. 'And where's Tiago?'

'I've really bad news on that front,' admitted Rick, feeling gutted each time he thought of his friend, which was every other moment. 'He sacrificed himself to buy us time to get away. He and Bob are prisoners of Oberon.' At least, he hoped they were. It was possible Oberon had killed them both in his fury at having let Merlin slip through his fingers.

'Oh Rick!' whispered Tabitha, both hands pressed to her lips.

'We'll get him back. We've got Arthur and Merlin now.' Rick said it as much to reassure himself as her.

Tabitha took a breath, suppressing her emotions until she could deal with them in private. 'Yes, yes, of course. Come, Linette, we've prepared a tent especially for you.'

Arthur jumped up onto a fallen stone, sweeping the campsite with his keen gaze. 'Young knights, we will meet for a council of war in one hour. I want double guard patrols from now on. Oberon knows we're free and he'll be looking for us.'

All the changelings were present for the council, though the inner circle of Rick, Roxy, Linette,

Tabitha, Edgar, and Simon sat with the adults and the pixies closest to the fire. Linette began the meeting by telling them what she and Tiago had been doing over the last two years. Her words reminded Roxy of just how out of kilter everything had become:

'I can't believe you are sixteen and Tiago's now thirteen. I'm getting left behind!' She didn't like being the youngest of the four of them; she and Tiago had shared that position, and that had been OK, but the gap had just got a lot bigger with her lagging like a middle-distance runner being lapped by the other contestants.

'He was looking forward to pulling your leg about it,' admitted Linette. 'He likes the fact he leapfrogged you. He's grown a lot too.'

Frost-E broke the glum silence that followed this reminder of Tiago and Bob's predicament by yanking Roxy's leg, forcing her backwards off the log she was sitting on. He clapped his hands, hooting with laughter. 'I see—yes! Leg pulling—very funny. But why does he have to be thirteen to do it?' the pixie asked reasonably.

Roxy, well used to her adoptive parents, brushed herself off and sat back down. 'I'll explain later, Frost-E.'

It began to rain. Merlin sketched a shape in the air and covered the henge with a magical shield.

'Excellent magician, isn't he? It's just like sitting in the centre court at Wimbledon with the roof closed,' said Natalia to Linette.

While the changelings had been catching up on the last two Earth years, Arthur was scowling at his old ally. The fact that they had been avoiding talking to each other since San Francisco had become embarrassingly obvious. Merlin had skated away as soon as he found himself near his old king. Linette guessed the reckoning was coming. Arthur stood up and called the meeting to order.

'Merlin!'

The wizard jumped. 'Yes, Arthur?'

'How long do we have before Oberon makes his next move against us?'

'Nothing is certain but . . . ' Merlin checked his watch. It was an ornate gold affair, finely engraved, with two dials—one for Earth, the other for Avalonian time. ' . . . We have time on our side—a commercial break, if you like—for us to make our plans.'

Arthur growled. 'You make no sense—as always you insist on talking in riddles and codes.'

'He means we have a lull in the battle,' explained Rick quickly before Arthur throttled the wizard. 'It will take Oberon a while to retreat and we have a hundred times longer.'

'So we also have time to settle old scores.' That sounded ominous. 'Do you still serve me, Merlin?'

Merlin stood up, aware all eyes were on him. 'I thought I'd gotten away without doing this bit,' he muttered. He walked round the table to his one-time friend. 'I have always served you, Arthur, as my king and our leader.' He bowed then held out a hand.

The king rose, a head taller than his old comrade. He looked at the hand once then drew back his fist and punched Merlin in the stomach—not too hard but just enough to make him double over, winded. 'That's for leaving me in solitary confinement for sixteen years.'

'Fair . . . enough,' wheezed the wizard.

Arthur put his fists on his hips, taking a commanding stance. 'I suppose you had your reasons?'

'Not good ones. Fear mostly.'

Arthur glared at his former ally.

Merlin held up his hands, warding off further blows. 'I thought if I brought you back, you'd die like all the others. I thought I'd mess up the prophecy. I preferred you alive, held in reserve, even if you were not free.'

Arthur folded his arms, foot tapping angrily. 'You always were too worried about our fate, Merlin Ambrosius. What happens to each of us doesn't rest on your shoulders. I've been living a life-in-death existence for years; I would have preferred to see even your ugly face than no one for all that time.' Arthur gave a heavy sigh, dropped his arms, letting go of the grievance. 'So, what have you been doing with yourself?'

Relieved to get past the initial encounter without further attack, Merlin shrugged modestly. 'Not much. Kick-started the Industrial Revolution and the digital age, had a few very entertaining chats with Newton and Einstein, helped unravel the human genome, oh and sorted out a few technical issues for NASA.'

Arthur frowned, his brow in deep grooves. 'I don't understand a single word you said, but I never did. It's all magical mystification to me.'

Merlin bowed. 'Some things don't change, your majesty.'

'So I've been learning.'

Daringly, Roxy bobbed up between the two men. 'Look, guys, and . . . er . . . your majesty, can we get down to saving Tiago and stopping Oberon, please?'

'I suppose you have a plan, Maid Roxy?' asked Arthur.

'Not really.'

'Oh but you do,' Merlin contradicted her.

'I do?' Roxy looked surprised to hear that.

'Yes. You've been working on it for days—or years

154

in Earth time—if your friends are to be believed. If we're going to take Tiago and Bob back and defeat Oberon, we'll need some major magical power behind us. We'd better get serious about rebuilding the Round Table.' Merlin scratched his chin, his brilliant mind already hard at work.

Arthur turned to the changelings gathered around him. 'Young knights, it is plain that Oberon won't take long to find us. He'll be throwing everything he has into the hunt—all those that he can spare from battling our ally, Queen Titania.' He nodded respectfully in the direction of the twins. 'We also have the issue of how to save our friends, Tiago and his familiar. I believe we can deal with both if we attack the enemy first before they come to us. We will make saving Tiago and his familiar our first blow against Oberon's power base.'

'How?' asked Rick.

Arthur ran a hand through his hair jerkily, pushing it back from his brow. After long years in solitary, he was awkward when having to explain himself to others. 'Oberon may try to bargain for our surrender with Tiago and Bob or execute them in some fashion. I would prefer not to sit digging in here to wait for that—the choice of how we would react might be too terrible, entailing losses either way. No, I think we should act swiftly, be on site before he even thinks to make a deal with us.'

'On site? You mean in Avalon?' asked Archer.

'Yes, I think we should bed down among the enemy and lead our attack from within his walls. That will give us the element of surprise. Merlin, is there any chance Oberon is back at his castle yet?'

Merlin checked his Avalonian dial. 'No, he's only had a quarter of an hour. Even if he is extraordinarily fast-thinking and with magical resources to travel at high speed, he can't have reached his fortress.'

'This gives us the chance to choose our battleground. We will go to Avalon.'

Rick heard Linette moan softly beside him. 'Problem?' he asked.

She nodded. 'What about my parents? I want to go with you and help—I won't be left behind but if I'm gone, I don't know, a few days?'

Rick nodded. 'Maybe. There's no knowing how long this will take.'

'That'll be almost a year! A year of my growing up they'll have missed—but I won't have grown up: I'll still be sixteen but technically I'll be seventeen.'

Rick rubbed his temples. 'I know. It complicates everything badly having to shift between the time zones.'

'We're not talking about a little jet lag but life lag.'

'You could stay here. You should think about it.'

'What—and leave it up to you lot to save Tiago and Bob? I don't think so.' She folded her arms, a mutinous expression on her face.

'You're going to have to choose one way or another,' Rick said, trying to be gentle. He wasn't sure what she would be able to do in Avalon in any case. 'None of us will blame you if you keep to Earth time.'

'Are you saying I'm not needed? Spit it out Rick: just because I can't walk, are you saying you'd prefer me to stay behind?'

'No!' He hadn't meant that, had he? Rick hoped he wasn't so stupid as to judge anyone on their physical abilities. 'I'm far more worried that you don't have magic.'

Their whispered argument had attracted attention. Rick realized that everyone close enough to hear was listening in.

Arthur gave them both an astute look. 'Squire, you and the maiden are at odds?'

Rick gave an awkward nod. 'It's just that Linette is the only one of us to have family and ties in this time period. I was suggesting she might like to remain here.'

'I see. We must protect the fairer sex, of course.' This remark provoked a snort from Roxy and a glare from Natalia. 'If they wish us to,' Arthur quickly amended. He was playing fast catch-up with twenty-first century attitudes.

'I don't need that kind of protection. I can't bear being left behind.' Now Linette was being honest. It was less about what she thought she could do for Tiago and more about having to sit wondering while the others were in Avalon; she'd done enough of that in the last two years.

Rick didn't blame her; he knew he'd feel the same. 'I get it, really I do. It's the fact that you can't do magic that's the biggest obstacle.'

Merlin sighed and threw a pebble at Rick. It hit him with a sting on the tip of his nose. 'I need a non-magical person as a neutral test subject. Linette is perfect.'

Rick wasn't sure he wanted his friend to become a lab rat either, but she seemed eager. 'You can make me magic?' she asked.

'Girlfriend, you already are!' Merlin said in a cheesy American sit-com voice.

Linette grinned and replied in kind. 'Oh gosh, thanks.'

Merlin winked. 'But yes, I can do that given enough time. We're lucky the changelings already have the capacity owing to their time as prisoners in Avalon—that'll speed the Table up nicely—but to calibrate it I need someone who has not got a speckle of quintessence—that's the stuff you call magic—and that, sweetheart, is you.'

'How much time do you need, Merlin?' asked Arthur. His tone was businesslike and direct compared to Merlin's meanderings. 'And where are you going to build it? I think the old Table has gone.'

'It's in Dark Lore, cracked down the middle,' said Rick.

'Phooey, I don't need that old hunk of junk. I'm looking at the perfect site as I sit.' Merlin crossed his ankles and leaned back on his log to look up at the rain falling on his roof.

'You're going to use Stonehenge?' asked Roxy.

'Any reason why not? It has the natural power connection, a little faulty but it'll do with a few adjustments. I like the dimensions—just right for our army—see how neatly we fit inside it. And thanks to its history, it has class.'

'Grand.' Roxy laced her fingers together and stretched them above her head. 'I can go with that.'

'Merlin!' Arthur's tone was a warning. 'I need your timetable for my plans.'

'What? Oh, yes. Hmm, I can start here but I really do need to drop by my laboratory in Avalon for a few bits and pieces. If you agree to be my assistant, Linette, we could make that journey together. You'd be immensely useful to me both here and there. But I understand if you have family reasons and want to duck out.'

'No, no, that's OK.' Linette glanced over to Natalia. 'If you wouldn't mind planting another explanation in my parents' minds?'

'Of course,' she replied. 'I've been doing the same thing to humans for a century now. How else have I lasted in my profession without anyone noticing I'm not getting older?'

'OK.' Linette looked a lot happier now her role was settled. 'Let's do that. I'm up for being the sorcerer's apprentice.'

'As long as you do better at it than Mickey Mouse,' whispered Roxy. 'No reading spells out of scary-looking books when Merlin's back is turned.'

'Got it.' Linette grinned.

'While you're setting up the Table,' continued Arthur, 'I will take a party and infiltrate the capital. We need to gather intelligence on where Tiago and Bob are being held and what plans Oberon has for them.'

Archer, who had remained silent until now, raised a hand.

'Yes, Prince Archer?'

'Cobweb and I must go back. Mother will have moved her people by now and we can help if we coordinate our attacks. That's assuming you are not planning to stop at a rescue?'

'No, indeed, that would be futile. Your father would just come after us. My plan is to make our rescue the first stage of our campaign and launch an attack at the seat of his power. At the very least it will prove to his courtiers that he is not invincible.'

'All the more reason to work together—you from inside the city, us from outside.'

The king nodded at the obvious sense of that. 'Squire, will you accompany the twins back to their mother and help with these efforts?'

'What?' Arthur's request caught Rick by surprise. He had been fully expecting to be on the team infiltrating the castle. 'Are you sure you want me there and not with you?'

'Yes, I want a man I can trust with our most important ally and, besides, if I remember correctly, you have a certain notoriety at the castle, seeing how you fled on Queen Mab's favourite horse last time you were there.'

Yeah, there was that.

'I was proposing a small team—myself, Maid Roxy and one or two of her pixie friends if they want to come. For now, this is reconnaissance, not combat.'

'Just Trix-E,' Roxy said quickly, anticipating the mayhem that the parents would bring. They could not stick to an agenda even if it meant possible capture.

'I'd like the other changelings to stay here and train in magical means of fighting. Tabitha, Edgar, Simon, can you handle that part? You must be ready when Merlin has the Round Table in place. The boost of power is enormous and you must be able to cope with it.'

'Yes, your majesty, we can do that,' Tabitha assured him.

Roxy glanced at Simon. 'Si knows about the difficulty of handling strong magic.'

The woodcutter's son flushed. 'Yes, I have been trying to master a few techniques to stop all my spells ending up as cudgels rather than scalpels. But to be honest, though I'm having some success, I'm getting more failures.'

'I'll give you a training manual before I leave,' said Merlin. 'I had to think up some exercises for Sir Bors, remember, Arthur?'

Arthur smiled fondly and rubbed his chin. 'Aye, I remember. He was like a thunderstorm after sitting at the Table, his strikes likely to hit random rather than chosen targets. We all learnt to duck around him.'

'But he improved after training,' Merlin added.

'Thank you, sir, that will be very helpful,' said Simon.

Rick was about to object that the changelings should not be left to cope alone when it occurred to him that they could handle it. He had been so used to thinking himself the eldest and most responsible of the changelings that he had forgotten that his time away had demoted him. Simon and Edgar were both now older in human terms; Tabitha had always been very mature for her age but now in her teens, was quite able to take on the challenge.

'And I'll come with you,' Natalia told Arthur. 'As half Fey I should blend in at the castle more easily than most.'

The king looked none too pleased by the offer, his save-the-lady gallantry barely leashed. 'If you are sure, my lady?'

'Very.' She folded her arms, giving the clear signal that there was no moving her. 'Tiago needs me.'

Arthur sighed. 'Then we'd best see to our disguises. We leave at dawn.'

Chapter 12

THE guards threw Tiago on the floor then slammed the door to his cell. He couldn't move, didn't even care that his face was rubbing up against some evil-smelling straw. The place stank of ... of—he couldn't identify the smell but it was acrid and overpowering, as he imagined the den of a wild animal would be if it had not been cleansed for centuries. He flexed his fingers, surprised to find they responded. He was so drained of magic that he felt as if his sinews had been unknotted, limbs limp like cooked spaghetti, bones fracked by the immense pressure of the pixie's machine. When he looked in his chest for the nugget of power that had always resided there he sensed only vacancy. That was the most frightening thing: the thought that he'd lost his magic for good.

'Fey bells, I was stupid trying to be a hero,' he muttered, spitting the straw from his mouth.

Water splashed on his face.

'I could have told you that myself, but then you didn't listen when I gave you a chance.'

'What?' Just when Tiago thought his imprisonment could not get worse, it nosedived from awful to disaster.

'I presume Oberon has a good reason for putting you in here with me? A new twist of the chain to make my time in his dungeons more unpleasant?'

It was almost funny to hear his own thoughts coming from his Mage father's mouth. Tiago rolled over and managed to sit, back propped against the bars. There was no natural light in the cell, just a dim firefly lantern hanging outside the cage door over the guards' table. Two ogres sat there, looking supremely bored with their assignment. One picked his teeth with a metal spike while the other threw a handful of bone dice on the table top. Malduc, Tiago's father and the defeated king of Avalon, stood by the single bed—a wooden frame with ropes rather than a mattress, a cup in his hand still dripping from the water he had thrown at his son. He was wearing the same robes that he had had on that day in the control room of the Fey reactor. Tiago did a quick sum—of course, it was only a week or so ago for him, not the years it had been on Earth. Malduc couldn't hide that his hands were shaking and his skin had a greyish cast, evidence that he too had been cannibalized for his magic. His long brown hair was matted, his beard untrimmed, but the hawkish expression of his face was unchanged.

'Hi, Dad. Miss me?'

Malduc put the cup down by a jug on the floor and sat on the bed. The two prisoners glared at each other, neither wanting to be the first to look away. Then Tiago realized how absurd it was to play such power games. He snorted, then buried his face in his hands.

'You won,' he said in a muffled voice.

'What?'

'I blinked first.' He wiped the mixture of snot and tears from his face with the bottom of his T-shirt. They'd kept his jacket. Fortunately they hadn't taken his Minotaur wristband but with Natalia on Earth he doubted very much the shield spell would work. He touched it with a fingernail. No, it felt dead—no magical hum as it had when he first tried it. 'Have you seen Bob?'

Malduc's silvery eyes glowed with vicious pleasure. Anything that hurt his son was fine by him. 'No.'

'I expect he's OK,' Tiago said, ignoring the malice and acting as if his father might care. That would annoy Malduc more than any other approach. 'They took him to give him food and water. The nixen will look after him. He'll probably enjoy being ship's dog.' That was a comforting picture: Bob standing on the poop deck, nose to the wind, barking at seagulls. Better than him sitting in this squalid cell waiting for a death sentence to be passed.

Malduc cracked his knuckles. 'I propose a trade, Santiago.'

'A trade?'

'News of what's happening outside this cell for information about what I've learnt here.'

Tiago knew better than to look too eager to make such an exchange. 'What in Avalon can you have discovered sitting here?'

'I know what's happened to our magic, for one thing.' Malduc's tone was cool but when he held out his hand, his fingers were quivering. 'See, not a spark.' Hating the evidence of his own weakness, he shook his sleeve down to cover up the signs.

Tiago didn't need to test his own power levels to know his magical battery was flat. He had a choice: he could give in to his terror and collapse in a screaming heap, or make a bargain with his enemy in hope of finding a way to escape. Pride also played a part: he couldn't let Malduc see how truly scared he was.

'OK, it looks like we are stuck here together for a while'—until the end—'and I don't mind telling you what's happening.' Some at least. 'You go first.'

Malduc shifted so that the ropes creaked. 'Oberon has had his feysicians develop a new device to drain magic from his enemies—the hard-to-get-to quintessence in the very marrow of all living beings.'

'Yeah, I met that.' The pain was still echoing in his bones.

'It explains how he has made himself so much more powerful than any other Fey. It might be the only thing for which I admire him.'

'Yeah, I can see it appealing to you—turning yourself into a vampire sucking out other people's power.'

'It is the next logical step if magic is to be eked out.'

'Hmm, turn on your own population. Why didn't I think of that? Maybe because I have a conscience?'

Malduc acted as if Tiago wasn't speaking his thoughts aloud. 'Magic under normal circumstances would flow back into the body of his victims.'

'That sounds hopeful.'

'But not if you are put in a dungeon surrounded by the magic-negating properties of dragons. We are being held in his dragon stable.'

'That explains the smell.'

'For some reason the dragons aren't here—or at least I've not heard any—but the carcases of old ones have been buried in the walls. Their bones prevent magic seeping in to us so we will remain powerless until we are removed from here. Now, I've given you a barrel full of information; your turn.'

Tiago told him about the battle on the Golden Gate Bridge. He made it sound as if the Fey King had come looking just for him and Linette; he could tell that Malduc realized he was missing out some vital pieces of the puzzle.

'What were you doing in San Francisco?'

'Oh, just hanging out.' Tiago massaged his temples; he had a crashing headache. 'Going to school there.'

Malduc's silver eyes glinted with something of their old cunning. 'I suppose it was nothing to do with a certain magician? There were rumours, you know. I went there at the beginning of the twentieth century to look for him but he was out of town. He missed the earthquake.'

'Er, how interesting. Can I have a drink?' There was only one cup.

'I suppose you may.'

Tiago wiped the rim with a clean patch of his T-shirt. The water tasted brackish but not foul. He took a gulp.

'Oberon's going to execute us in public.'

Tiago spat out the mouthful.

Malduc smiled. 'At the Fey Games. You know about them?'

'Yes, I was told that the Roman Emperors got the idea from the Fey. You pioneered the idea in your reign. So what are we up for: gladiatorial combat?'

'Ha, if only! No. The Games were far more than that—processions of defeated enemies, ball games, sea battles in flooded arenas, wild animal fights, throwing troublemakers to the lions. All these and more.'

'Which event are they putting us in?'

'Do you have to ask? We are marked for destruction, Santiago. Whichever he puts you in, you end up dead.'

Tiago hugged his knees. He had known even as he ran at Oberon that he was going to stand little chance of coming out of this alive. Maybe part of him had hoped for a miracle, a rescue. Yet Oberon was using him as a hostage, leading his friends into a trap. He should hope they didn't attempt such a thing. 'I wish he'd just get it over with.'

Malduc flexed his capable fingers, digging dirt from under his nails. 'That's not how public entertainment works—even on Earth they know that.'

Tiago tried to find a silver lining to this very dark cloud. 'We . . . we could work together. Come up with a strategy to defend each other.'

'Yes, we *could*.' Malduc's tone indicated that he had no intention of doing anything of the sort.

'Or you could hope to get away by leaving me as bait.'

'Yes, I could.' Malduc's tone was much more positive.

'OK. I see that I don't face just one enemy then.'

'My boy, that should have been plain from the moment you were born. You can trust no one, rely on no one.' Malduc's eyes were so cold. There was no humanity in him; his glare was that of an alien species with no interest in anything but his own survival. Looking for aid from him was like asking a leopard to take your side. Added to this was the grudge against his son for stopping his rebellion. The cell gave him a chance to settle that score. Tiago knew that Malduc was succeeding in getting his revenge on him, which was to make Tiago even more miserable than he need be. He had to fight back for his own pride.

'You know, Dad, you are one seriously sad *hombre*. At least I have good mates out there seeking to help me. I bet you never made a single friend while you were on Earth. Don't bother tweeting: no one would follow you.'

Malduc gave a hollow laugh. 'You are . . . ' Malduc paused, seeking the right word. 'You are very amusing and spirited. At last, a glint of strength that suggests you are my progeny.'

Tiago wasn't letting him get away with that bit of self-congratulation. 'Any of the good stuff in me—that comes from *mi madre*. If I die like a selfish coward, that's all you.'

Malduc frowned. 'Then you better face death like a Mage, proud of your heritage.'

'I will—if you at least try to help me. If you don't, I'll make sure everyone knows it's down to you that I lack any dignity—I'll do my utmost to spoil your name for all eternity.'

Malduc gave him a fleeting look of approval. 'You bargain when you have nothing—that is excellent. I will consider your suggestion.'

'Yeah, you do that, Dad.'

Silence fell in the cell, broken only by the rattle of the dice and the occasional grunts passing between the guards. Tiago didn't like the fact that he now had time to contemplate the messed-up nature of his relationship with his father; he felt better when the exchange of insults, threats and news distracted him. Tiago realized it was idiotic to feel sorry for himself. The assumption that parents were supposed to care for their children absolutely did not apply to Malduc. He saw his son only as a resource. Then again, he saw everyone and everything in the same light; Tiago wasn't getting special treatment. It would've been nice though to have just a hint of love from his father—the kind of love Linette had from her parents.

Uncomfortable hunched on the ground, Tiago shifted his arms and the Minoan wristband tumbled to his pulse point. At least he had one person back on Earth, someone who did care like a parent should. Natalia had been fierce in her promise to defend him. He was far better off for family now than he had been two years ago. And he knew as sure as the sun would rise tomorrow that his friends, including Natalia, would be moving mountains to save him. That was what Oberon wanted, but the thought still warmed Tiago.

The ogre nearest the door turned his head. Something was scuffling at the gap underneath. He got up with a creak of his joints and ambled over, making a big deal of unlocking it with a key taken from a heavy ring of assorted sizes. He cracked it open and stuffed his head in the gap, foot blocking the way.

'What ya want!' he bellowed.

There was a yip followed by several growls.

'If you must. Not got orders to stop you.'

Bob slipped between the ogre's legs and squeezed through the bars, jumping into Tiago's arms. Tiago buried his face in Bob's fur, stupid, silly happiness swamping him.

'Oh you infuriating hound,' Tiago murmured, 'you should have stayed away—should have stayed safe.' But of course Bob wouldn't, no more than Tiago would have left Bob had he been the one imprisoned.

Bob licked Tiago's chin.

'Yeah, I'm OK. See who's here?'

Bob sniffed at Malduc and whined. The last time they'd met, Malduc had taken Bob hostage. Funny how the boot was now on the other paw with Malduc the prisoner and the dog free to leave.

'My feelings exactly. Still, seems we've got to put up with him. Where've you been?'

Bob couldn't speak, quite, but from the intense look in his brown eyes and the smell of salt Tiago could put the salient facts together: Bob had been with Litor and spent the time worrying about his master.

'Oberon took my magic. I'm a wreck.'

Bob cuddled close to Tiago's heart, listening to reassure himself no other damage had been done.

'Feeling a bit shaky but old Dad there says it's reversible if we get out of this dragon bone cage.'

Malduc gave him a disgusted look. 'I don't think that's likely, do you? You should tell your dog to run while he still can.'

Tiago hugged Bob. 'But he won't. He loves me.'

'Then he is as bad as you. Only fools love others.'

Tiago didn't feel the need to reply. The Mage Fey was one hundred per cent wrong. If Malduc dismissed love so easily, he was the one who was a fool.

Chapter 13

ROXY checked her disguise for any chinks. Her family of pixies had developed a clever charm that cast a glamour over the wearer for as long as the power lasted, which they estimated to be about an hour. Frost-E had made one that turned Roxy into a pink-haired pixie cousin of theirs, Toast-E.

'This is grand.' Roxy admired her new appearance in the full-length mirror Miz-Begotten had sourced from a department store in Salisbury. Toast-E had a wild style of dress, clashing colours and layered fabrics like a tornado in the dressing room of London Fashion Week.

The pixie matriarch tweaked Roxy's bubblegum-pink hair. 'It's better than the normal glamour spell. It leaves you free to use your power for other kinds of spells.'

'Like what?'

Miz-Begotten grinned.

'Don't tell me you disguise yourself when you go collecting? Who's been caught on CCTV thanks to you?'

'No one you know. I made myself look like those women who appear on all the paper money. There appears to be a lot of them. Frost-E rather liked the blond hair of that man in the newspapers— you know the one who rides a bike in London?'

'You mean the mayor?'

'What's a mayor?' Miz-Begotten wasn't to know what that meant and Roxy didn't feel up to the task of explaining. 'We did wonder why we were asked to sign pieces of paper by that party of school children. Is he famous?'

'Not as famous as the Queen. You could have chosen two less high-profile people to mimic.'

'But it is very useful: people are so interested in what we look like they don't notice what we take.'

Two young trolls accompanied by Frost-E walked into the tent where Roxy was changing. Blue-skinned with a mane of rough fur, the troll cubs were among the uglier examples she had seen of that species.

'Natalia?'

The female one on the right raised her paw. 'Gorgeous, aren't I?'

'Next stop: the cover of *Vogue*.'

Natalia deactivated her charm, shrinking back to her normal elegant looks. A second later Arthur joined her.

'Thank you, pixies,' said Arthur. 'These disguises work very well.'

'Brilliantly,' added Natalia. 'No one with any sense would think to engage a troll cub in conversation—they are even denser than the adult variety.'

Trix-E was the last to arrive in the tent. She delved in the patchwork bag over her shoulder, checking her kit. 'I've packed some spares for when those charms wear off. The key will be to make sure you are away from prying eyes when the switch is required.'

'What happens when that point is reached?' asked Roxy.

Frost-E rubbed his nose. 'You'll notice a flicker— a little wearing at the edges like a fraying piece of material.'

'Or a ladder in a silk stocking,' added Miz-Begotten. 'The ladder will get worse until the real you pops out.'

'Like a snake shedding a skin,' concluded Frost-E. 'It's rather fun to watch.'

'But I don't advise doing it in front of Oberon.' Miz-Begotten did a headstand and waggled her feet in the air—a sign she had nervous energy to burn.

'So, are we all set?' asked Arthur.

They'd already said their goodbyes to those staying behind. Rick and the twins had headed north at dawn to make a doorway close to Titania's camp. Merlin, Linette and Gordon had gone west to Wales to be near Merlin's secret laboratory before doing the transfer. The wizard had said he would send some animals through to keep the balance. The changelings were working hard on their exercises, Frost-E and Miz-Begotten promising to keep an eye on them and ensure they lacked for nothing.

'Yes, I'm good to go,' said Roxy.

'Family huddle!' announced Frost-E. He pulled his daughter, Miz-Begotten and Roxy into a group hug.

'Look after each other.' Frost-E kissed their noses.

'Don't do anything I wouldn't,' added Miz-Begotten.

That gave them a wide field of possible behaviours, most of them criminal.

'We'll do our best,' promised Trix-E.

They came out of the tent to find their pixie wagon ready for them. Roxy and Trix-E were going to enter the city as pedlars so a cart of brightly coloured goods and charms had been prepared for them. The two horses in the traces were the ones who had accompanied Rick and Roxy on their adventure to reclaim Arthur. Dewdrop, a grey mare, stood patiently; Peony, the high-spirited stallion who had once belonged to Queen Mab, was pawing the ground. His distinctive strawberry-tinged coat and straw-coloured mane had had to go; the pixies had rubbed a dull brown dye into his hair, making him look unremarkable.

'Peter!' growled Arthur. A multi-coloured beak peeked out from among the packages. 'I'm not risking you—you have to stay here where you are safe.'

The response was the puffin equivalent of a raspberry. Roxy laughed.

'I don't think you are going to win that argument,' said Natalia. 'Besides, he adds a touch of whimsy to the pixie wagon—it helps the girls blend.'

Arthur turned to her. 'But what if someone recognizes him?'

'Your majesty.' Roxy dug the puffin out of his hiding place and cradled him in her arms. 'He was only seen in the battle with Morgan for a split second. I doubt she knew what hit her. The chances that she will notice him and make the connection must be very slight, whereas he can be very helpful flying ahead to warn of problems on the road.'

Peter purred his approval.

Arthur threw up his hands in exasperation. 'Very well, you can come.' He pointed his finger at the puffin, jabbing the air to reinforce his command. 'But you must follow orders—my orders!'

Peter settled in Roxy's arms with a smug expression.

Three robins flew in and perched on the tailgate of the cart.

'What now?' Arthur had the look of someone who knew his careful plans were coming undone.

'These are my familiars,' Roxy admitted. 'Well, actually, there was a whole flock of them but I suggested they choose three of their number to visit Avalon with me. They'll be handy for getting into places we can't go.'

'That's all very well but do they know that time passes differently there?'

'Yes, but none of them have chicks so they are happy to make the journey.'

Arthur hooked his thumbs on his sword belt. 'Does anyone have anything else they need to tell me? Any more stowaways?'

Silence.

'Then we will depart. Miz-Begotten, please make the door so that it opens onto a place where we will be undercover. I'd like to save using the charms until absolutely necessary.'

'Spore Forest?' suggested the pixie.

Trix-E grimaced. 'I suppose that's the best idea.'

'What's wrong with Spore Forest?' asked Roxy.

'It's the hunting ground near Oberon's castle but not a pleasant place. It has grown up in the last few years since the king began feeding his magic into the ground near his capital to raise some natural defences. Some say the magic is sick, twisted. We pixies avoid it.'

'Then so will others,' said Arthur. 'Take us there.'

Miz-Begotten wove the spell, spreading it like a net of rainbow droplets between two upright stones of the circle. The gap in between shimmered, time and place bending and folding into a passageway. 'May your fingers be ever nimble!'

'And the road clear before your feet,' finished Frost-E.

Roxy settled into the seat next to Trix-E, who picked up the reins and gave the horses the order to move out. The wagon clattered over the uneven ground, through the doorway, and crossed into Avalon.

Linette, Merlin and Gordon planned to reach Merlin's secret laboratory by making a Fey portal in the centre of the amphitheatre at Caerleon Roman fortress in South Wales. It was the location of the castle that had once been called Camelot and Merlin had used it many times over the centuries to make the crossing to Avalon.

'Are you sure this is a good place to release reindeer from the Fey realm?' Linette could hear the hum of the not-so-distant M4 and it seemed rather suburban to her.

'Oh, they'll be fine,' Merlin replied breezily. 'They can graze here for a day or so until someone works out what to do with them. It'll give the local newspapers something to write about.'

Linette wasn't so sure the news would stay in Gwent. It seemed like the kind of story that would go viral. 'And they're normal reindeer, right?'

'Oh yes, apart from their ability to fly.'

'You're joking?'

'Where do you think the Santa Claus legend comes from?' Merlin paced out the dimensions of the portal and put two rocks in place to remind himself of the aperture.

'But normal reindeer don't do things like that!'

'There are more things in heaven and earth, Linette, than are dreamt of in your philosophy.' Merlin tried to look wise.

She folded her arms. 'You stole that from *Hamlet*.'

'Well, in Avalon, creatures can fly. Just look at Gordon here.' His eyes twinkled. 'It's life, Linette, but not as we know it.'

'Not very original. That's *Star Trek*.'

'Rumbled. I thought your generation couldn't tell a hawk from a handsaw.'

He was teasing her now. '*Hamlet* again. Will you stop testing me?'

'Just checking you're up to being my apprentice.' He started weaving his spell.

'And if I fail to recognize the quote, you'll say, what? *You're fired!*'

He paused and the doorway shimmered to nothing. 'That's familiar but I can't place it. Who said that?'

'Doesn't matter.' Linette didn't want him getting any ideas from television about how to train his apprentice.

He resumed his spell and completed the doorway. 'Gordon, take a sniff out the other side and give us the all-clear.'

Gordon trotted through the doorway and returned almost immediately. He barked once and headed back.

'That means it's all quiet in Hildre Fjord. He'll round up some reindeer for us and when we've counted seven, we'll go through and collapse the portal.' Merlin zipped up his hiking jacket. Linette realized he was wearing boots rather than his usual sandals and had pulled on a bobble hat.

'Did you forget to tell me something?' she asked.

'Hmm, what's that? One . . . two . . . '

Two silver-coated reindeer bounded through the portal looking very alarmed. Gordon's barks echoed in the doorway.

He chucked her a pair of gloves he had been about to put on. They swamped her hands. Uh-oh.

'Three . . . four . . . five . . . six . . . seven.' The small herd of reindeer circled the amphitheatre once and then headed for the gift shop rather than staying to crop the grass as Merlin had anticipated. He shrugged. 'Oh well, somebody else's problem now. Let's go.'

Linette crossed between the stones, entering Avalon into the teeth of a bitter snow-bearing wind. Merlin clearly wasn't a details person if he forgot to warn her about the climate.

'Your lab better be very close!' she shouted above the howl of the storm. She could see nothing in this blizzard. The snowflakes were larger than on Earth, disks of lacy ice cut-outs that spun in the air like manic Christmas decorations.

'Don't panic.' Merlin tapped the map system on her chair, feeding in the coordinates. 'It isn't far.' He pointed to a building on its own not far away. Linette couldn't see it clearly as the air was thick with flakes.

The chair hummed into action, whisking her over the top of the deep snow as smoothly as a hydrofoil crossing a bay. She could just make out the iron-grey water of a fjord and herds of reindeer huddled in any shelter from the wind. Gordon loped back to them, snow settled on his head like a jaunty cap. He shook it off, his sombre face lit up with canine joy.

'Trust you to like this.' Linette hugged her arms to her sides.

Gordon woofed his agreement and bounded forward, heading for the laboratory building, which Linette could now see looked like the gingerbread house from a fairy tale. The roof appeared to be made of frosted biscuits and the walls of pink-and-white striped candy. Chocolate buttons surrounded the windows; toffee-apples grew in the flowerbeds.

'Hardly inconspicuous,' she shouted to Merlin through cupped hands.

He laughed. 'But does it look like a laboratory to you?'

'Absolutely not.'

'Then mission accomplished.'

With a sign from Merlin, the door melted away like ice-cream on a hot plate to let them pass, before refreezing in the same space. Inside, there was none of the whimsy of the outside, not a stick of rock, wisp of candyfloss or smattering of chocolate powder. It was all business—glass, white walls, and as high-tech as his HQ in San Francisco.

'Welcome to my laboratory.' Merlin stripped off his coat. 'Now, let's build ourselves a Round Table.'

As the train presented too much temptation to the twins to misbehave, Rick, Cobweb and Archer flew to Edinburgh. The tall Fey attracted a lot of attention at the airport thanks to their striking looks, arrogant manner, and amusement at human habits such as queuing. Rick had to haul them back more than once before they got into a fight with the party of football supporters at the security check.

'We wait our turn,' he said tersely, then smiled apologetically at the big guy Archer had tried to elbow past. 'Really sorry. They're from . . . um . . . an Icelandic rock band. Don't understand our culture.'

The man's face changed from irritated to interested. 'Cool. What's the name of their group?'

Rick's mind blanked.

'Eyjafjallajokull, after our favourite volcano,' Archer said smoothly.

'I'll look you up on YouTube.'

The queue shuffled forward and the man went through the metal detector.

'How did you know about that . . . that volcano?' asked Rick, unable to even pronounce the first part of the name.

'It's the site of a Fey reactor.' Used to the routine now, Archer stripped off his rings and silver belt. 'We get extra power when it erupts. It's doing very well for us so far this century.'

Archer stepped through the detector.

Rick followed, but set off the alarm. Dang it, he'd forgotten Aethel. Normally he reminded her to change discreetly into snake form under his clothes so she was not picked up by the device. Neither of them wanted to find out what showed up when she passed through the X-ray. The security guard waved his metal-detecting wand at him.

'Step aside for a moment, sir.'

Aethel was currently sitting around his neck in torc form. Rick casually adjusted the collar of his shirt, tapping her with a fingernail. He hoped she got the message to transform and slither out of sight. From the tickle at his nape, he guessed she was on the move, amused by Rick's difficulty.

'Did you empty your pockets?'

'Yes, I thought I did.' Just forgot about my magical snake.

The guard passed the wand over his front. As he moved to the back, Aethel slid around Rick's waist.

'Ah . . . ah.' It tickled!

The guard stopped and gave him a suspicious look. 'Problem, sir?'

'Ah . . . ah-choo!' Rick faked a sneeze. 'Sorry. That one caught me out.'

The man stood back. 'You're fine. Go through again and see if the machine catches anything.'

Rick passed back through the gate, thinking it was strangely like a Fey portal. The machine kept silent.

'OK, on your way, lad.'

Cobweb and Archer waited for him.

'What was that all about?' asked Cobweb, taking his arm.

'Aethel.'

The snake slid to his wrist and curled round to make a bracelet. She shimmered back to gold before someone spotted her and started a panic about snakes loose at the airport.

The Spore Forest was every bit as unpleasant as its reputation. Roxy had been expecting a tangle of trees but instead found a thicket of giant fungi growing in boggy ground.

'Beware the Death Traps!' called Trix-E.

'What in Avalon are those?' asked Natalia, struggling to untangle her shirt from a hooked frill of fungus growing out of the earth like an oversized oyster shell.

'Exploding toadstools. They lie hidden in the mud—look, there's one over there, half poking out.'

Roxy saw a great round grey fungus the shape of a lily pad. When below the soupy soil, she would only notice it when her shoe sank into the fleshy part. 'What happens if you tread on it?'

'They release clouds of stinging spores that eat through skin like acid, inducing madness, then death. Horrid, but standing still is not an option either: the wagon is already sinking.' Trix-E clicked encouragement to the horses and they heaved, hooves splashing in the puddles. Arthur and Natalia pushed the back. Roxy spread dry ferns and anything else that could help the wheels get a grip. She was already having second thoughts about the wisdom of their choice to come into Avalon here.

'Do we know which way we are going?' asked Roxy, wiping mud off her cheek.

'I'm trying to find the track,' explained the pixie. 'It emerges from the forest and joins the main road into the castle quite close to the checkpoint. That way you shouldn't need to have your charms in place for too long.'

Roxy stumbled, missing a Death Trap by a hair's breadth. 'I doubt anyone will have made a path here.'

'You'd be surprised: hunters, smugglers, those who don't wish to be seen.'

'People like us, you mean.'

'There are more opponents to Oberon's rule than you might think.'

The wagon hit some firmer ground and began to make better progress. Roxy's robins flew a little in front of the horses, marking what they judged to be a safe path. Peony and Dewdrop trod carefully and the walkers followed in the ruts the wheels made in the soaked earth. The water as it seeped back into the tracks had an oily surface. It gleamed with rainbow colours in the faint light that penetrated between the umbrellas of the thick mushroom canopy. If this corpselike forest was due to Oberon's magic, then something had gone seriously wrong with it.

'Whyever would anyone let a forest like this grow up on their doorstep?' Roxy wondered aloud. The atmosphere was stuffy and hot, reminding her of a tropical greenhouse. Large gold and green beetles buzzed in her ear, not leaving even when she swatted at them.

'It does have tactical advantages,' replied Arthur. He was facing the unpleasant conditions stoically, not bothering to pause and pick off the insects and leeches attaching themselves to his body. 'No enemy could live here so he need have no fear of opposition setting up camp on his doorstep.'

'Not unless the enemies are fungi-eating frogs. I can't imagine anyone else enjoying this.' Roxy flicked a gobbet of mould from her hand.

'It's the natural habitat of the hobs,' Trix-E called from the wagon.

'That figures. They smell the same.'

'But it's worse than I remember,' said Trix-E. 'It feels like the magic is tainted.'

'That's what I was thinking. Not less magic—just *wrong* magical power,' said Roxy.

A breeze rippled through the forest, stirring the mushrooms. Roxy felt grateful for the fresh air on her face, but only for a second. With a groan and a tick-tick-tick, the fungi started releasing spores. Orange spiked balls the size of a man's head puffed out of a crop of parasol-shaped toadstools.

'Protect the horses!' Trix-E drew the hood of her coat over her face. 'These ones blind you if they burst in your eyes.'

Arthur leapt to the front of the wagon, taking his shield off his back as he sprang. It was inhabited by a dragon from another realm, a spirit Pen Draig, guardian of Aethel, who could be seen as a gold wire decoration on the surface when dormant. Dipped in dragon tears to make it invulnerable, the shield could withstand the stinging spores. Arthur positioned himself ahead of the horses, and dragged his scarf bandana over his mouth, leaving only his eyes exposed. Moving with the cool fluidity of a martial-arts expert, Arthur wielded the shield to knock the spores away. He judged each thrust and turn carefully—too much power risked bursting them. He almost missed one but Peter squawked a warning and he repelled it so no spore reached the horses.

The breeze died down and the toadstools stopped their release. The robins flew back, cheeping excitedly.

'The road!' Roxy cried. 'They say it's just ahead. You were right—there is one.'

'Did you doubt me?' Trix-E grinned.

'Nope—I'm really not going to answer that.'

The wagon bumped up onto the firmer surface of the smugglers' road. It was quiet, no other vehicles in sight.

'Busier at night,' observed Trix-E. 'Only law-abiding pedlars like us use it during the day, of course, and there aren't many of those.'

'Time for the charms?' asked Natalia.

'We'll come out of cover about a quarter of a mile down the track that way.' Trix-E pointed to the east. 'It's risky but let's save them to the last moment. We don't want them to start flickering as we wait to enter the castle.'

They activated the spells as they exited the cover of the tall fungi. There was no sudden end to the forest. Gradually, the toadstools shrank to smaller, less scary specimens; shrubs and trees took over where the fungi had given them room.

Then they too petered out and the first fields and orchards came into sight. Roxy climbed up beside Trix-E; Arthur and Natalia in their guise as troll cubs trudged behind them. No one would question the two species travelling together as they were known for getting on well and putting up with each other's peculiarities.

'Uh-oh,' said Trix-E as they rattled out of their side road onto the main way into the city. 'Looks like we've arrived at a busy time.'

The carriageway was heaving with Dark Folk. They weren't moving with the patience of people knowing that market day would wait for them; they were rushing towards the gate, pushing and shoving, like human shoppers on the first day of the sales.

Trix-E whistled to a pixie family who were entertaining the passers-by with their acrobatics.

'Hey, my friends, what's going on?'

The matriarch of the group completed her handspring then jumped up onto the wagon. 'What've you got there?' She was pointing at Peter.

'I'll tell you if you answer.'

'The Fey Games are starting. There's the triumphal procession first. Oberon's going to make an example of that old king, Malduc. Display him in chains behind his chariot.'

'Why?'

The matriarch shook her head. 'I can't fathom why the Fey do what they do—full of spite and malice against each other. Give me a pixie any day, hey?' She winked at Roxy.

'Oh . . . er . . . yes,' Roxy quickly agreed.

'Needless to say, we're steering clear. Money to be made out here. Word of advice: I wouldn't go in there myself. The Fey get very bloodthirsty at the Games.'

'Thank you, but we've already agreed to meet the rest of our family inside to set up our stall.'

'Hah! Don't say I didn't warn you. So, how much?' The matriarch's hand darted out and clamped around Peter's beak.

The Arthur-troll grunted a protest.

'What?' Trix-E hadn't expected the pixie to want to buy him.

'He's not for sale,' Roxy said in a clear voice. 'He's my familiar—a puffin.'

The matriarch let go at once. Even pixie thieves respected the sanctity of familiars. 'Accept my apologies, little one. Interesting choice.' Peter tucked his beak under Roxy's arm to reinforce the claim. 'Who are you? I've not heard of a pixie girl with such a familiar.'

'I'm Toast-E Lightfingers and he and I have only recently joined up. He comes from the islands in the north.'

The matriarch's eyes glinted with sudden intelligence. 'You've been up there, have you? Nothing to do with a certain queen? Not her.' She jerked her head at the castle in disgust. 'But the other one.'

'Why do you want to know?' Trix-E held her hand loosely in her lap, finger and thumb in a circle.

The matriarch glanced downwards and formed the same shape with hers. 'Now I understand what you're about. Good luck. If you need help getting away, we'll still be here for a few more days. Games last a week. The ball game today— water battle tomorrow.'

'Much obliged to you for the hint.' Trix-E clicked her tongue and the horses started moving.

'Not all of us are to be trusted,' the matriarch added in parting. 'Don't forget that.'

Chapter 14

ON the rocky hillside outside the dungeons, the ogres pushed Tiago onto a wooden cart made of rough-cut planks, his hands bound behind his back with rope of twisted dragon sinew.

'Stay there,' the commander growled.

Bob dodged the guard and jumped up beside him. The terrier tried to gnaw the rope but gave up with a yelp—there was a good reason why dragon sinews were used on prisoners in Avalon.

'Leave it, Bob. I've got nowhere to go anyway, not without being caught.' Tiago was just grateful for a breath of fresh air. The dungeons were below the level of the dragon stables and he'd not seen daylight for hours—he wasn't sure how long. As his eyes adjusted, he could see the king's castle across a narrow bridge—a fantastical palace of pinnacles and spires in white marble. It looked like it had been moulded rather than built. The closest human building he could think of was the Gaudi cathedral in Barcelona—but this castle took impractical architecture to new extremes, a mad man's maze. It had to be for show—an expenditure of magic to impress the onlooker with its extravagance.

One part did look inhabited: the middle was dominated by a tall tower that curled upwards in diminishing spirals—Oberon's private quarters. A flag flew from the top proclaiming the king was in residence. Bits of the tower veered off in perilous protrusions, marble striped with grey and red. Something looked very wrong, like gangrene setting into a once-healthy limb.

Two ogre guards emerged from the dungeons leading their second prisoner by a rope tied round his neck. They took this off and prodded Malduc to step up beside his son.

'Oh, lovely. Humiliation as well as death. How original,' sneered the Mage.

'You know what's happening?' Tiago asked. His knees were shaking, from fear as well as magical depletion siphoning off his strength.

'Oberon's decided on a triumphal procession. I am the main attraction. I suppose I should be flattered. But a tumbrel—how eighteenth-century of him! I expected better.' Malduc closed his eyes and swayed. 'Nothing.'

'What do you mean: "nothing"?'

'I had hopes that magic would seep back once out of the cage but it seems we are still to be deprived of our natural power.' His brow creased in a frown. 'I wonder why.'

'Dragon-sinew ropes?' suggested Tiago.

'I'm not blind, boy! I've considered that possibility. The ropes will prevent magic coming near our hands but I'm surprised they are that strong. I would have expected my head and feet to be out of their range.'

'Then maybe the magic itself is getting weaker?'

'You know, that might well be it.' He shot Tiago an approving look. 'A clever suggestion—another sign of your blood running true. Earth is not holding up well in its part of the bargain that underpins the exchange. Parts of Avalon are turning into wasteland and there is just not as much power as there once was. The stuff Oberon steals from his donors comes out warped—it doesn't make good building material.' He flicked a glance at one of the gangrenous turrets.

The cart lurched forward, pulled by an ogre standing in for an ox. Malduc steadied himself by jostling his son. Tiago fell against the side of the cart but Bob grabbed his trouser leg and stopped him toppling out.

Scared at what lay ahead, Tiago turned to his usual distraction: arguing with his father. 'I know you don't like me, Dad, but if you could cut out the cheap tricks? It's just getting old.'

Malduc sniffed, lifting his chin in disdain. 'That infers I actually spare you any thought to dream up tricks. I assure you I don't.'

The cart bounced over the bridge, the ogre swearing at the potholes in the road, but he got no sympathy from his fellow guards who paced either side. Looking past the stocky ogre on the left, Tiago caught glimpses of a waterfall tumbling from the cliff top. Its spray formed a rainbow over their heads and down the ravine; silver-white birds weaved in and out of the arc. Tiago snatched at the memory of such beauty, holding it in his mind. He feared it might be the last pleasant vista he would see.

They passed through an iron gate into a minor courtyard of the castle. The procession was assembling here: groups of musicians, dancing troupes, soldiers in full dress uniform. Their arrival caused everyone to fall silent. Malduc regarded his audience with wry pleasure.

'Glad to see they are still afraid of me.'

'Don't kid yourself, Dad. They're just struck dumb by Bob's good looks.'

Malduc turned his eyes to the sky. 'Tell me, Heavens, what did I do to deserve my final hours to be spent with this annoying boy?'

'Um.' Tiago pretended to think. 'Had me with my mother? Tried to take over power, thus cheesing off the most powerful Fey in existence? Failed to make friends and influence people? Do you want me to go on?'

'Your irritating abilities are almost magnificent, Santiago.'

Tiago chuckled, experiencing a tiny prickle of hope. His dad was a nightmare, but oddly, he felt closer to him sharing this tumbrel than he ever had. 'Changed your mind about working together in the arena?' It would be some comfort not to have to fight alone.

The wicked amusement on Malduc's face faded and he now looked grim. 'Don't hold your breath, Santiago. I will do what I think gives me the best chance of surviving. I advise you to do the same.'

As fatherly advice went, it was severely lacking in the warmth department, but probably correct.

'I consider myself warned. Thanks for that.' Tiago's mood darkened as his hope faded.

A blast of trumpets stirred the procession participants back to their duties. They began filing out in order through the archway.

'Oberon will join us at the last moment, I would guess. I wonder how close they will let us come to him?' From the eager glint in his eyes, Malduc was considering his options.

'Not close enough for you to succeed in an assassination attempt so I'd forget that. What would you do, in any case, with tied hands and no magic: headbutt him to death?'

'I wasn't thinking of me. Your dog is at liberty.'

How dare he! 'Don't even mention it to him. Bob is not a killer.'

Bob tucked his muzzle between Tiago's knees, blocking his ears.

'Pathetic,' muttered Malduc.

Their cart took its place in the middle of the procession, flanked by two parties of Oberon's crack troops, ogres with iron muscles commanded by Fey with harsh expressions. Their smart blue and silver uniforms made a sharp contrast to the grubby state of the prisoners, not that Tiago was too fussed about looking his best to die, but he could tell it bothered Malduc. It was typical of Oberon not to grant them a last request of a wash and brush-up. After time in the dungeons, they both looked like scarecrows in contrast to the gorgeous uniforms of the guard. The procession swept out of the courtyard on to the broad way that led to the main gate. The road was paved with stones that had seams of pyrite, aptly called fool's gold, running through them; the cobbles shone in the sunlight making rivers of vain hopes. Hedges clipped in the shape of Dark Folk lined the way, decreasing in size from the tallest Fey to the smallest pixie. The grass was mown into wavy lines like a sea encroaching on the castle walls. It was all too much for Tiago. There was not a bit of scruff, no random feature allowed.

'I think he's trying too hard,' Tiago said to Bob. 'When someone tries to impress you with his palace like this, you can tell he's insecure.'

Bob yipped an agreement.

'But an insecure leader is the most dangerous sort,' said Malduc.

A new fanfare blared from one of the towers, blown on silver horns that jousted with the sunlight. A golden chariot rolled out from the shadows.

'Yawn, yawn, yawn, here comes the big Fey himself,' Malduc muttered sarcastically.

'Not met him yet?' asked Tiago.

'Not since my exile, no. He doesn't do prison visits. Leaves that up to Morgan. She's the one who likes to come and poke you through the bars.'

'Speak of the devil . . . ' Oberon had two females either side of him in the chariot: one was his new wife, Queen Mab, dressed in a putrid shade of pink; the other was Tiago's old commander at Dark

Lore training camp, Morgan La Faye, in severe black. Oberon himself was wearing crimson robes. They clashed horribly with his wife's lacy bell-shaped dress.

'Red! How boring. I suppose it is all the better to hide the blood he'll spill,' commented Malduc. 'He's so predictable. Oberon doesn't really understand what it is to give a show of power; he falls into all the clichés.'

'And you were so much better until you ... what was it now? Do remind me. Oh yes ... lost power?'

'Mock all you like but my reign lasted for much longer than his will. You mark my words.'

'I would if I thought I'd be alive to see them come true.' Tiago swallowed, throat dry. He really didn't want to die, but no clever escape suggested itself.

Oberon steered his chariot to the head of the column of soldiers some distance from his prisoners. He glanced once in their direction to see the captives were in place but did not dignify their presence by paying them any more attention.

'Move out!' called the sergeant-at-arms, a Fey commander decked in silver armour.

The procession started, the ogre pulling the cart having been replaced by a team of mules with platinum coats and blue eyes. Long ears twitched in the racket made by Oberon's entourage.

'I suppose we're lucky he didn't make us pull it ourselves,' Malduc observed as the lead mule let out a honking bray at the application of a switch to its rear by its handler.

They passed under the archway. Tiago looked up and glimpsed the wispy figures of sylphs flying in a wavering formation like migrating snow geese, providing air cover for their king. The noise suddenly got much louder as they hit the streets of the city beyond the gates. The buildings here echoed in miniature the pinnacles and towers of the castle but there were places where magic had failed and walls had crumbled into slumped heaps. Temporary buildings put up in the gaps mostly looked twisted and unstable—ugly, diseased forms of the original designs like fungi growing on a once-healthy tree. Crowds thronged the thoroughfare, packed against the sides to make way for the procession. They cheered the dancers and the musicians, applauded the king for giving them the free show, saving their jeers for his captives. Tiago himself did not come in for many insults but Malduc had not left behind any friends when he went into exile and some enemies had long memories.

'That's for my father!' howled one Fey woman. She jerked back her arm and chucked a cabbage at Malduc. He ducked and it sailed past to hit the ogre guard. Her action encouraged others. People began picking up any bit of street rubbish they could get their hands on—stones, fruit and vegetables, potted plants stolen from windowsills, gutted fish and a few sparks of elfshot magic. Tiago hunkered down in the bottom of the cart with Bob; Malduc stood tall, pretending to be oblivious to the missiles that struck him. Tiago had to admit that he displayed grit.

The guards had had enough—largely because they were more often than not the ones who got hit. 'Shields up!' ordered the chief ogre.

They struck the pikes they were carrying against the cobbles. Bolts of light shot from the top of each; they arched over, forming a wall between the prisoners and their attackers. After a few objects bounced off and hit the crowd, the onlookers gave up the game, hissing and booing the guards for spoiling their fun.

Tiago got to his feet, shaken by the force of the crowd's malice. Bob brushed off the worst of the debris with his nose. 'Thanks.' He hugged the dog.

Bob licked his face and proceeded to eat the fish.

They rumbled round a corner and out into the avenue leading to the arena. He must have seen pictures of it before but nothing could prepare him for the shock of encountering it for real. This was the place he was going to die. Four pyramids, each with four sides and a flat top, surrounded the games area. A broad flight of ceremonial steps ran up the centre of each; stone benches formed tiers either side. It looked very familiar and very ancient when compared to the castle.

'You see the resemblance, do you?' observed Malduc. 'It's no mistake that Earth's Aztecs used this design for their buildings; I introduced it to them on one of my earlier visits. Of course, that was a few centuries before I came back and led the conquistadors to their capital.'

'Why?' Tiago was shocked to the core. He hadn't realized his father was responsible for the destruction of his mother's people.

Malduc shrugged. 'I needed the gold.'

Tiago shook his head at Malduc's callousness. 'And before the Aztec pyramids, you built these ones?'

Malduc smiled bitterly. 'I am well aware of the irony. I made this my entertainment capital, having my main palace at Dark Lore. Oberon chose to build his castle next door as this was one of my creations he always coveted.'

Tiago tried to find comfort in the fact that he was going home in a twisted way. He had no memories of his earliest years in Mexico before being taken to the orphanage but he'd always wanted to visit and discover more of his mother's culture. Tragic that it was under these circumstances. He'd had so little time—barely started his life. Sensing his control was beginning to crack, Tiago found it was easier not to look at the faces in the crowd. He tried to distract himself by watching the clouds shifting over the tops of the pyramids. But then Bob suddenly started barking, his stubby tail thrashing Tiago's leg. His heart leapt: Bob was giving the signal that meant friends.

Attempting not to appear too obvious about it, Tiago scanned the crowds lining the avenue. Bob's quivering attention was focused on a pedlar's stall where a blond-haired pixie was selling her wares to those who had become bored of the spectacle. Her companion, a pink-haired pixie girl, had her eyes fixed, not on Malduc as everyone else did, but on him. Two troll cubs stood at her back. But there was something odd about these three: their appearance was faded at the edges, wobbling out of focus. He couldn't tell which of his friends they were, but it didn't take a genius to guess they were using a glamour and it was on the blink. They didn't seem aware of the danger they were in; once his cart had passed the crowd would turn and see that their disguise was failing. He had to warn them.

'Bob, go!' He toed the dog off the back of the cart. Bob ducked and dived between the legs of the crowd.

'Sending your familiar to safety? How touching.' It was formulated as a sneer but Tiago could sense a grudging respect beneath his father's comment. 'I suppose you are now truly on your own.'

Tiago shrugged, not so sure of that. The wristband began to hum against his pulse point. So, Natalia was in town. Hope returned but so did the added fear that his friends would suffer trying to save him.

Malduc turned to face their destination proudly. 'It would have been a pointless sacrifice, that dog joining us in there.'

Tiago hugged his empty arms to himself. 'A sacrifice, yes, but not pointless. You wouldn't understand that.'

The cart trundled into the shadow of the nearest pyramid, entering the holding pens at the base. The rest of the procession continued on to form up in ranks on the flat performance area so Oberon could review his troops, flags rippling viciously in the wind. Tiago imagined the pennants ripping and shredding his mood to pieces as they gloried in his date with death.

'This is where you stop,' said the ogre chief. He pointed at two separate cages.

'Lovely—a room of my own.' Malduc entered his enclosure as if it were a palace. Tiago could do nothing better than emulate him.

'Fab.' He backed up to the bars so the ogre could remove his bindings. 'I'm really digging the wooden-pallet-and-straw thing you've done with it. Your interior designer should get a raise.' He was rewarded with a snort of laughter from Malduc.

'Yes, and don't forget my morning call,' called Malduc as the ogres filed out, slamming the holding pen shut.

Great. They were in a cage within a cage. The only way out led to a killing field.

'You can't get the staff these days.' Malduc tested the pallet and stretched out.

Tiago rubbed his knuckles across his eyes. Without Bob he felt naked. '*Mi padre*, sir, do you think we have a chance?'

Malduc paused. 'Put it like this, Santiago, no one has yet escaped the arena. I suggest you make your peace with that fact and enjoy the time remaining to you. That's what I intend to do. I'm going to entertain myself with working out how to annoy Oberon as much as possible before I die—take him with me if I can, fight my way out if I get my chance. But don't fool yourself there will be a happy ending to your story.'

Tiago clenched his fingers around his wristband. He wasn't ready to give up hope, as Malduc suggested. Not yet.

Chapter 15

'**G**OOD morning. Lovely day for it,' observed the hiker descending the path from Arthur's Seat on the edge of Edinburgh, his legs splattered with mud. His map, hanging in a plastic folder around his neck, beat time with his steps.

Cobweb was taken aback to be addressed by a grimy stranger, not understanding that different rules applied to humans as soon as they donned walking boots or picked up a dog leash. 'A lovely day for what?' She speared the man with an icy stare.

'Oh, er, for stretching your legs, of course.' The man resettled his backpack and picked up his pace to get out of their way. 'Have a good one.'

'Stretching my what!' spluttered Cobweb.

'Thanks—you too,' called Rick, drowning out her indignation. He gave what he suspected was an over-friendly wave to compensate for Cobweb's rudeness. He waited until the hiker had turned the corner behind a jutting rock. 'OK, this will do. No one else in sight. Can you make the door here?'

Archer nodded. 'Naturally. I'm not sure of our mother's exact location but I have a fair idea where Cerunnos' camp is.' Archer began sketching the doorway. 'Once we get through I'll be able to sense her more accurately.'

Cobweb jumped onto a flat-topped stone and gazed out over the city of Edinburgh. The castle sat on its volcanic plug of rock in the centre, settled in for a long vigil like a nesting bird, surrounded by low spreading undergrowth of higgledy-piggledy streets. The North Sea sparkled in the east; the Firth of Forth cut into the countryside to the north.

Rick joined her, admiring the view. He understood cities that grew up around fortresses; they spoke to his Anglo-Saxon soul. Most cities of his era had been about protection, people coming together to watch the walls and guard their goods.

'Can you tell me more about your mother's ally, Cerunnos?' Rick asked Cobweb. 'I'd prefer to be prepared when I meet him.'

'What do you know?' She glanced behind to see how her brother was doing with the spell. Archer was making progress but not yet ready to call them through.

'I've heard that he's some kind of wood sprite. Looking at human legends, he's often described as a man with a stag's head.'

Cobweb crossed her arms, foot tapping impatiently. 'That's a garbled version of the truth. He's more than an ordinary sprite. A better word would be "spirit". He *is* the wood and he's definitely not a man. He is a hold-over from earlier times—times before us.'

'I thought the dragons ruled before you.'

Cobweb shrugged. 'The older ones, dragons and wood spirits, they are said to have occupied the same land, not talking in terms of rule, just living. I think it was something akin to Earth before humans arrived—animals co-habiting but no single species being dominant.'

'It's done!' called Archer. The doorway wavered between his outstretched arms like a net curtain of magic blown in a breeze.

Leaping from the stone together, Rick and Cobweb stepped through the rainbow arch of the doorway. Archer followed and unwove it behind them. They had come out into a pleasant glade in Deepdene Forest, but it felt much further in than

Rick had gone before. Long meadow grass grew in the clearing, butterflies dancing above the waving seed-heads; deciduous trees—Fey oak, chestnut, elm—were scattered across the landscape, not in thick suffocating clumps but in groves. A few sheep wandered the grass, oddly out of place with all the Fey beauty—the swaps sent over in place of the changelings a while ago. The flock had found a good spot for their exile under Cerunnos' protection.

Archer slapped Rick on the shoulder as he came to stand alongside. 'Cerunnos keeps his land well, doesn't he? He allows forest fires and animal grazing to stop it getting too overgrown.' He pointed ahead. 'We'll find his camp that way.'

As they walked through the long grass, Rick felt the peace descend on him like a soft cloak dropping on his shoulders. It was exquisite here—deep down fresh and somehow clean-spirited. It wasn't magical—not in the Fey sense—just completely true to itself: a landscape that liked what it was and meant to stay that way.

They passed through a gap in a long green tree-topped bank about the same height as Rick's head. There was no building marking Cerunnos' camp, no gate. He only knew he had stepped into the middle of it when Titania emerged from the trees, her hands held out to her twins. With primrose-blond hair and a pale green dress, she hardly looked old enough to be the mother of two teenage children, but the Fey were always deceptive in their appearance to human eyes.

'My darlings, you're back! I'm so pleased you're safe.' She kissed them both. 'I heard earlier this morning that you had been in a battle with your father on Earth somewhere far to the west. I've been so worried.'

'It was OK,' said Archer with a grin.

'What is this "OK"?' She tweaked his chin. 'I see bad human habits are rubbing off on you.'

'It's been fascinating, Mother. You won't believe how extraordinary humans are.' Cobweb bounced on her toes, eager to share her traveller's tales. 'They put their rubbish in bins and have special people to collect them in these wonderful machines—wonderful except for the smell. They growl and eat up the refuse like dragons.'

And that was the high point of everything he'd shown her on Earth, thought Rick, rubbish collection?

'Yes, the way the humans have adapted without magic is an education in itself.' Archer beckoned Rick forward. 'We've brought Elfric Halfdane back with us. He is to act as liaison with his people.'

Rick bowed. 'Your majesty.'

The queen inclined her head. 'I trust you left your allies well?'

'Yes, thank you, ma'am, most of them at least. And we have Merlin so can expect to make quick progress now. But I'm here because two were taken in the battle with Oberon. We're trying to free them but we will need your help.'

Titania tucked her hands in her wide sleeves. 'Is this a half Mage, Santiago Dulac, and his familiar that you are talking about?'

'You've news?'

'I have sources in the palace—a well-placed pixie who knows him, and you, she says.'

That could only be one person. 'Shreddie?' Rick had always felt that the pixie who had accompanied them to Earth felt fondly towards Tiago, Bob and Roxy at least, even if she was less keen on him.

Titania whipped out her hand and put her finger to his lips. 'Please don't mention her name again. She would be in grave danger if you were overheard.'

'Sorry.'

'I've been considering what we can do for your friend, but he is destined to participate in the Fey Games with an old enemy of ours, Malduc of Misty Lake. It will be difficult to save Santiago while containing the threat the Mage poses to all Fey.'

Rick could see that she had bigger strategic considerations than a single boy but he was determined to push for all the help he could get. 'Arthur, Roxy, and two other friends have gone to the city to do what they can for Tiago and Bob. Maybe they'll have some ideas about a rescue. Arthur sees it as the first blow in the battle against Oberon.'

Titania looked sceptical. 'Few survive the Games—and none that the king wants dead. That is rather their point.'

Rick was reminded again of the chasm between him and the Fey on sport. The Fey were far more like old human civilizations than present ones. 'There always has to be a first time.'

'Then we will be ready to help if possible.' She waved her slim hand to call her Fey attendants forward. They emerged from the trees and Rick was encouraged to see that their numbers had grown since he last saw them all in one place after the battle of Deepdene Hunting Lodge. 'We will talk more about this later, Elfric, but now it is time to introduce you to Cerunnos, our host. We are here on his invitation and he must accept each newcomer before you can stay.'

The approaching Fey broke into two files and formed up around them in a circle, an army of hundreds. They all waited in silence, the expectation building. Rick's mouth went dry and he cleared his throat nervously.

The steady beat of hooves preceded the appearance of a great stag from the forest. At first glance, the beast looked white-grey, but then it seemed red or brown, as if its coat was going through all the possible seasonal variations at once. Two antlers reared out from its forehead, golden tinged, but they too changed—growing and receding from autumn splendour to new growth of spring. It stood the height of a shire horse and looked equally strong. Liquid brown eyes gazed at Rick with piercing intelligence, long lashes sweeping down as it blinked. The air around the stag seemed to hold a golden promise, the scent of honey and blossom.

'Cerunnos?' murmured Rick but, of course, it was.

Archer went down on one knee, a gesture quickly copied by Cobweb and then Rick. The stag waited. Rick glanced up and saw that it was standing completely still, head raised as if listening for the rumour of distant trouble. He wondered if he had been found wanting. How did the Fey communicate with Cerunnos? He did not seem the sort of creature to whom you poured out your story in words. In fact, he reminded Rick most of the dragons he had met.

So you find me. The voice came inside Rick's thoughts. It did not feel like an outsider butting in as it had with the dragons he had spoken to, but something that had always been there but Rick had been too slow to realize. Rick didn't need to be told; he understood that Cerunnos wanted him to be still with him, nothing more complicated than that.

A long moment passed.

You may stay. I will help.

Rick lifted his gaze to Cerunnos' face. A sensation stole through him like releasing a pent-up breath. He could completely grasp why the Fey, not known for their humility, respected this creature. He was beyond them—something better and finer than any other Rick had met, with the possible exception of the spirit Pen Draig.

You think along the right path, Elfric. May I see the little one? Aethel.

Rick held out his arm and Aethel shimmered into life. She was fizzing with excitement, much as she had when the Pen Draig had first emerged from Arthur's shield. Cerunnos dipped his head and touched her with his nose. Tiny wings split from her spine and fluttered rapidly in the air like the beat of a dragonfly. She launched into the air and zipped around Cerunnos' head, proud of her new ability.

I give her a gift. She has these pinions in spirit form but I thought you both would enjoy seeing her fly.

Aethel arrowed upwards and attempted a loop-the-loop.

Catch her, Elfric! warned Cerunnos.

Seeing she was on the brink of ploughing into the Earth, Rick dived like a wicket-keeper, snatching her up before her ill-judged manoeuvre ended in disaster. She wriggled in his hands, not at all put off and eager to go again.

Enough, little one. Rick could sense Cerunnos was highly amused. *Practise baby steps before you try something so ambitious again.*

Aethel fluttered from Rick's chest to wind in Cerunnos' antlers like a coronet, rising and falling as they grew and shrank in their seasonal rhythm.

'Are you also from the spirit realm like Aethel and the Pen Draig?'

Yes indeed.

'Does that make you a what . . . a god?'

Cerunnos laughed. *No, human child. We have been called such but we are merely beings that material creatures fail to understand and cloak with divinity. The true Creator is beyond all of us. We come from the spirit realm because we enjoy the experience of corporeality.*

Cerunnos was saying that they liked a holiday from the eternity of spiritual existence, decided Rick.

The stag caught the thought and chuckled. *More a gaining of wisdom.*

'I thought the spirit realm beings could only live in objects, not in living creatures, like my torc and Arthur's shield.'

Cerunnos nodded. *True. For most of them. But I am special among my own people and have learnt ways that few others know.*

'You're a wizard?'

If you wish to call me that. We in our realm are a purer form of the quintessence. A spark of us lives in you in this world and on Earth. Where we live, all is magic.

Rick sensed that Cerunnos was moving from their private conversation to opening up their thought speech to all.

My friends, you must all listen now. Rumours in the natural world say that Oberon has devised a method of draining the magic from living creatures. He has been stealing the power for years. I feel the corrupt magic staining this land.

The onlookers gasped.

'But to take someone's magic without their consent is forbidden!' exclaimed Titania. 'It is a crime punishable by the severest penalties.'

Archer and Cobweb looked sick to hear their father's latest cruelty.

He has persuaded others by saying he is driven by necessity. This is a great threat to all and must end. Those like me who are of the spirit realm would not usually intervene in the fleeting battles of this place but this is an exception. Oberon has to be stopped. You may count on our help.

'How do you know this?' asked Rick.

The stag closed his eyes, veiling their dark depths. *I feel the distress in the quintessence. It is different from other forms of matter in your worlds as it has consciousness as part of its structure. When forced from an unwilling subject it takes part of that person with it. This can be healed if the magic is later released but Oberon is hoarding the magic, keeping it for the time of shortage that will soon arrive in Avalon thanks to Earth's destruction of its green power.*

'You mean our father is stealing the people's spirit?' Archer asked, aghast.

Piece by piece. If he repeats his process too many times on the same subject the damage becomes irreparable, a scar in the consciousness that cannot heal. And worse, it is their screams and pain he is storing up for future use and that will only result in a warped dark magic. Already Avalon shows the signs of his sick energy, forests twisting from their original purpose, lands turning to deserts and dustbowls, buildings taking perverse shapes.

And this was the madman who had Tiago in his prison?

'We must stop him.' Rick paced restlessly, rubbing his wrist where Aethel usually sat to comfort him. He wished she hadn't defected to Cerunnos.

We will. Do not be afraid. Cerunnos' whispered vow soothed Rick's jagged feelings. *We must act quickly. Already the king is turning his mind to massing his political enemies into camps to be a power source for him. The only thing preventing him is the fear they would use their power against him before it can be drained. He thinks to scare them into compliance by making an example of the Mage leader, Malduc—and your friend too—as sacrificing an innocent makes those contemplating rebellion fear for their families if not themselves.*

The crowd's alarm swelled. Many here had relatives at risk of the same fate.

'What would you advise?' asked Titania. 'We are not yet strong enough to take on Oberon in his palace and no one has ever escaped the arena.'

You cannot face Oberon alone and win, that is true, but you are not without allies. The human knights are preparing, as Elfric told you. But you need more than warriors. You need the dragons.

'Who hate all Fey,' interrupted Cobweb. 'They'd rather have their talons plucked out than lift a claw to save us.'

Rick sensed Cerunnos was rather entertained by Cobweb's irrepressible manner, which was fortunate because most often Rick felt like strangling her. *They wouldn't be saving you; they'd be destroying their enemy. I propose a truce so you can work together. Your other issues must wait until this more immediate problem has been dealt with—or have you not understood the linear time in which you exist?*

'And you will negotiate this for us?' asked Titania.

I will. Elfric, you and Aethel will join me.

'Are we sure this is a good idea?' asked Cobweb dryly. 'Won't they just eat Rick if they don't like what they hear?'

Titania frowned. 'I trust Cerunnos.' But she didn't look too certain.

Rick tried to believe the wood spirit knew what he was doing too but each time Rick had tried to work with the dragons they had ignored his pleas. The only exception had been when the spirit Pen Draig had been present and she was on Arthur's shield, nowhere close to protect them.

Still, they had no choice but to try.

'I'll come. But how do I travel?'

On my back. We have a long journey and only that way can I carry you swiftly enough.

Archer cupped his hands to give Rick a leg-up onto the stag's back. Cerunnos felt warm and incredibly soft, more alive than any creature Rick had ever touched. Each hair bristled under Rick's hands, tickling his palms with flicks of energy.

Hold on tight.

Cerunnos leapt and the world blurred.

Chapter 16

'NOW where the hex did I put it?'

Linette was not encouraged to discover that Merlin, arguably the most brilliant mind the world had ever seen, was a clutter magnet. His storeroom was the antithesis of his clinical laboratory where every surface was clear. It was only clear, she decided, because he had chucked everything into this cupboard without bothering to file or classify it.

'Can I help?' she asked.

A boot with wings sailed past. 'Nope, almost there. That layer was from the seventh century.' A helmet with extendable horns clunked on the floor, missing Gordon by a whisker. Linette wheeled her chair further back as it was getting positively hazardous by the door but Gordon stayed put.

'Ah-ha! Eureka!'

That sounded hopeful. But so had the six other similar shouts, which had preceded him producing some artefact he had forgotten he had. Merlin emerged from the cupboard and tripped over the Gabriel hound stretched across the entrance. He tumbled, falling heavily on his side as he concentrated on preserving the object in his hands rather than his dignity.

'Blasted dog!'

Gordon licked his face.

'Did you find it?'

'Yes, yes.' Merlin got to his feet and held out his discovery. It looked smooth like a crystal ball but inside it appeared to have the many facets of a cut diamond.

'What is it this time?'

'A bit of frozen magic—mine from the fifth century. I used it to store the information about how to build the Round Table.'

So he really had found it! 'You mean like a blueprint?'

'A little—but the difference is that once we bring it out of its freeze, it will begin to build the table as well. I'm trying something like this on Earth without magic—computers that will make other computers—but it is much easier with magic.'

Linette reached out and touched the bubble—it felt cool under her fingers but not dead, like a creature in hibernation, a fish burrowed deep in pond mud for the winter. 'Your rival, Malduc, made a Round Table but he turned it into a sphere. He said it was better with more dimensions, not a flat surface.'

'Did he?' Merlin's eyebrows shot up. 'Holy moly, he took a risk there. There are some technologies that should not be tried as getting them wrong could be disastrous.'

'He came very close to blowing us all up in both worlds.'

'Exactly. The mark of a good scientist is knowing when to stop as well as where to start.' He breathed on the ball. 'I'll start with a small trial table so we can calibrate it to a neutral human, by which I mean you.' He winked and placed the magic on the lab bench. They both stood back. The ball melted and unfolded, something like watching a board game set itself up, though the pieces were far more complex.

Linette edged closer. 'Can I touch it?'

'Yes, it's safe. Take a good look and tell me what attracts you.'

She raised the level of her chair so she could see the surface of the workbench. The magic had settled into the shape of a silver circle, graven with pictures and names in elaborate detail. It took a while to make out what they were as they were tiny, symbols and signs all weighted, she was sure, with significance and meaning. Heraldic shields, the names of Arthur's knights, mythical beasts, flowing lines and numbers, runes and hieroglyphs. 'How does it work?'

'Hmm, how can I explain it? I suppose you could say you are looking at the code I use to programme the magic.'

'And the people's names?'

'They were part of the original coding. To make it work it is vital we find the changelings who have the right profile to fit the names—a modern match. I could start again but we don't have time to do that.'

'Malduc did it with whole armies.'

'Another sign of his recklessness. So tell me, which calls to you?'

Linette wasn't sure she felt at all warrior-like. Surely she had nothing in common with any of Arthur's men?

Merlin sensed her hesitancy. 'Let your heart decide, not your brain.'

A hush fell in the laboratory, the air crackling with latent magic. She took a deep breath and just looked, trying not to guide her choice by her reason. Her fingertips wandered the surface, tracing a name here and a shape there. Her touch rested on a figure sitting by a stream. It was one of the simplest shapes there but yet it felt right. 'This one.'

'Ah, the Fisher King. Yes, yes, that is excellent. A great choice, Linette.' Merlin smiled broadly at her. She felt she had just passed a test he had set.

'Fisher King? Who was he?'

'A wounded man in a wounded world.' Merlin's eyes were misty with memory. 'He was guardian of the grail in our heyday—but that's another story. His strength came from overcoming difficulties, rather like you.'

'Me?'

'I'd say the slipper fits.' He winked.

Linette felt a warm swirl of embarrassed pride in her chest to hear his praise. She had always thought she just did what was necessary but if he wanted to make that into hero material, then who was she to stop him? 'So I take his place at the Table?'

'Yes. Now, hold your finger to the symbol you've chosen and I'll run a little cycle of the table. It will give you a short burst of power, nothing that you shouldn't be able to bear.'

Linette pressed her right index finger on the engraving. Merlin waved his hand over the surface, bringing the etchings alive with silvery light. The disc grew warm, humming with power. Linette felt the static and crackle as if she were standing under an electricity pylon in her world. Her finger prickled with pins and needles; it was almost painful, certainly uncomfortable. She bit her lip, determined not to flinch.

'Enough.' Merlin passed his hand over the machine again and the glow ceased. 'How do you feel?'

'OK.' She flexed her hand.

'Anything changed?'

'No . . . wait: I can feel something in my chest. It's like I've got a fish bone stuck in my throat.' That didn't sound very heroic but it was what she felt.

'Not a fish bone—a grain of magic. Try drawing on it.'

Tiago had been training her for this moment. Linette closed her eyes and held out her hand, palm upwards. She imagined a flame forming. She opened her eyes. Nothing.

'You kept it in your head. You have to release it. That's the difference between imagination and magical power.'

OK, learn to let it go. Linette took a breath and blew—making the gesture physical, which came more naturally to her. The air as it passed over her palm took on a shape—a tiny glittering candle.

'Awesome!' Merlin applauded. 'I've not seen someone breathe magic like that but I suppose it makes perfect sense. The movement of air is that which is unseen being felt on our skin so it was a good place for you to start. I'm just sorry we don't have more time for your training; your unconventional approach would be most rewarding.'

Linette marvelled at the tiny light she had made. It still burned on her palm. 'Did you get what you need?'

'Sure did. I'll just feed the data into the programme and then we can get back to our friends.' He took out a little stylus and cut a new groove on the table surface, making delicate little flicks with the pointed end.

Linette could feel her magic running out. The flame guttered, fading to nothing. 'It's gone.'

'You only had a sip. We'll be doing the equivalent of dunking everyone in the ocean when we get this running full-scale.'

'Will it hurt?' she asked, remembering the prickly feeling.

'It will stretch you rather than hurt, like steeling yourself to jump out of a plane with a parachute—terrifying then exhilarating. There: all done.' He tapped the table and it rolled itself up into the crystal ball again.

Linette braced herself to go back out into the snow.

'Wait up: just thought of something.' Merlin dived back into the cupboard and threw her a thick velvet cape made of midnight-blue velvet strewn with silver star clusters. 'One of my old ones.'

'Beautiful.' She wrapped it around her shoulders and put up the hood. It was exquisite, curling round her like a hug.

'It's been magically primed to repel the weather so no more problems for you outside.'

'Thanks. You don't mind me using it?'

'That old thing? No. I last wore it at Glastonbury. I don't think I'll wear it again. Too many memories of being knee-deep in mud and suffering.' He headed for the door, crystal ball tucked under his arm.

'Was that last battle of the old Round Table so terrible?'

Merlin looked surprised. 'I was talking of the music festival. I'm getting too old to camp.'

'I should've guessed.' Linette beckoned Gordon. 'Come, let's go.'

The dragons had chosen the jagged peaks of Fanglin Mountains, far to the north, as their lair. Barren summits, wooded slopes, highland meadows for flocks of deer, crags for mountain lions: it was a paradise for their species. The air smelt clean, untainted by the over-perfumed, cloying odour of the mis-worked magic of Oberon's realm to the south.

Cerunnos slowed, leaping lightly up the mountainsides to land in the midst of the sunbathing reptiles. Spread out on the rocks to warm in the cold bright sunlight, splashes of crimson, emerald, ebony and cobalt on the creamy quartz rock, the dragons looked unprepared for their arrival. That was until Rick's old nemesis, the Stormridge, cracked open one black eye, and Rick knew they were expected. The dragon's skin looked healthy, a silvery mail blending to a salmon-pink belly, iridescent with the natural oils that polished its armour, far better than the dusty grey captive Rick had first met in Oberon's stable dungeons.

Old one. The Stormridge lifted its head off its paws to nod to Cerunnos, a trail of smoke drifting down like a drooping moustache. *It has been very long since we last met.*

The other dragons raised their heads one by one until Rick felt he was the focus of at least sixteen pairs of stony eyes. Hungry eyes.

Cerunnos stamped the ground with his front hoof. Though on the surface he may appear like one of the deer the dragons were fond of eating, Rick knew there was absolutely no chance they would mistake him for quarry. Cerunnos was no more edible than the mountain.

Human, bearer of the little one.

Rick realized the Stormridge was addressing him. Sensing Cerunnos wanted him to dismount, Rick slid from his back and bowed to the gathered dragons. Aethel unwound from the stag's antlers and crossed to wind round Rick's neck, offering protection to her chosen human.

We know why you have come. But we do not agree with your solution. Why, Old One, do you side with these warm bloods? Would Avalon and the other world not be better off without them?

Rick held his temples: the Stormridge was projecting a series of memory flashes, of Avalon before the Fey evolved to be the dominant species. Herds of deer ran across the plains; many-coloured dragons flew in the air. Spirit beings, Cerunnos' kin, danced in glittering shapes above the dragon-gatherings like constellations of stars. The coming and going of the spirit beings between their realm and that of the dragons was slow-moving, like ice ages that came and went on Earth. The Fey, meanwhile, lived in woods, streams and oceans, small tribes of wanderers, beneath the notice of the bigger species.

In fact, Rick realized, the dragons' world was more than a little boring. Centuries of the same—no art or music, no friendships or fun. Even the pinnacle of that civilization—the communion between dragons and spirit creatures—would have been like living in one very long solemn religious ceremony.

So you understand me, Cerunnos whispered to Rick's ears alone. *I am here to bring joy, not just to exist. Dragons are not much interested in that quality, unlike you humans, unlike the Fey even at their darkest.*

Cerunnos turned his attention to the Stormridge, who was waiting for his reply. From where Rick stood, his branched antlers framed the dragon's jaws. *Leader of Avalon's dragons, I believe we will never see eye-to-eye on the Fey. Still, there is much we can agree on. This twisted magic must cease.*

Yes! The dragons all raised their snouts skywards and blew out a corona of flame.

Oberon must be overthrown. Cerunnos' voice rang out, a stag calling a challenge to all rivals.

The fire rocketed upwards again, the dragon sign of assent.

And we will retake Avalon at long last! said the Stormridge, breathing out an arc of flame.

Cerunnos shook his neck, antlers rocking from side to side.

Sparks floated down to rest on Rick's hair and shoulders. He brushed them off, aided by Aethel, before he was set alight.

No. You make no place in your plans for the Fey, said Cerunnos. *That I cannot allow.*

The dragons dipped their snouts, not daring to refuse so powerful a being but also withholding agreement.

You once regarded this place not as your land or their land but as our land. Since when did dragons talk like the Fey?

We are nothing like the slave masters! spat the Stormridge. The scale-spikes that usually lay flat against its brow bristled with indignation.

Yet you have adopted their attitudes in your long captivity. Did you forget that no one inherits the right to the land; we only borrow it from our children?

Rick shifted uneasily, wondering what he was doing here. He didn't like the feeling he was little more than a visual aid of the enemy for the dragons. Even though he had helped them on several occasions, he knew they bore him no gratitude. That was another attitude of which the dragons had scant conception.

Why should we help with Oberon? Why don't the Fey clean up their own mess? asked the Stormridge. *I could give my word that we will remain here, neutral, until this war is over. Will that do, Old One?*

That wasn't enough, thought Rick in despair. The changelings and Titania's small band of renegades just didn't have the shock power of a dragon squadron. Without them, they would never gain mastery of the skies.

Aethel's tongue flickered in Rick's ear, a sign of her impatience.

'Yes, I know, legless, we can't hang around: Tiago needs us right now. It looks like the dragons are going to refuse to help.'

With a little shake of her body, she unfurled her new wings and shot up into the air. The dragons sighed with pleasure to see the little spirit creature flaunt her new skill. Then she broke into a series of hisses and trills that Rick had never heard from her before. He didn't understand them but the dragons seemed to follow her easily. Her appeal did not appear to be going well as her audience looked merely gently amused by her antics, like adults watching a child perform a party piece. Annoyed now, Aethel landed on the Stormwing's muzzle and blew a shower of sparks right up its nostril. It sneezed, dislodging her. With an indignant hiss, Aethel retreated to Rick.

Cerunnos nudged her with his nose, well pleased with her.

The spirit dragonet wishes us to intervene because she loves you, boy, said the Stormridge. *An odd emotion, this love. We dragons rarely feel it but she is full of this sensation, ties binding her not just to you but to those you call friends. We can see them—they are like magical threads but made of another substance.*

This is what she is learning on her visit to this realm, said Cerunnos. Aethel's reflection glowed in his brown eyes, a bright spark of gold. *You dragons are pledged to protect the spirit beings, are you not? That alliance is as old as your race.*

The Stormridge sank back on its haunches, exposing its pale underbelly. *But you ask us to stretch this alliance to defeating Oberon on such flimsy grounds as love?*

That is exactly what we ask. The little one's guardian, the Pen Draig on Arthur's shield, endorses the request. As do I. Cerunnos shook his thick neck, light flashing from his pelt as if he had so much energy he could barely contain it.

The Stormridge puffed a cloud of grey-blue smoke. It found it hard to deny three such requests, but it clearly had little relish for what was being asked of it. *We dragons will consider but our decision cannot be made quickly. There is too much at stake, too many vows we have made in the past never to aid the Fey or their allies also to be weighed.*

'But we don't have time.' Rick bit back his complaints, knowing they would have no more effect on the dragons than gravel thrown at plate armour. 'I can't wait—please, Cerunnos, you must see that. My friend might be dying right now!'

The stag bent his head, closer to Rick, breath smelling of sweet grass. *I must stay and convince the dragons. Without them, you might only save your friend for you both to face defeat.*

Cerunnos was right—of course, he was right—but Rick couldn't bear to sit while dragons debated. He knew his place was with Roxy and Arthur—not here, miles from the action.

Aethel flapped, hissed and snapped like a saucepan of popcorn.

If you so demand, said the Stormridge. *I can do that much without discussion.*

'What have you asked it?' Rick asked as Aethel preened herself.

She wishes to return to Deepdene. One of the children will take you. The Stormridge nudged the closest of the two black dragons, Girax or Jontil—Rick couldn't tell them apart.

'Do you mind if I go, Cerunnos?' Rick asked.

Your part is done here. Aethel's love is proved to them beyond doubt as they see how you work together. That is better than many words of argument that I could bring to them. Go now. I will join you as soon as I may. Cerunnos dipped his head and brushed his nose over Rick's hair, a kind of stag blessing.

'Thank you.' Rick bowed to the Stormridge. 'For the lift.'

I do it for the dragonet, not for you.

'I know. Still, you have my thanks even if you don't want them.' Rick turned to the crouching dragon and realized the Stormridge was going to exact a small revenge even by granting this favour. 'I don't suppose there's a saddle?'

The flight back to Deepdene forest was terrifying but swift. Of course there was no harness; they were symbols of dragon slavery. The black dragon enjoyed knowing its human rider was clinging on for dear life as it dipped and soared over the treetops and crags. Rick was convinced it was taking some of the turns more sharply than was necessary.

Finally they spiralled down to land in a clearing near the camp. He slid gratefully off the dragon's back. 'Thank you.'

The dragon gave a snort of disdain and took off, knocking him down in the backdraft of its wings. Human-dragon relations hadn't progressed very far but at least he hadn't been eaten, thought Rick.

'And I have you to thank for that, don't I, Aethel? If I had known, I would have played my trump card much earlier when I was still a dragon-keeper.'

Aethel waved her agreement and curled round his neck for the walk back to camp.

The scene that greeted them was like something from an old tapestry. Titania reclined on a pile of strawberry satin pillows, listening to a singer in a white and gold mask. In her hand dangled a goblet of honeydew. The twins sat back-to-back, Archer reading a book, Cobweb polishing her sword blade. The sight of such relaxation when Rick was so wound up stung like the splash of salt water in his eyes.

'Your majesty,' he said crisply with a curt bow. 'I would like to join Arthur in the city immediately. The Games begin soon.'

Titania put down her goblet and rose to her feet, the signal for all her court to rise. 'Is this not rash, Elfric? You will not wait for Cerunnos? How fares his mission?'

Rick rubbed the back of his neck. 'I'm not sure. We're halfway to persuading the dragons but I'm not convinced they will give up their grudge against the Fey to stop at overthrowing Oberon. They'd be happy to get rid of all of you.'

Titania pressed her long fingers together. 'But Cerunnos pleads our case?'

'Yes. He's really clear that the bad magic has to go or we'll all suffer—dragon, Fey and human. But while he's doing that, I could go in an advance party to back up Arthur.'

Titania shook her head at his unspoken message. 'You think I am not doing enough—I can see it in your face, Elfric. Just because I know I have to wait here does not mean I have been idle. I've sent word already to those loyal to me who live close to the capital. I cannot go myself as I must wait here to speak to our new allies.'

Cobweb coughed. '*If* the dragons are our friends and not another enemy. I wouldn't mind getting out of frying range myself.'

'That's not why I want to go!' Rick knew his tone was snappish but he felt insulted at the idea he was fleeing the dragons.

'Quite.' Titania glared at her daughter, reproving her for her discourtesy to an ally. 'You want to be on hand for your friend—I understand that. And I will not stop you. Indeed, it would be useful for one of my commanders to go south with you and take control of the volunteers. They've been told to muster at the Games as part of the crowd. Kind of Oberon to provide an excuse for large numbers of people to gather in the heart of his kingdom, would you not say?'

Those nearest laughed at her ironic tone.

'But now we've learned that he is stealing our magic, I wonder if his purpose is not much darker?' The laughter died. 'We must warn our friends. We cannot allow him to drain so many.' She tapped her fingers to her lips. 'So whom shall I send and how shall you travel?'

Archer stepped forward. 'Send us, Mother. They'll rally more easily to one of your blood. We may even to able to persuade some of Father's guard to our side when they see that both Cobweb and I support your cause rather than his.' He glanced at his sister. 'And Cob does want to put some miles between her and the dragons.'

'I'm not scared of dragons!' fumed Cobweb, angry to find her own jibe turned on her.

'You should be,' Titania said severely. 'No one is safe. Stay or go: both are dangerous. Those who stay will soon follow; all of us will see combat. Yes, you are right, Archer: I will send you with Elfric, along with fifteen of my personal guard.'

'Thank you, your majesty.' Rick felt a sense of relief that he had got his way more easily than anticipated.

'I suggest you travel in the disguise of the royal choir from Alta Jewel—we have their robes as they defected to my side a month ago. Oberon is not yet aware of their changed allegiance. Is that not so, Malinel?'

The singer—one of the choir, Rick now guessed—bowed to his queen. 'It would be our honour to supply you what you need. It is an ancient tradition that we always perform in public wearing masks so as not to distract from the beauty of our music. That will make your passage easier.'

'Excellent choice,' agreed Archer.

'Until they ask us to sing,' muttered Cobweb.

'Do we travel Earth-side?' asked Rick, wanting to hurry this along.

'There is the question of the balance with so many of you going. It may take too much time to get that right.' Titania looked pensive. 'Go by the Dew Track. There's a small station not far from the eaves of the forest. If my griffins fly you as far as the station, you could then travel swiftly onwards, arriving before the Games start.'

'But isn't the Dew Track reserved exclusively for Oberon's favourites?'

Cobweb huffed in annoyance. 'Rick, when are you going to get over your sticking to the rules? We just take a bubble and use it—we don't ask permission.'

These twins had happily stolen a mainline train and driven it to Scotland, so he should have expected that.

Titania raised her hand. 'No, Cobweb, you will do no such thing. That will merely result in you reaching the other end and being arrested.' She smothered a smile as her daughter pouted in disappointment. 'My point, Elfric, is that as far as the guardians of the Track are concerned, the Alta

Jewel choir still number among Oberon's favourites. You are urgently summoned to entertain the king at the Fey Games and have the royal order to prove it—or will do, thanks to my forgers.'

'When can we be ready to go?'

'Within the hour. I'll order the document to be prepared immediately. I suggest you go with Archer and Cobweb and find yourself some robes.'

Rick bowed. As they retreated from Titania's presence, Cobweb caught him by the elbow. 'Any good at singing, Rick?'

'Not great. You?'

'Awful. Can't carry a tune to save my life.'

'Then we'd better hope it doesn't come to that then,' added Archer dryly.

Chapter 17

THE sleepy guards on the Dew Track station scrambled to attention when they saw the Alta Jewel Choir climb the ladder to their platform high above the ground. Everyone in Avalon knew the king's favourite entertainers. They were famed for their distinctive light blue robes figured with unique musical notation, and white facemasks decorated with swirls of gold. They enjoyed a special mystery as it was known that once dedicated to their craft, the singer never showed their face again in public, burying their identity in the unity of the choir.

That was if the guards bought their act, thought Rick, crossing his fingers.

Titania had handpicked the fifteen Fey who

accompanied them. All were tall and elegant, at ease with the instruments they carried. They also happened to be highly trained warriors, instruments converting into deadly weapons. Rick was the odd one out if the guards cared to examine him too closely. Shorter than the others, he wore his human clothes and a sword under his robes, keeping to the back where he was likely to attract the least attention.

'Singers, what are you doing here? We were not told to expect you,' said the smaller of the two guards, a rough-haired Fey who looked as if he had some pixie in his ancestry. It would make sense that Oberon posted the less-than-impressive recruits in this backwater.

'We were summoned to Oberon's castle from our musical retreat in the Hartshorn Hills,' replied Archer, naming a small range to the east that bordered the forest. 'You are our nearest station on the track.' He handed over the carefully prepared royal summons. Titania had brought a real scribe and supplies from the household when she went into exile, so the forger had done an excellent job. Only Oberon himself would know it wasn't his hand.

The guard stared at the paper so long, Rick was beginning to wonder if he could read.

'The king's signature! Look at that, Danty! I'm holding the very paper his hand has touched!'

Nope, it was worse than not being able to read; the guard had an incurable case of hero-worship. Unfortunately, the second guard was less easy to impress. He was a full-blooded Fey but unusually slovenly in his appearance, dirt under his nails and hair in need of a wash.

'How do you know it's the king's, troll-brain? These people could be pretending to be the choir. Not showing us their faces are they?'

'No, but don't you see, that's how we know it's them.' The small guard was bobbing with excitement. 'The Alta Jewel never show their faces once dedicated to their singing. Ladies, gentlemen: you honour us with your visit to our humble station.'

'You have no reason to suspect us,' continued Archer smoothly. 'All we want to do is arrive at the Games on time.' He studied his nails, eyes flicking up once to the taller guard. 'Of course, if you wish to send to your superiors for authorization, then we may have to mention to the king why we were not there when he called us to sing.'

The brighter one knew it was more than his job was worth to be responsible for a delay. He picked his nose and grinned. 'Off you go then, you high and mightinesses. Don't let a lowly minion like me get in the way of such musical greatness.' He stepped back and waved them through the entrance of the station. 'We only have these old carriages at your disposal as you didn't give us warning, but I'm sure you'll not mind, seeing how eager you are to get to your performance.'

Fey technology copied its practices from nature so the principle of the Dew Track was that the bubbles of magic ran down the rails, mimicking dewdrops on long blades of grass. A new carriage on the track would shine with rainbow lights like a soap bubble; these greying vehicles looked fit only for going down the plughole, not along the soaring silver track. Dew Track accidents were frequent events thanks to the insane velocities at which they travelled.

'These will do,' said Archer, pressing his boot on Cobweb's toes before she could protest.

'Don't mind old Danty; he's not been the same since he got bitten by a werehag. Sorry there's nothing better,' burbled the small guard. 'They may not look much, but these old bubbles are the best—a more thrilling ride than the new ones. Eighteen of you, are there? Just got enough then.' He loaded them in one by one, each bubble getting increasingly dilapidated. As the last in line, Rick got the worst. He could see gaps in the magic fabric. 'I'll release you in ten-second intervals. Should give you a chance to do some racing if you've a mind.'

The guard pulled a lever. The first ball plummeted to the track below the station, squishing slightly as it hit the rails, and began the rapid slide along the tracks. Rick could see Archer strapped in to the suspended seat, taking the swerves and spins in his stride. Not so Cobweb: Rick could hear her screams as the second bubble dropped down. Thanks to the mask, he couldn't tell if she was loving or hating it. Seeing his turn approaching, he reached down to strap himself into his seat, only to find the belt broken. If he didn't anchor himself to something he'd end up at the palace jumbled in pieces.

Danty tapped on the bubble. 'Changed your mind, singer? Want to stay and give us a tune while we order you a new one?'

Rick shook his head.

'Your funeral.' The guard shrugged.

'Aethel?' Rick whispered.

Understanding what was needed, the snake unfurled from his wrist under the cover of his robe and stretched across his lap, hooking head and tail in the loops. She turned back to metal.

Just in time. Rick's carriage plunged to the track below like a conker from a chestnut tree. The chair creaked, barely doing its job of cushioning the movement. The carriage began rolling forward, gathering momentum. The speed pressed him back, vibration shaking him to the bones. He approached the first of the big loops.

'Feyyyybells!' shouted Rick as the bottom seemed to drop out of his world.

When Rick reached the huge terminus by Oberon's palace, he stumbled quickly out of his carriage, heaved up his mask and was promptly sick in a flowerbed.

'Never. Again.' His legs were shaking; cold sweat beaded on his brow.

The attendant, a cheerful pixie in a red uniform, didn't seem too surprised to find his passenger suffering from motion sickness. He slapped the wobbly surface of the bubble. 'Who did you annoy then, my friend, to put you in this? I'm amazed this made it. Can't have been renewed for centuries. Better send it straight to maintenance.' He gave it a prod, and the carriage weaved its way to the end of the line and dropped into the vat of magic, turning back to unformed magic until it would be called on again to take shape. The pixie turned away, chuckling.

Rick shifted the mask back so it covered his face. He stood up and found the choir gathered, watching him with distant curiosity like people at a zoo observing a particularly intelligent chimpanzee pour tea.

He gave them a wave. 'Don't worry about me—I'm fine.' Just dying by inches over here, he added silently.

Archer took him at his word rather than his body language. 'Good. We have choir practice in thirty minutes.'

'Choir practice' meant rendezvous with their Dark Folk allies.

Rick wished he could take the mask off. His skin still felt clammy from the ride. 'I'll be with you in a moment. Just catching my breath.'

'So we see.' Cobweb threaded her arm through his, showing she at least had developed some ability to sympathize during her time with humans. 'Don't worry, we all feel grim when we first ride the Dew Track. "No gain without pain", isn't that what your species say? What kept you?'

Rick thought back to the hair-raising ride, the feeling that at any moment his dewdrop carriage was going to shoot into the air and dump him on the ground far below. It was only when he worked out that the way he moved in the chair helped direct the rollercoaster progress, slowing for bends and speeding up for loops, that the journey smoothed out somewhat. 'I'd not been on one before. Took a while to get the hang of it.'

'It's one of my favourite ways to travel. I almost caught Archer on the big loop over the Blackore Mountains, but he made up time on the Trailtop curve.'

Rick really wished she wouldn't rehash the journey; even the name of those tricky spots made him feel sick again. 'We'd better go.'

Cobweb helped steady him on his feet, then removed her grip on his elbow. The choir was known to walk smoothly in formation, not stagger chummily along arm in arm. Rick took his place near the end of the column just behind Cobweb. Archer led the way down from the station. Unlike the little outpost near the forest that had only a ladder to reach the platform, this terminus had a spiralling ramp descending to ground level, broad enough for the crowds who came to the city. There were many stations in the huge settlement that had grown up around Oberon's palace but this was the finest. It also happened to be closest to the arena. Rick could see it through the windows on the opposite side to those that looked out on the palace. The flags were flying from the pyramid tops. He hoped that did not mean that the Games had already started.

He edged up alongside Cobweb. 'Can you tell me exactly what goes on in the arena? Have the Games begun?'

'The early heats. Not Tiago's match.'

'What are the Games? I only know that almost everyone dies.'

'They're very exciting,' she began enthusiastically, but then had second thoughts, 'but not for those who take part. I hadn't ever really considered that. I always thought they were just criminals deserving punishment but they're not, are they? I suppose they'll have to stop when we take over.'

'Why do you find them exciting?' Rick asked.

Cobweb twirled her hands. 'It's not the death part—though I suppose that does add to the tension; it's the skill we like. In the ball game they're playing today, there's one rule: get the ball through the key, that's the stone with a hole in it. How you do it is up to you—cheating, speed, foul play—anything goes. The contestant who scores the most gets to choose whom he kills. They keep going until there is a winner; then he or she may take their place in the rolls of glory written on the walls of the arena.'

'That's the prize—get your name on a list?'

'And honourable execution and burial. Very few are pardoned as they were already condemned before being entered in the Games.'

Rick's memory nudged him. 'I've heard of this before—they did this on Earth too. The Aztec culture had a game in an arena like this one. They played in teams, the winners being a sacrifice after the other side was eliminated. I think they may have used the heads of their enemies rather than a ball.'

Cobweb turned her shoulder to him; her attention was really caught by that. 'How cruel!'

Rick regretted proving again that humans always managed to outstrip the Fey for ways of making others suffer. 'I guess that your old enemy Malduc introduced it there when he was in exile.'

'I think he started it here too. It was one of the things that Father kept when he took over.'

Trust Oberon to choose one of the most horrible aspects of Malduc's reign to preserve.

'But why do it?'

Cobweb shrugged. 'The people like it—without death it would lack drama—wouldn't be enough to satisfy them. Some even enter for the honour. It offers those who are under sentence of death a chance for a final flourish, to go out with style. Occasionally there is the chance of earning a reprieve if your performance pleases the crowd.'

Rick felt sick and this time it was nothing to do with the Dew Track. 'Tiago is not that kind of person. He won't want to win a game like this.'

'Then we'll have to hope that in the early rounds no one thinks him a big enough threat to choose for the kill, won't we?'

Tiago sat in a corner of his cell watching the participants in the early heats of the Games prepare. Oberon had emptied his prisons to entertain his people, dragging in all those who had offended him over the last year since the previous slaughter, and the pens under the arena were full. Malduc and he were being saved for the grand finale; these victims were being sent out as warm-up acts and returning in diminishing numbers.

The crowd roared. That meant someone had scored—or been killed: the sound was the same. His insides twisted in knots. He was keeping his grip only by the merest fingernail of self-control. Tiago worried for the mermaid he had seen towed out last round. How could anyone expect a sea creature to get anywhere in this competition? Then again, maybe they didn't: an easy bone thrown to the baying spectators.

Earlier, in a lull between heats, Malduc had explained the aim of the game to Tiago and warned him that there were next to no rules. Tiago didn't want even the fake glory of winning so intended not to make the slightest effort. He was going to be looking for a way out, not to score in some savage contest.

The contestants in that heat came back, prodded into their cells by the ogre guards. The mermaid was still with them, looking flushed and happy. She bared her razor-sharp teeth at Tiago as she was carried past.

'Who died?' called Malduc to the chief guard.

'Argh, that stupid drac from the South Seas. He should've held his shape and carried on pretending to be a pixie. He should've taken a proper look at his opponents.'

The drac were able to shape-shift, actually becoming other forms, unlike the glamour magic used by other Dark Folk. In their natural state, they were small lizard-skinned creatures adapted for living in shallow water and rivers.

Malduc didn't seem too bothered at the news of the first death. 'A basic mistake; he deserved to die.'

Sorry though he was for the drac, Tiago had to weigh up the winners, knowing he would be up against them. 'Did that half-ogre, half-Fey soldier win?' The guy was enormous, arms the span of tree trunks. Tiago had picked him out as most likely to score.

The guard laughed. Malduc gave Tiago a sneering smile.

'What?' Tiago asked.

'He's far too slow.' Malduc shook his head. 'Anyone with the simplest understanding of the game would see that.'

'OK, clearly I don't get it. Tell me who won.'

'The mermaid, of course. If the ball ever came near her, her tail would decide the rest.'

'Yeah, and the merpeople hate the drac almost as much as they hate the nixen. It was a certainty that she'd slate him for the first kill: that's why he shouldn't have dropped his shift. It was his only advantage but I thought he'd stick with it.' The guard tapped on the bars. 'You win that bet, Mage; shame no point in giving you your winnings.'

Malduc waved it away. 'See it as a tip for your continued favour.'

'If it's any consolation, I'll put it on you for your name going up on the wall.'

'Much obliged. It would help of course if that certain item I mentioned reached me before I went into the arena.'

The ogre scratched his stomach. 'I'll see what I can do.' The guard shuffled off, banging on the bars to wake up any of his charges who were managing to rest in this hellish place.

Tiago met Malduc's eyes. 'That's cheating.'

'Cheating's allowed.' Malduc settled down cross-legged on the floor, eyes closed in meditation.

'Out there it is, but you said nothing about cheating before you got into the arena.'

Malduc opened one eye. 'I made the rules up; I think I am well within my rights to change them. I have no intention of going down easily—or going down at all. Oberon made a big mistake putting me in my own game.'

Tiago gripped the bars, letting his head hang between his arms. This was madness. What did he care if Malduc cheated? He should be welcoming it, because anything that upset the ordinary running of the game could be the crack through which he might be able to escape.

The wristband on Tiago's arm caught the light, reminding him that he should not despair. Malduc wasn't the only one with a surprise up his sleeve.

Chapter 18

ALMOST two months had passed on Earth in the twelve hours Linette and Merlin had been away in his laboratory. They came through the Fey portal to find no trace of the reindeer at Caerleon so had to summon by magic one very surprised polar bear from Cardiff Zoo and send it over in Linette's place to restore the balance.

'Will she be OK?' Linette asked as the bear ambled through to her new life.

'Oh yes, she'll have a fine time.' Merlin finished setting up a glamour showing an illusory bear still in the enclosure, set to run until nightfall. They would be long gone from Wales when her disappearance was noticed. Merlin had summoned one of his company cars to drive them back to

Stonehenge. He took the chance to catch up with his business from the passenger seat. He talked to his managers and fired off a few emails, humming happily. It took Linette a while to work out he was singing 'Frosty the Snowman'.

Merlin called over to his driver. 'Moston, put us down here.'

The chauffeur touched his cap and drew the limousine to a stop. He unloaded the bag of equipment they had brought back from the laboratory by the side of the road and drove away. When the car was out of sight, Merlin turned to Linette.

'Our friends have been busy since we left.' They stepped through the protective glamour to see what had been done to the camp in the two months. The changelings hurried to greet them, dodging between the clutter that had taken over the space in the centre of the stones.

'Is that a tomb effigy?' marvelled Linette.

'Yes!' Miz-Begotten climbed out from behind it. 'William Longspée, Earl of Salisbury. We thought he'd make a nice target for our archery.'

Merlin dropped his head in his hands.

'You should see what else they've taken.' Tabitha bit her lip. 'Without Trix-E to rein them in they've got a bit out of hand.'

The pixies must have taken almost every landmark of note from the surrounding towns and villages: a market cross, several statues, church clocks and weathervanes. They hadn't stopped at architectural features: the middle of Stonehenge now had a floral display worthy of the Chelsea Flower Show. And a dentist's chair.

She raised a brow at that.

'Don't ask,' whispered Tabitha.

Frost-E jumped on the chair to show it going up and down.

Merlin clapped his hands. 'Right, people, gather round.' The changelings shuffled into a circle. 'We can't take any more risks attracting human attention. These things have to go back.'

Frost-E hugged the chair and wailed. 'Noooo! That's sacrilege.'

'NOT because of human ideas of property rights,' Merlin reassured him, 'but because we have something far more important to do and I need the space. You want to be a knight of the Round Table?'

Frost-E fell back in the chair, tripping a lever so that his head dropped below his feet. 'We can? Us pixies?'

'Sure—everyone is welcome at our Table. I'm no pixiphobe.'

'Count us in!' declared Miz-Begotten.

'Then you take this stuff back and give me a clear work area. Anyway, what were you thinking: stealing tombs!'

'But he's pretty.' Miz-Begotten stroked the earl's mail-clad arm.

'He also belongs in Salisbury cathedral. Take him back—he wasn't something that could legitimately be stolen. You dishonour a dead man's bones.'

The pixie paled. She kissed the effigy's nose. 'I'm sorry, Mr Earl. You go back at once. Frost-E, take the other end.'

Linette watched the pixies begin hauling the tomb away. 'I'm surprised you've still got anything to call your own, Tabitha.'

She shrugged. 'We make regular raids on their tent. They expect it.'

With the pixies busy relocating the stolen goods and the changelings removing their tents beyond the stone circle, Merlin soon had a space cleared for his round table mechanism. He didn't activate it immediately but stood alone in the centre of the henge, waiting for everyone to get back. Night had fallen; the stars came out against a moonless sky. Linette had a sudden revelation that the easy-going man she had become used to over the last few days was only a fraction of the real character, an iceberg tip. Even dressed in jeans and T-shirt he looked mysterious, echoes of his druid ancestors and Mage mother.

But he didn't quite look the part of the legendary Merlin. She knew what she had to do. Directing her chair forward, she held out the cloak he had lent her.

'Here: you need this.'

Called from his reverie, he looked down at it and smiled. 'Yes, I do believe you are right. Thank you, apprentice. Stay with me and watch.'

'Won't I be in the way?'

'Not at all.' He swirled the cloak so it settled around him, then dropped his hand to rest on her shoulder. He raised his voice to his audience of changelings and pixies. 'I summon to the Round Table all true knights of King Arthur. Stand ready to defend your kingdoms and your people.' He took the ball of magic from the bag. Instead of putting it on a surface as he had in the laboratory, he threw it straight up in the air. It rose swiftly then stayed hovering at the apex of its flight.

'The time has come for the Table to awake.'

A bolt of power shot from his fingers and hit the ball. It split open, releasing a glittering shower of lights. The sparks danced and whirled, roped and span. The movements were similar to the unpacking of magic she had seen at the lab but this time written against the night sky. That trial table had seemed solid; this one hovered overhead, a flying saucer made up of heraldic beasts and scrollwork. Names fizzed out against the stars: Sir Lancelot, Sir Gawain, Sir Bors, Sir Kay, the Fisher King, Queen Guinevere, the Lady of the Lake—all who were mentioned in legend as allied to Arthur had their place.

Merlin looked up and nodded with satisfaction. 'Good, the power here is strong enough to sustain it. We can connect directly into the magic grid that feeds Avalon.' He turned to Linette. 'Now all we need is Arthur and the rest of our recruits. This will only work if we have warriors who match the original knights; we can't have an empty seat.'

'Can we not run it now?' asked Linette. 'See if some of us fit?'

'We already know your seat.' The sign for the Fisher King burned more brightly than the others. 'But I can't run it at this strength without the king. Arthur is not just needed for his brawn, no matter how often I may have told him that. He and I stabilize the Table for the knights when it's in operation; his leadership, my skill—it's all part of the underlying equation. No, we have to wait.'

'And if they don't get back?'

Merlin grimaced. 'Then we'll be in a whole lot of trouble. It would still work but not very well— not enough to make us fit challengers to Oberon's forces. We'd be bugs splattered on his windscreen.'

'Great.' Linette shuddered at the image. This had always been a fairly desperate plan but the chances of it succeeding seemed as thin. 'What shall we do then?'

'We wait.'

Chapter 19

'THEY'VE got magic detectors,' murmured Trix-E as Roxy, Arthur, Natalia, Bob and the pixie shuffled closer to the front of the crowd of people edging into the arena. They had left Peter guarding the cart and horses tied to a post just outside the ticket barrier. 'They're going to sense your charms.'

Roxy peeked over the heads of a large family of claurichauns, malicious cousins of the more numerous leprechauns. Dressed in green and draped with what in the human world would have been called bling, the eager clan popped up and down like meerkats standing on their burrows.

'Will we be in time?' squeaked the smallest, a

shockingly ugly child with a pink face and tuffs of brown hair. Hard to tell if it was a he or a she.

'Of course we will, what's-your-name, as long as these security people hurry up. What are they playing at—holding up us ticket holders!' The claurichaun jumped on the shoulders of his wife, who buckled under his weight. 'Oi! What's the fuss all about? Some of us want to get in before it's all over!'

His answer from the ogres on duty was a growl.

The sylph in front of the claurichauns, milky skin semi-transparent like wet silk, turned to them, her annoyance plain. 'It's the new security procedures,' she grumbled. 'The king is here and they're expecting trouble.'

'Trouble?' The claurichaun rubbed his hands. 'We like trouble, don't we, kids?'

His twenty-four children all shouted 'Yes!' and 'Sure do, Pa!'—or variations of the same answer. They then started juggling their hats and generally making a nuisance of themselves—one mass of annoying claurichaun youngsters all equally irritating and indistinguishable.

That gave Roxy an idea. 'Trix-E, can we reset the charms to be like them?' She nodded to the family in front.

Trix-E caught on quickly. She grappled in the depths of her bag, muttered something and pulled out three blue feathers. Arthur (in troll shape) nodded his approval. 'Good thinking, Maid Roxy. Perhaps Bob can provide a distraction?'

Trix-E got out a charm in the shape of a pine cone. 'This might help. Wait till we're near the front, Bob.' She slipped the cone into his mouth. 'Then bite down.'

The claurichaun father reached the checkpoint and immediately began protesting at the scandalously long wait and how he had a mind to ask for a partial refund of the exorbitant price he had paid to bring his entire family to the games. He then took offence when the ogre asked for every single one of his chains and bracelets to be passed under the magic detector. It was going to take for ever if they did the same to every child; Roxy was banking on them getting bored of the idea and waving most of them through.

'Now!' whispered Trix-E.

No one but the pixie knew what was going to happen, not even Bob, who was a trusting soul. He bit down and brilliant blue bubbles erupted from his jaws. They exploded with a snap and a crack. He tried to capture one but it dragged him upwards so he was flying above their heads. The crowd oohed and aahed, heads turned upwards. Roxy almost forgot to make use of the distraction until Natalia nudged her. They switched charms

and mingled with the teeming crowd of claurichaun children.

'Help!' called Trix-E, waving to the ogres. 'The
charm malfunctioned. Catch him, will you?'

Ogres were the most alert guards in Avalon but
they shared the Dark Folk's fondness for familiars. They quickly organized themselves to spread
out beneath the floating dog. While they did this,
Roxy, Arthur and Natalia slipped through the
security gate with ten of the claurichaun kids. It
was a mark of how huge the family network was
that none of the real children recognized them as
interlopers.

'You can let go now, Bob!' called Trix-E. 'They'll
catch you.'

With a yelp, Bob released the bubble and
dropped into the nearest ogre's arms. The crowd
at the checkpoint gave a cheer. The ogre grinned
and bowed.

'Here's a free charm for each of you, with my
thanks,' said Trix-E, pressing into the ogre's hand
the last spells from her bag.

'Thanks, pixie. Be more careful, little one.' The
ogre ruffled Bob's fur. He then checked that Trix-
E's bag was empty and waved her through.

Once at a safe distance from the checkpoint, by
the stands for food and drink, Roxy spotted Trix-E
scanning the group of claurichaun children for her

friends. Arthur tapped the pixie on the shoulder. She turned to find them back to their ordinary sizes. Saving the last power in the glamour charms for an emergency, they had risked their real appearances, Arthur's face hidden in the hood of his cloak and Roxy's under a wide-brimmed hat. Natalia didn't need a disguise as she looked more Fey than human. The only people she had to avoid were those few from Oberon's family that would recognize her.

'Let's take our places,' said Arthur in a low voice. They filed down the stone ledge to their seats, making their way past family groups with picnics, ball-game enthusiasts dressed in the colours of their favourites, and a dozing troll.

The shell in Roxy's pocket hummed. Trying not to look too conspicuous, she pulled it out and held it to her ear.

'Hi. We're here.' Rick's voice. A hag Fey scowled at her. It was considered bad manners in Avalon to use spelled shells in public places.

'Yes, Mother, I did remember my wolfsbane medicine.'

'I take it you can't talk right now.'

'That's right—we've got good seats. Southern pyramid—row six.'

'We're just below the Royal Box.'

Roxy shaded her eyes to look across at the

pyramid on the western side. The seats were occupied by royalty and favourites. She couldn't imagine how Rick had got there—until she saw the choir with one member holding something to the side of his head like he had toothache.

'I see.'

The hag jabbed her in the side with a bony elbow. 'Pixie, can't you read the signs? No talking! It's for security.'

Roxy tugged her hat lower on her brow. 'Sorry, Mother, can't talk now. I'm in my seat and we are supposed to have deactivated our spells as we came in.'

'That old hag giving you grief.' Rick must have spotted her. 'I won't risk you any further but know that we're standing ready to back you up. There are more sympathizers spread out across the audience. Be alert for our chance—I'm sure Malduc will do something to upset the smooth running of the Games.'

'Yes, love you too, Mother. Bye.' Roxy slipped the shell back in her pocket.

'Hope you're not going to talk on that thing all afternoon,' huffed the hag. She made a great show of tucking her knucklebone necklace deeper into her bodice, daring the pixie to try and take it. 'Young people have no manners.'

'Wouldn't dream of it,' murmured Roxy.

The trumpeters blew a fanfare and the noise of the crowd subsided so that only the cries of a few ogre cubs could be heard. The doors to the prisoners' pens opened and the participants walked out in a string, bound together by dragon sinews. Roxy felt a lump in her throat as she saw Tiago at the end, much smaller than the other participants. Malduc was next to him, striding briskly as if he owned the arena. An ogre followed on behind, carrying a mermaid in his arms. Strangely, the appearance of this sea creature was met with the loudest cheers.

The trumpets rang out again and Oberon stood up, a slash of gold and crimson among his courtiers, many of whom were dressed in white. Morgan and Mab stood out, decked out in black and pink respectively.

'My people, my queen and I are delighted to be able to bring you a special gift. As you will know, these games were begun on the orders of the deposed king, Malduc of the Misty Lake—' On cue his henchmen started the crowd hissing and booing. Malduc stared straight ahead, acting as if his attention was on more important matters and the people around him far below his notice. That only inflamed the audience to worse threats. The hag next to Roxy joined in the jeering enthusiastically.

'Murderer!' she screamed. 'Kill him! No mercy!'

Oberon held up his hand, smiling indulgently. 'Thank you, thank you. I too feel the wrongs he has done you—I feel your pain.' He clapped his hand to his chest, the spot where Roxy doubted any feelings existed but self-interest. 'Malduc has been captured in a wicked plot to destroy Avalon and now will face the punishment. What more appropriate than to pit the inventor of the game against his own? He will participate in this final round.' The crowd whistled and shrieked their approval. 'But there is more: I am changing the rules today. The one who kills him and survives will go free—a full pardon!'

There was a gasp in the arena as the crowd absorbed this rare news. The contestants in the roped line jerked to attention. Tiago took one look at his father and dropped his head.

Oberon smiled. 'But Malduc must be the last to die—that is the only condition.'

There was a murmur through the stands and then the beginnings of a cheer. It grew in strength as the spectators worked out that it would add a delicious edge to the competition.

Oberon held up his hand. 'In the unlikely event that Malduc himself emerges winner, I will be merciful: his name will be allowed on the wall.' His gaze screwed his enemy to the spot but Malduc did not deign to look at him.

Oberon was giving his rival a slender hope of survival but Roxy doubted Malduc would be allowed to live whatever happened.

The king hadn't finished. 'There is a second gift in today's competition—Malduc's own son—that pitiful specimen at the end of the line. One look at this half human and no doubt many of you have laid bets on him being among the first to die. So to show you the true nature of Malduc—he who once thought himself worthy to sit on the throne—none may choose to kill the boy but if his father allows. If he refuses, another will be picked. This means if the son survives to the final three, it will come to the decision: will Malduc choose to sacrifice himself for his son? If he does choose the half-human over himself, the boy goes free.'

There was an exclamation of shock and surprise as the crowd absorbed this new twist to the familiar formula. Oberon was trying to steer the final to a three-way showdown with the death of Tiago as the concluding flourish, a sacrifice that would prove to everyone how evil his father was.

Now there was a reaction from Malduc: he turned his head slightly to look at Tiago, frowned, then returned to his impassive stance.

Did Tiago stand any chance of being saved that way? wondered Roxy. She glanced at Arthur. His eyes gleamed like faint stars in the depths of his hood. He shook his head. No, Malduc would not choose for his son to live—his selfishness would not allow himself to be dishonoured. If he had a choice of his name going on the wall or his son's life, his legacy in cold stone would win out over flesh and rebellious blood.

Arthur leaned down and whispered in Roxy's ear. 'Never fear, Maid Roxy. Oberon thinks he is orchestrating this match but do not forget Malduc's own plans. He does not look like a Mage who has come here to die.'

'Participants, you understand what is at stake?' called Oberon.

The prisoners, apart from Tiago and Malduc, bowed. Roxy quickly assessed the opposition: a half-ogre, half-Fey warrior with ragged leather armour; two nixen whose skins looked grey after being away from water so long but their teeth were still razor-sharp; six Reiver Fey, bandits who preyed on travellers in the Blackore Mountains, all of whom had been battered by prison but continued determined; a troll whose only expression was confusion—he probably still hadn't understood what he had done to be there; and the mermaid. How could the people bear to watch such stupid slaughter? Many Dark Folk hated the Games as much as she did but unfortunately there was still a majority who thought them a just punishment.

'Then let the game begin!' called Oberon, sitting down with a swish of his robes.

With a drum roll, four sylph flew in holding the ball in a net. It was perfectly spherical, pale grey like the moon. As Roxy watched, it changed hue, becoming in turn the red planet, Mars, giant Jupiter, blue Earth, ringed Saturn, cold Neptune, finally hot glowing Sun. It shrank and grew as it became each in turn.

'What do they have to do with it?' asked Roxy in a low voice. Those around her in the crowd had their attention fixed on the arena, eager not to miss a second of the action, so there was little chance of being overheard.

Trix-E leant across Arthur. 'They fight to get it then they have to put it through the key—that's that carved stone ring in front of the Royal Box. The trick is that the ball will only go through on the Earth phase. You have to keep it out of the hands of the others until it turns to the right planet. And if you are holding it when it turns to one of the outer planets or, worse, the Sun, you'll get your fingers frozen or burnt.'

They had to get Tiago out of there at once—and the others too if they could be saved. This was just barbaric. 'Arthur! We've got to do something!' Her voice had risen above a whisper. She turned her comment into a cough as the hag glared at her.

Arthur waited for the hag's interest to turn to the game again. 'We can't make a move yet without being crushed. I hope your friend is quick enough to work out the flaw in Oberon's rules.'

'What flaw?' Roxy hissed. The rules had seemed straightforward to her—all ending up with death for everyone but the winner, and that wouldn't be Tiago as he didn't stand a chance in the arena.

Arthur rubbed his right hand over his left wrist thoughtfully, strong brown fingers bearing many battle scars. Tiago had Natalia's bracelet still—they could see it. 'What if Tiago were the one to score and chose not to kill anyone?'

Utter confusion—confusion they could use. 'But he won't win, will he?'

'I think he might—with a little help. Bob?'

The dog sat up on his haunches.

'Have you been following what I've been saying?'

The dog yipped.

'Then you know what to do.'

Bob jumped down the terrace of seats and wiggled under the barrier that stopped the ball rolling out of the arena. He bounded across the sandy arena to Tiago, deftly ignoring the attempts of the ogre guards to stop him. Tiago scooped him up and appeared to be scolding him. Bob licked Tiago's ear to silence him. The boy folded up on the sand and cuddled the dog, head bent over him.

The crowd murmured, whispers of concern for the familiar rippling through the ranks.

Roxy's shell vibrated.

'What in Avalon is Bob playing at?' hissed Rick. 'That wasn't the plan!'

'Saving his master.' Roxy blinked back tears— she was torn between relief and horror to see that Tiago was no longer alone. She cut the connection before the hag could complain.

Chapter 20

THE sylphs released the ball, still in its Sun phase, letting it fall to the sand. It landed with an explosion like a landmine going up—that was the first clue Tiago got that touching the ball was not going to be straightforward. A molten sphere, it hissed and fizzed, no one daring to approach it.

'Does it have a set order or are the changes random?' he asked Malduc, hoping his father would at least share this much with him.

'It may seem random but there is a pattern.' Malduc circled, keeping out of the way of the other participants. He knew he was safe until the end. Not so Tiago.

'Bob, Arthur really wants me to try this?' Tiago

shot a look into the crowd to where Arthur and the others were sitting.

Bob yipped.

'I suppose we did rescue him for a reason. I just hope he isn't counting on me winning.' Tiago ran his hands through his hair, trying to knuckle some sense into his brain. He hated being here, hated this stupid contest, refused to think that he might be dead in a few minutes. At least no one had protested the fact that his familiar was helping him.

The ball shifted to Saturn, one of the easier phases to handle as you could hold onto the rings. One of the Reiver Fey grabbed it and skimmed it to his brother like a frisbee. On the next pass it changed to the gas giant Neptune, hitting the Reiver in the stomach, turning his tunic to ice.

'Get it off me, get it off me!' shrieked the bandit as the cold burned through the material. The ball turned to Mars and fell to the sand—to be scooped up by the ogre-Fey.

'Now would be a good time to participate,' said Malduc smoothly, standing behind Tiago with his arms crossed.

Trick or tip? Tiago had no idea but decided he had at least to try to obey Arthur's order to score. He dodged forward, Bob at his heels. The ogre-Fey was weaving between the others, Mars tucked under his arm like a rugby ball. The crowd began to cheer his daring run.

'Bob, trip him!' said Tiago.

But Bob was too far away—the mermaid was there before him. Though she could slide smoothly like a snake, she was still limited in how far she could move in the sand, not able to leap like the others. Sensibly she waited by the best spot for taking a shot at the key. As the ogre-Fey pounded towards her, she flapped sand in his face, bit his ankles in the shark-snap of her jaws and dragged the ball from his arms. The ogre-Fey rolled on the ground in agony. With a powerful flip of her tail she kept the ball bouncing until it began to shift. Tiago was almost level with her but it had turned to Jupiter and he swerved away: no one wanted to get near that gas giant. The mermaid seemed not to be bothered: she continued to bounce it like a basketball off her tail. That fish mail of hers had to be armour-plated. Everyone else stood back, waiting their chance. But it didn't come. The ball began to change again. Thwack—the mermaid hit it towards the key. She hadn't even paused to see if it was Earth but it sailed through, landing with a soft thud on the far side, the blue planet now visible.

The crowd roared their approval.

How had she known? Was it always Jupiter before Earth? Then it sank in: her goal meant someone was going to die.

The trumpets sounded.

'Players, stand still!' called the referee.

Oberon stood up. 'Mermaid, you have won this round. Whom do you choose to eliminate?'

The mermaid licked her lips, her eyes going from player to player with a hungry gaze. Her grey eyes came to rest on Tiago.

'He'll do.'

The crowd cheered, realizing that this was just the kind of vicious twist in the drama Oberon had planned for them; the mermaid knew how to play along with the script. Tiago shuddered. *Come on, amigos, time to bring on the cavalry surely?*

'Mage, shall we kill your son now?' asked Oberon.

Two ogre guards ran from the sides and took Tiago's arms. They forced him to kneel on the sand. Bob was restrained by the sylph referee, the creature's airy body making him almost impervious to the nips and bites of the dog. Tiago dropped his head. 'Mage, what is your answer?'

Malduc folded his arms, refusing to look at his old rival.

'We demand your answer, Mage.'

Malduc savoured his brief moment of power, the life and death decision. 'Not yet,' he declared.

Tiago slumped forward.

'Then I give the choice of the kill to my dearest wife.' Oberon turned to Queen Mab. 'Whom shall I eliminate for you, sweetness?'

She fluttered her heavy eyelashes at him, today a bright orange colour. 'I don't like the half-breed—the ogre-Fey. He offends me.'

'Then he is gone.' Oberon thrust his palm towards the ogre-Fey. A shaft of pure white light shot from his hand and struck the player in the chest. The victim threw his arms wide in shock, then burst into flame—and was gone. Just a pile of ash. Two claurichauns ran on with a shovel and removed the grey heap with practised efficiency as the crowd cheered their sovereign's ruthlessness.

That could've been me, thought Tiago. What were his friends waiting for?

'OK, mutt, I have to tell you: I'm not rating my chances that highly anymore. So, here's my last request. If I go down, get clear. No heroics, agreed?'

Bob stared at him defiantly.

'Agreed?' Tiago said more firmly.

Bob whimpered.

'And just so you know, you've been my best friend and I love you, OK?'

Bob howled.

'Enough of that. We're not going down without a fight, so the next round is ours. We're gonna show these guys that we have so moved on from ancient games; football is where it is at.' Tiago brushed off the sand and checked the laces on his human-made trainers were tied. 'I hope you guys are fireproof.'

Malduc came alongside, still looking supremely calm.

'So, Dad, thanks for not killing me,' Tiago said sourly.

'I do not wish you harm, Tiago, but my mercy will have to end soon. That makes me sad but . . . ' He shrugged.

'Yeah, a Mage's got to do what a Mage's got to do when he's faced with a completely mental game—I get it. Can you at least tell me one thing: why was Mars a good moment to join in?'

Malduc paused, weighing up the benefits of revealing some information. 'Mars is the second-to-last change before Earth. What you get in the middle is random but so long as you hold on to it, you get the chance to score.'

Tiago tapped his forehead in a salute. 'Thanks. And this time I mean it. I don't suppose you are going to continue this cooperative mood and tell me what you're planning?'

'Of course.'

Tiago's jaw dropped.

'I plan not to die.'

He'd known it was too good to last. 'Don't we all.' Tiago walked away to find a better spot to get to the ball.

The sylphs put the globe back into the net that suspended it over the arena. This time they released it when it was in a Pluto phase. It fell with a crack, waves of what looked like dry ice billowing from where it touched the sand. Next it shrank, becoming a warm lemon colour—Venus. One of the nixen ran to pick it up but dropped it with a scream, his hands raw with burns. Time for a little foot action.

Tiago jogged forward through the players waiting for the ball to turn to a cooler phase. Trainers made contact and did not burst into flame—great news. Dribbling the ball up the pitch, he knew enough not to take the ball anywhere near the mermaid. He chipped it past the lumbering troll and rejoined it on the far side. A defensive line of Reivers bore down on him just as the ball shifted to Mars.

'Bob!' he shouted, passing over to the dog running on the wing.

Like a champ, Bob stopped the ball with his flank and nosed it past the other nix.

'Pass it back.' Tiago did not want his faithful hound to get a muzzle full of whatever planetary horror came next.

Bob scampered through the legs of the troll and flicked it back to Tiago—just as it turned into the

Sun with a whoosh. The players fell back but Tiago realized that he was in a position that gave him a decent chance of taking this like a penalty once the phase was through. He could see the mermaid squirming nearer.

'Not today, Fish Girl.' He cracked his knuckles. 'C'mon, c'mon.'

The flare of the Sun faded, the shimmer of blue beginning. The mermaid moved more quickly than he expected, side-winding like a snake, hands outstretched. As the tips of her fingers reached the surface, Tiago ran and booted Earth through the key.

'Yes!' He punched the air—all that goal practice at school paying off.

The crowd roared their approval.

The trumpets blared and the familiar instruction to stand still was issued. Bob ran over to Tiago and sat at his feet.

'What now, mutt? Did Arthur say? He doesn't really want me to try to win every round, does he?'

Bob cocked his head sceptically.

'So I'm to kill someone off? No, I can't. I won't.'

Bob's tail wagged furiously.

'So that's the plan.' Tiago ran his grubby fingers over his face. 'Flipping ancient kings. Could've sent clearer instructions.'

Oberon held up his hand for silence. 'Human

mongrel, you have done well. You may now claim your reward. Whom do you wish to kill?'

Tiago chanced a look over towards Roxy and his friends. He'd seen what had happened to the ogre-Fey; Oberon may not take being refused well. His fingers went to the wristband, ready to activate.

'King of the Fey,' *not my king*, 'I have made my choice.' His voice sounded very feeble in the huge arena even though he was shouting.

'And that is?' Oberon opened his hand, ready to strike.

'I choose no one.' He cleared his throat then repeated, 'No one is my choice.'

His words were echoed as the audience picked up on what he had said, trying to work out how that fitted in the rules.

Oberon dropped his hand and made a fist. 'That is not an option.' He took a breath, summoning up a fake smile. 'But a very good jest. Mage are known to be tricksters, are they not? Make a proper choice. Come now. I'll even let you kill your father if you like.' He flicked his fingers towards Malduc.

'No thanks.' Tiago put his hands on his hips. 'So what you going to do about it?'

Malduc chuckled. For a second they exchanged a look of understanding, a brief moment of family feeling. 'That's my boy—disrupt the usurper's games.'

The crowd began to boo, not liking the delay to play. Morgan stood up and whispered something in the king's ear. He nodded once.

'If you break the rules, then we break ours. We kill you. Simple.'

Hoping to drive him clear, Bob sprang and hit Tiago in the chest even as Oberon gathered his elfshot.

'Looks like we're getting two birds with one stone!' laughed Oberon. He hurled a bolt of power. Tiago saw it coming directly at them, a shaft of white light, blinding in its intensity. Curling round Bob, Tiago slapped the wristband, adding a last-minute prayer that Natalia's magic could withstand her uncle's. The elfshot struck the shield and fractured, jagged bits of power flung in all directions, causing players and guards to hit the sand. All but Malduc: he whipped out a dagger from a fold of his robe and held it up like a lightning conductor so it attracted a splinter of magic. As the power shot down the dagger haft, he transformed it into a sword, skewering the ogre guard who rushed to disarm him.

'This game is over, Oberon!' shouted Malduc. He stuck the sword into the ball, now in glowing Sun phase, and heaved it in Oberon's direction. The ball hurtled towards the Royal Box, beginning to lose height. If it didn't take out the entire court, it was going to do serious damage to the masked choir just underneath. They were already leaping out of the way.

Tiago uncurled. What now? He was stranded in the middle of an arena with no magic and no weapon while pandemonium raged about him.

'Not good,' he muttered to Bob. 'This is really not good.'

Chapter 21

RICK had gambled on Malduc making a move they could use, but he hadn't bargained on it arriving in this form.

'Incoming!' yelled Rick, pushing Cobweb out of the path of the ball as it scorched its way to their position. It smashed into the ornate hoarding of the Royal Box, burning right through to set the structure on fire.

The choir vaulted the low barrier in front of their seats in to the crowd below. The arena was in utter confusion, audience heading for the exit as soldiers swarmed in. Rick made his way against the flow. He could see Tiago and Bob dodging ogre guards who were attempting to herd the prisoners back to their pen. Malduc stood alone, repelling attacks but taking every opportunity to absorb stray magic power through his sword. He was replacing the energy drained from him the quickest way he could.

Archer took out a sycacopter soldier who plummeted onto the unforgiving stone of the terrace. Rick jumped the barrier and landed in the sand of the arena. It was almost impossible to know who was fighting on what side: the Reivers had banded together with the nixen; the mermaid was on her own biting or swiping anyone who approached. Forget them—find Tiago and Bob.

He heard Bob before he saw the pair. Following that clue, Rick sprinted across the pitch, dodging his way past obstacles, and joined Tiago and Bob under the key—a good spot as it offered a little protection from spells coming from overhead.

'You OK?' Rick asked, tearing off his mask and dumping his robes. He drew his sword.

'*Hola, amigo,*' Tiago ducked a low-spun spell—it bounced from the sand and hit the wall behind him. 'Glad you could make it.'

'Happy to be here.' Rick deflected an elfshot with his sword. 'Aethel?'

His dragonet shivered into life and took off, clawing at anyone who came too close, releasing tiny bursts of flame.

'Wings? Since when?' Tiago dived and rolled, grabbing a whip from a fallen ogre.

'Since Cerunnos. Long story.'

The Alta Jewel choir formed up around Tiago and Bob, Archer using his bow to keep attackers at bay, Cobweb joining Rick taking on the swordsmen.

'What next?'

'We get out of here.'

'I'm totally on board with that.' Tiago cracked the whip, releasing a cloud of sparks from the magically charged thong, much to his own surprise. The mermaid, who had been creeping up on them half buried in the sand, fell back with a shriek.

Roxy dived through the ranks of the choir and barrelled into Tiago. 'You're safe!'

Tiago drove off the troll who was about to fell her with his axe. 'Not sure I'd call it that.'

'Words, later,' Rick said, gritting his teeth as he took an elfshot on his sword, the collision jarring his bones.

Roxy spun round and cast a spell to make a magical net. 'Good point. Focus, Roxy.' She threw it over two soldiers who were running towards them. With a yank she had them on the ground.

'I haven't got any magic.' Tiago cracked the whip again.

Rick took a quick survey of the battle. Arthur had just beaten his ogre opponent with a masterful display of swordmanship. His impromptu army had been swelled by the resistance fighters hidden among the spectators. A family of pixie acrobats had thrown off their cloaks and were making excellent use of their skills to outmanoeuvre their opponents. Fey and sylph, nixen and part-ogre—all kinds of Dark Folk appeared to be battling on their side. Queen Titania's network had done its job sending out word that they would need support.

'Malduc!' roared Arthur, 'come join us!'

Tiago's father cut the throat of the hobgoblin that lunged for his neck, pushing it aside. 'Why should I, human?'

'We can offer you sanctuary on Earth.' Arthur wiped the sweat from his brow.

Malduc's mouth turned down in a sneer. 'Unlikely. You can't make a doorway here—I designed the place with a spell that collapses such easy escapes.'

Arthur nodded as if he had expected just such a thing. 'And Oberon's cut off all exits. At least with us, you stand a chance.' It was true: while they were in control of their patch of the arena, Oberon's troops were six deep at each exit and rapidly taking control of the terraces. The king himself had mounted a griffin and was directing his forces from the air.

'*Mi padre*,' called Tiago, 'please, you could help us!'

Malduc's eyes flickered once from Oberon to his son. 'I'm not going back into exile so you can forget your offer. And I never help, Santiago.'

The griffin swooped down onto the sand, claws digging into the earth, landing between Malduc and Arthur's army. Sycacopter soldiers followed, a stinging swarm that took all the attention of the defenders. Oberon stood up in his stirrups, then turned to Malduc, letting his troops tackle the larger body of resistance fighters.

'I should have got rid of you long ago, Malduc.' Oberon urged the griffin closer to his old enemy. He held his seat superbly as it loped, front bird talons and back lion paws giving it an uneven gait. Cinnamon-tufted tail swished the air angrily; beak snapped, echoing its rider's temper.

'Yes, you should.' Malduc readied himself for the coming assault, hands taking a firm grip on his sword hilt.

Oberon launched an elfshot—a hissing fireball. Malduc swung the sword but thanks to some twist in the magic could not absorb this like he had the others. Frowning, he took the next best option and thrust it back. The king snatched it from the air, letting the spell burn in his hands, gathering in strength. 'I always had far more power than you.'

'Raw stolen power: you've lived off warped magic for years,' mocked Malduc. 'Only now do you make your dirty secret public.' He whipped up the dust of the arena and spun it into Oberon's face. Oberon blasted it away with his elfshot.

A black griffin landed softly behind Malduc, Morgan La Faye in the saddle. She came up behind the Mage. Oberon smiled, his eyes sliding to his most loyal commander.

'Watch out!' shouted Tiago.

Malduc started to turn, but too late: Morgan raised a thin silver dagger and stabbed him in the back. He hunched forward with a huff of air expelled from his lungs.

'No!'

Rick grabbed Tiago before he made the fatal mistake of leaving the cover of the defenders to run to Malduc.

Oberon approached his fallen foe and kicked sand in his face. 'Not so hard to kill in the end, were you? You should have taken Arthur's offer—at least you would have lasted a few minutes longer with allies at your back.'

Malduc twitched, his hand still trying to heft his sword at his enemy.

Oberon stood on his wrist and picked up his weapon. He threw the sword to Morgan. 'Keep it—a trophy.'

'Thank you, my lord.'

Oberon stooped over Malduc, hand on the Mage's chest, his gauntlet equipped with suckers that latched on like leeches. He muttered a few words and power began transferring between the two, the last sparks of the dying Fey's store ripped by his enemy. It looked ugly—a vampire king stealing the very essence of his victim. The air around him thickened and clotted with diseased power. Tiago swayed, resting a hand on Rick's arm to stop his legs crumpling from under him. Bob howled. Natalia shouldered her way past one of the Fey choir and hugged Tiago, holding his face against her chest so he did not see the body being dragged off.

'You shouldn't have seen him die like that.' Rick's heart squeezed painfully when he saw the shocked gaze of his friend.

'I . . . I . . . ' Tiago couldn't find the words. They all knew that Malduc had been a disaster as a father but Tiago had not entirely managed to give up hoping that one day this would change.

Rick grappled for something comforting to say. 'He . . . he wouldn't have wanted to live unless he ruled.'

Tiago brushed his sleeve over his face. 'I know.' He pushed away from Natalia.

Oberon wiped the sand off his hands in a

dismissive gesture. 'Now for this rabble. Guards, finish them off!'

'Pox, pox, pox!' hissed Roxy. 'What next?'

'I was hoping we could've made the door by now.' Rick winced as Aethel just missed being swatted from the air by a griffin. He knew he should have more faith in her but she was not used to her wings and some of her evasions were more luck than judgement. 'But you heard Malduc: the arena blocks that spell.'

'Fire-throwers!' Tiago pointed to four huge cauldrons being raised to sit on the top of each pyramid. Oberon's troops were pulling back so they would not be caught in the river of fire.

Oberon slashed his arm down, signalling them to begin. His griffin took off, taking him out of range.

Glowing white-hot, the liquid splashed from the cauldrons. Streams of molten material flowed down the steps, bearing down on their position. In a few seconds they would be swamped like a boat going under the falls at Niagara.

'Take shelter by me!' roared Arthur. He slammed his shield onto the sand, summoning the Pen Draig. She twisted rapidly from the surface, her beautiful dragon body of golden wires taking shape. Spreading her wings, she surrounded the group of huddled freedom fighters as if she were guarding her nest. Aethel hissed and whistled, landing on her back. The fire splashed against the Pen Draig like waves on a cliff, forced to fall back. The Fey shot bolt after bolt of magic at her but none made any impact as she was spirit, the magical quintessence itself, so their shots were no more than breezes on her skin.

In the shadow of her wings, Arthur knelt among his followers—a strangely quiet space in the midst of battle, vaulted like a chapel. 'My friends, I would welcome any ideas for how we can get to a place where we can make a door.'

'We are not enough to fight our way out of here,' said Archer, stating what everyone knew.

'Bit of a rubbish rescue if it means you all die,' muttered Tiago. Rick knew he was feeling bad that his situation was the reason they were all in this hole.

Cobweb stood up, her head brushing the underside of the Pen Draig's wing. 'I smell dragon.'

'We're sitting under one—of course you do,' said Roxy.

'Not this sort—our sort.'

The Pen Draig's wing moved back like a fan furling. Overhead they could all see a squadron of dragons spiralling, led by Rick's old nemesis, the Stormridge. So Cerunnos had persuaded them!

Just as Rick had that thought, half of them split off and dive-bombed the castle, ripping through the magical walls of the building like paper, throwing masonry, tiles and contents crashing to the ground. They were aiming at the parts of the palace most infected by polluted magic, the dizzying impossible peaks and twisted turrets. He was no longer so sure of their purpose here.

'Are they here to save us or attack?' asked Cobweb, having the same doubts.

The troops lined up on the high ground became aware of the danger above. They turned their arrows and elfshot upwards but that was no help against the magic-proof dragons. Soldiers at the northern entrance to the arena also reversed their formation, fighting those arriving behind.

'Reinforcements!' shouted Cobweb.

But how to join up with Titania's army? They were trapped on a small patch of sand surrounded by a bubbling moat of white-hot magma.

Then a stag appeared in the northern gate, stepping through Oberon's soldiers as if they were no more than saplings. Cerunnos kept going, hooves treading lightly across the firepit. He lowered his head and let his nose touch the surface. Ice flowed from his breath, causing the lava to turn to a sheet of obsidian, black volcanic glass.

'Forward!' Rick shouted, leading the way across the bridge Cerunnos had made. The Pen Draig continued to cover them, flying overhead with

Aethel at her side. They fought their way through the last soldiers in the gateway and joined up with Titania and her people on the far side.

'Make a door!' yelled Rick.

Archer grabbed Cobweb and pushed to the front, already muttering the spell as he ran.

The Pen Draig slipped down like a vast silk scarf folding back onto Arthur's shield. Aethel landed on Rick's shoulder and coiled round his neck. Roxy's robins perched on her head, tiny claws anchored in her hair. Trix-E whistled to summon Peter and the horses from their hitching post.

'It's ready—I'll hold it this end!' shouted Archer.

Arthur went first, followed by his allies. Rick caught a glimpse of Titania urging her people to go through behind the lead party.

'What about the balance?' Rick asked Archer.

'It will have to hold for the moment—we have no time to fix it.'

They came out onto Salisbury plain. Thanks to Archer's skill, he had brought them to a field in sight of Stonehenge. It was the middle of the night but the stone circle was glowing.

'Merlin's work,' said Arthur, running up the slope.

The army streamed through the archways made by the stones, but there were too many for all to fit inside. Titania ordered her people to stay back before joining Arthur and his allies in the circle.

Merlin was standing ready in the centre of the ring, Linette and Gordon by his side. He grinned.

'Excellent timing. We thought we were going to have to start the party without you.'

'Where's the Round Table?' asked Arthur.

Merlin gestured overhead. 'Waiting for you. If I could have the scrying glass—that's always the finishing touch.'

Roxy dug in her bag and handed it over. Merlin breathed on it and tossed it up into the air. It hovered and then burst open like a flower, petals shining the warning of the attack heading their way, glimpses of the feverish eyes of Oberon, sick with polluted magic, the taut white face of Morgan, the human-hating Fey troops, squadrons of sycacopters. 'I take it you come with danger snapping at your heels?'

'Exactly.' Arthur gulped water from a flask Tabitha passed him. 'Queen Titania—Merlin; Merlin, Titania.'

The wizard bowed low, digging deep for forgotten courtly manners. 'An honour to see you on Earth, my lady.'

'Where do you want us?' Rick asked.

'For this to work, all places at the Table must be filled with the right kind of magic carrier. Arthur, your place is prepared. As for you others—the changelings and allies who will serve as knights of the Round Table—they need to find theirs.'

Rick looked round the circle and saw that his friends from Dark Lore were waiting for a signal. Arthur strode briskly to the king's seat. His symbol—a dragon's head—flared brightly, welcoming him back.

'I know mine,' said Linette, moving beneath the Fisher King, Gordon trotting at her side. Merlin stood opposite Arthur under his star symbol. Three places filled but many still were empty.

'How do we know?' Roxy asked Linette.

'You'll know.'

Roxy gazed upwards. 'OK, then I think I should . . . I should go here.' She walked to be under Sir Gawain's name. The robin symbol flickered and then blazed more strongly. 'Yes, this is my place.'

Tiago shrugged. 'I always knew mine—Sir Lancelot du Lac. He must have meddled with my Mage ancestors at some point—distant cousin.' He whistled to Bob and they took their place together.

Simon frowned then his face cleared. 'I think . . . yes, I think this is mine. Sir Bors.'

The little Arabian boy, Ahmed, practically skipped to Sir Gareth's place, a huge smile on his face as the symbol lit up to greet his magic.

Tabitha bowed her head, hands together, before moving quickly to the place of Sir Bedivere, the faithful knight. Seeing her safe, Edgar then strove to Sir Kay's spot, foster brother to Arthur, another staunch knight.

'My lady?' Arthur bowed to Natalia. 'I think you also know where you should be.'

With a blushing nod, Natalia stood at his side under the symbol for Guinevere.

That left two places—the Lady of the Lake and Sir Galahad.

'Come on, Rick, it's obvious,' called Roxy. 'We always knew you were the contender for the most perfect knight.'

Rick strode to the spot that had been calling him. The sign glittered with joy to have its knight in his rightful place.

'But the Lady—who can fill her place?' asked Arthur. 'She was from the Other World.'

'Not one "who" but many,' said Merlin. 'That is the place for your Avalonian allies that serve under your banner—the pixies.'

Trix-E and her family cartwheeled to take the final opening.

'My table is complete.' Arthur caught them all in his proud gaze. 'We will fight with the power of both Earth and Avalon behind us. Merlin: now!'

On his word, Merlin activated the table. It floated down from over their heads to settle on them so that they were within it, swimming in the magical energies it released. Rick felt the power seeping through his skin as he was immersed in a bath of pure enchantment, swept in the tide, dragged under with the currents coming from two worlds. Before his magic had always felt like a hard diamond in his chest, now he was fashioned into one huge gem, radiant with power. It both hurt and felt joyous at the same time—the birth of something new. Symbols and names wove before his eyes, waves on the sea of magic, but he never felt lost as he was anchored by the strength of Arthur and the wisdom of Merlin. Just when he felt he could take no more, the glow began to fade, the table lifted from them as softly as a cloud of mist rising from the earth on an autumn morning.

'Welcome, knights,' said Arthur, confidence in every gesture. He drew his sword from its sheath, letting the light flash on its name. Excalibur, ablaze with magic. 'Let's change history,' he looked across at Merlin and laughed, '—again.'

Chapter 22

LINETTE struggled to find the words for what she was experiencing. At least her friends had had a few years to get used to magic but it was a complete shock to her system. The energy inside her was not alien—if anything it made her even more herself. When she reached for the power, it felt like a song she had to sing, a picture she had to draw, a laugh she couldn't suppress. Her skin tingled. She was too scared to cough or sneeze in case some of the power escaped.

Tiago was closest to her so was the first to catch her marvelling expression. 'Like it?'

'I didn't know.' Desperate to feel a human touch within this whirl of enchantments, she held out a hand to Tiago, which he took and gave a squeeze.

'You've had this all your life? It's amazing. How do I manage it?'

Tiago seemed to be glowing with the stuff himself, his eyes a brighter silver, his hair electric, floating rather than lying flat. 'Tricky thing is, Linette, I've not had this much at my fingertips before so I'm not sure of the answer. I fear that if I let it go like I normally would, I'd take out everything—flatten the place like a hurricane.'

Linette rolled her shoulders. Arthur, Merlin and Titania were in conference, their seconds-in-command at their shoulder. She was at first surprised then pleased to see that Rick stood beside Arthur, the king's first commander. That felt right. 'I bet Arthur wished he had more time to train us.'

'My guess is that focus is the key thing. Spells work when you bring your inner thoughts and shape the magic to your idea.' Tiago flourished his hand and a box appeared on his palm. 'I'm holding that shape in my mind. Then you move it to the next stage.' He blinked and the box sprang open, a burst of tiny fire-flowers like confetti. He let the shape fade and rubbed his chest. 'That was way harder than usual because I could feel all the supercharged power dammed up inside wanting out.'

'I tried once with a little power—at Merlin's laboratory. I had to breathe it out—I mean that literally.'

Tiago gave in to the laughter that welled up inside him. 'If that's what works for you, go with it, *amiga*. Shame we don't have time for the Magic for Beginners course but Oberon won't give us it. He'll be on us like fleas on a dog.' Bob thwacked his tail against Tiago's leg, releasing a shower of stinging sparks. 'Cut it out, mutt, you know that was nothing personal.'

Last to arrive from Avalon, Archer raced into the stone circle. 'Oberon's coming.'

'Already?' asked Cobweb, chucking him his bow, which she had been minding.

'Yes.' Archer snatched it from the air and turned to share the news with the commanders. 'I was going to let the doorway fold but Cerunnos said not to—he promised to hold it and stop the balance being disrupted. It means he won't make the fight but he said he felt keeping space and time collapsing was a higher priority.'

Cobweb laughed at his dry tone. Even Arthur smiled.

'But before I left, I had the chance to see our father gather his forces. He's abandoned the palace to the dragons for now and he's decided to go after us first.'

'Thank you for this news, Prince Archer.' Arthur leapt onto a stone so he was head and shoulders above everyone. 'Friends, allies, this is our hour.

Prepare yourselves.' As he spoke his clothes shimmered and transformed into magical armour, a dragon etched on his breastplate. One by one the changelings did likewise, adopting protection fitting their skill, light armour for archers, heavy for those who fought with close-quarter weapons. Rick wore a full suit, complete with sword and lance, Peony in matching gear of polished steel. Rick mounted, as did Arthur on Dewdrop—the only two cavalry among the changelings. Roxy created a golden mail shirt for herself and a crossbow. Tiago summoned a bronze breastplate and helmet, looking like a figure from a Greek vase, legs bare to allow him freedom to run and jump. Natalia stood tall and stately in her light armour, a long sword at her hip.

Everyone seemed to know what to do—everyone but Linette. That wasn't good enough. *You didn't get to this point, all charged up and nowhere to go.* She ran through her options. She could not match the agility of those on foot but she did know how to ride. Concentrating on her chair, she blew a bubble of magic, letting it surround her. The chair shifted, transforming, wheels flattening to become flanks, struts criss-crossing to form a chest, head and legs. It became not flesh and blood, but a moving creature like the huge puppet horses she'd seen used for a stage show— even better as it needed no one to manipulate it.

Thanks to her magic and Merlin's skill in construction, it now answered to her thought.

Tiago watched her open-mouthed. 'That is so cool, Linette. I want one.'

She gave herself a mental pat on the back. 'I'm as surprised as you are—this magic thing really rocks.'

Roxy and Rick joined them. Peony nosed Linette's mount and received a very horse-like response.

'I'm totally green with envy,' admitted Roxy.

'I was just saying the same thing.' Tiago clapped his arm around the shorter girl. 'Come on, Rox, us foot soldiers better get in position.'

Rick held out his hand for Tiago to shake. 'Good luck.'

Roxy put hers on top of theirs, and then Linette leaned over to add the final hand.

'Hey, this is like one of those cheesy "all for one and one for all" moments—you know, musketeers?' said Tiago.

'Works for me,' said Rick with a grin. 'Keep safe or I'll be furious—that's an order. I didn't haul you out of San Francisco Bay,' he looked at Linette, 'and you out of the arena,' he cuffed Tiago lightly, 'to lose you on Salisbury Plain.'

Tiago hit him back on the leg. 'Ain't gonna happen. Bob and I—we're feeling pretty invincible.'

'Just don't get too confident. We have power but so does Oberon—all stolen from hundreds—thousands—of other people.'

Roxy gripped their fingers hard. 'Love you guys. Don't do anything stupid.'

'You too.' Rick dropped his hand and bent down to kiss her on her forehead where he could reach. Linette suspected then that there was something just a little special going on between her two friends. Tiago grinned at her, sensing the same thing.

Pretending not to notice their knowing expressions, Rick settled back in the saddle and clicked his tongue to Peony. 'Come on, Linette, we should go to Arthur.'

Chapter 23

UNDER King Arthur's flag, Rick arranged the army with Stonehenge at their backs, giving cover to their archers. They were under orders to move round the stone circle to face the enemy once they knew which direction he would come from—or directions if Oberon decided to split his forces.

Aethel perched on Rick's shoulder, wings beating restlessly.

'Remember you're still vulnerable,' Rick told her. 'You may be a little spirit dragon but your bodily form hasn't been dipped in dragon tears like your guardian on Arthur's shield.'

Linette urged her horse nearer. 'What's on the shield?'

Rick had forgotten she'd not been with them when the Pen Draig had been visible. 'Aethel's guardian came from that realm and inhabits Arthur's shield like Aethel does my torc. In that realm's terms, Aethel's still young—still vulnerable—just a baby really.'

Aethel hissed in his ear indignantly.

'Don't you sass me, legless. I'm serious—you get hurt and your guardian will not be pleased with me.'

A flock of robins flew in from the east where the sun was beginning to show above the horizon, twittering the alarm. Rick raised his sword, pointing to the dawn. 'Oberon approaches.'

'Merlin: keep the table running or we're all—' began Arthur.

'Up the creek without a paddle—I know, I know.' Merlin headed back to his side of the circle. 'Later, peeps.'

Arthur turned to Natalia. 'Did he just say what I thought he said?'

'Oh yes.' Natalia smiled. 'I think he said that to annoy you so you have an extra reason to want to survive and take him to task for it.'

'So that's why he does it. And there was me thinking he was the most irritating wizard in existence.'

A second flock arrived from the south, warning of an approach from that direction.

'Commander, the army is yours,' said Arthur to Rick. 'Remember what I've taught you. I have to hold my place at the table to keep the magic strong, so you have to be my eyes and ears on the field.' He beckoned some of the strongest Fey soldiers from Titania's bodyguard to take their positions protecting him.

Rick scanned the battleground, urgency not giving him time to be overwhelmed by the responsibility. 'Queen Titania, will you take our right flank?'

The Fey queen nodded. 'With pleasure.'

'Sir!' said Ahmed, gesturing to the north. A line of ogres was cresting the hill, long shadows slanting sideways.

Rick was not surprised to see that Oberon had thrown everything he had at them, bringing all his available armies to Earth. 'Archer, will you lead the defence on that side?'

Archer nodded and led a detachment of Feys and changelings to block the ogres, Tabitha, Edgar, Simon and Ahmed among them.

A single bird flew from the west and landed on Roxy's shoulder.

'He's sent a pack of hobs that way to scoop up any of us who flee,' Roxy translated.

'As if any of us would flee,' snorted Cobweb before hurrying off to join her twin.

'Do we go meet them?' asked Roxy.

'No.' Rick could see the moves clearly in his mind, like anticipating an opponent in a game of chess. 'We don't want to get too far ahead of our forces and present him with a way to split us up. We'll engage him there.' He pointed to the place a stone's throw ahead where the road forked to go past the stone circle.

Oberon's forces appeared out of the morning mist like wraiths, seemingly barely there. The oblique shafts of the sun made it hard to focus but Rick thought he could make out Oberon and Morgan mounted on griffins.

Peony pawed the ground, hot breath snorting.

'Not yet.' Rick checked the stallion. 'Wait until you see the whites of their eyes.'

Sweat trickled down Rick's neck, one hand clenching his lance, the other holding the reins.

'The griffins first, Linette,' said Rick.

Shouts and cries erupted on their left flank as Archer engaged the ogres.

'Charge!' shouted Rick.

Spurring Peony, Rick crouched in his saddle, holding the lance steady. Tiago and the other foot soldiers ran alongside, spears on shoulders, swords held out ready to strike. A volley of arrows whistled overhead, taking out a couple of warriors in Oberon's advance guard, but that was only a few leaves in a forest. Rick urged Peony faster. He knew that Roxy had his back with her cross-bow and there was no one he would trust more to be watching out for him. He glanced sideways: Linette was matching his pace. She didn't have a weapon to direct her magic—there hadn't been time to teach her that, but she had no trouble throwing sheets of flame like someone shaking water from their fingers.

The sight of his friends all hurrying to meet their enemy put Rick's heart in his mouth. He had to remind himself that this wasn't a battle about muscles and physical size; this was a fight to see who had the stronger magic. The smallest pixie with the greater skills stood a better chance than the biggest ogre who relied on his brawn.

A sycacopter Fey swooped down on him from the right. Aethel launched and struck, burning the warrior's wings with a crisp blast, her dragon-fire defeating any repelling spell he had put on his harness. Rick blasted an arrow from the sky before it could strike the dragonet. He caught a glimpse of Tiago going one-on-one with the leader of the nix, Prince Litu. A troll lumbered in between him and Linette. Rick took the creature on, exchanging sword blows. The troll held his dull steel blade with some skill, his magic-powered strikes jarring with every swipe. Rick danced Peony round him, taking jabs at the troll's unprotected sides, meeting the sword only when he had to. The contest was taking too long—he had to ensure Arthur and Merlin were protected so the Round Table continued to work. Time to call on his magical reserves. Rick found the power almost too eager to rush from him. His elfshot blasted the troll ten feet in the air and brought him crashing down on six Fey running to attack.

OK, that taught him: next time quit playing and start working the Round Table magic sooner.

When Rick had a chance to look about him, he found to his dismay Oberon and Morgan had got past him. Arthur was fighting them both, the guards he had kept with him already fallen. Malduc had been slaughtered in a two-pronged attack— Rick refused to allow that to happen to Arthur. He pressed Peony through the massed armies, the chance of battle bringing him up on Oberon's side. He lowered his lance and aimed for the griffin, knowing that the Fey King would be more strongly armoured with magic than his mount.

Channel the power through the lance. Channel. Focus, he told himself.

The world narrowed to one screeching tawny mount, clawing at Dewdrop's eyes.

The impact unseated Rick but his lance stuck in the flank of the griffin, then exploded in a shower of white sparks. The griffin went down—a mortal wound. Oberon rolled quickly off the ground and drew his sword, leaping upon Rick before he knew what was happening. The blade arced towards his neck but Aethel was there before it— turning back to gold torc at the last second. The sword cut deep into metal but Oberon could not withdraw it.

Fury filled Rick. He exploded to his feet, sword and torc falling still intertwined. Rick hurled an elfshot at Oberon's chest. As he did so, he glimpsed out of the corner of his eye the Pen Draig unfurling from Arthur's shield, coming to the aid of her child. Even though Arthur was fighting Morgan, he threw his shield to the ground to cover the wounded Aethel.

Rick's missile hit the Fey King's magical defences. Shocked by the impact, Oberon staggered but quickly recovered. He couldn't reach his sword under the Pen Draig so he whirled his arm, sending a lash of fire at Rick's neck. Now Rick understood just how powerful the Fey King really was. It caught, burning against Rick's skin, pulling him almost off his feet. The touch of the magic made him feel sick, like he was being forced to drink polluted water.

'Die, human!' sneered Oberon. He tightened the noose with a vicious twist as, with a flick of his wrist, he speared one of Titania's Fey soldiers who was rushing to the rescue.

There was no way to undo the fiery thong—Rick had to master it. Sending his own power down the leash, he stopped holding back on his huge well of magic, focusing it through this one small connection. It gushed, sizzled and foamed like a geyser erupting, throwing Oberon back.

As Rick broke free, there came a cry of triumph from Morgan. She took advantage of Arthur's lack of shield and drove her sword into his side. He slumped over Dewdrop's neck, red droplets staining her white coat. Morgan raised her blade to finish off King Arthur but Natalia dashed into the gap and caught the sword on hers. At a disadvantage between the two mounted fighters, Natalia was swiftly driven back by the griffin's beak snapping at her eyes, claws raking her thigh. Yet her intervention gave Arthur the moment he required to summon his last strength. He rammed his sword into Morgan's chest—the power of Excalibur cutting the threads of the enchantments and letting the point sink into the Fey's heart. Pure Round Table magic streamed in through the wound, burning out the rotten power that Oberon had been feeding his commanders. Morgan shrieked with ear-splitting fury. She fell from the saddle and writhed on the ground, only to have her own panicked griffin step on her neck, abruptly silencing her cries. Enemy conquered, Arthur slid from his saddle, ending up beside her. Neither moved.

The supply of Round Table magic spluttered and failed. Rick was thrown back on his normal levels of power with a disorienting jolt.

Dewdrop and Peony took charge, herding the griffin away before it could do any more damage to the fallen. Natalia rushed to Arthur's side to pad his wound and use what healing spells she knew. Rick could not help—he had a bigger problem on his hands. Oberon was up and ready for a second strike. Rick blasted him with his strongest elfshot. Oberon repelled it and returned with an even greater detonation of power. Rick knew he was outclassed and now his Round Table magic was no longer being refreshed, he was no match for the energy Oberon had been stockpiling.

Then Roxy ran up beside him, joining her elf-shots to his.

'Get back!' warned Rick.

She gave him a reckless grin. 'I never could obey orders.'

Linette spurred her horse to the far side, battering Oberon with waves of fire, each one getting weaker as her magic ran out. Tiago leapt the body of the fallen griffin and threw his spear, forcing the

Fey King to stumble. Still Oberon withstood them, even though he now faced four young knights.

The Pen Draig whirled around them, Aethel in her claws.

How is she? asked Rick, desperate to know his friend still lived.

She hurts. She tells you to . . . the Pen Draig's voice in his head warmed with amusement *. . . finish this.*

I wish.

Then do so. Send Oberon's stolen magic back to its owners. Unknit the power from his frame.

That was one of the simplest charms a magic wielder learned, necessary to repair the many mistakes of the beginner. But Rick only knew how to call back his own power.

If you let Oberon take yours, then summon it, I promise you it will be the crack that breaks the dam holding the stolen magic within him.

You'd better be right about this.

The Pen Draig spun in a dizzying circle, petal-like scales of magic raining down on their heads. Oberon brushed them away, shuddering at their touch. The young knights felt refreshed, like a cool drink in the midst of combat. Rick took that as the reassurance he needed.

He didn't have time to warn his comrades what he had in mind. On the next blast of elfshot, Rick let it slip under his guard and strike him on the chest. It was like willingly laying on an anvil and letting a troll blacksmith hammer his breastplate. He didn't have to feign the collapse back—but he did pretend to be unconscious. It was almost impossible to lie still knowing he was all but unprotected from Oberon's revenge.

'Rick!' screamed Roxy.

'Stupid human,' spat Oberon, stamping on Rick's wrist and taking his sword. 'Get back the rest of you or I will slit his throat.'

Rick thought for a moment that he was going to leave it at that but then Oberon knelt and pressed his gauntlet against the point his elfshot had struck. Rick felt his power leave through the gap like water sucked up a straw. How much was enough?

Now, nudged the Pen Draig.

Rick flung himself into action, gripping Oberon's wrist with one fist, the other hand plastered over the Fey King's nose and face. He sent the strongest undoing spell he knew through the contact of skin to skin. It was like they became two magnets—he couldn't lift his hand even if he had wanted as the power reversed and poured back into him. Oberon dropped Rick's sword and struck him around the head with his mailed fist, trying to loosen his hold that way, but Rick could've told him it had gone beyond his will in the matter. He regained his full power but he could feel other kinds rushing on behind. They streaked from Oberon—a huge blast heading straight for Tiago, knocking him off his feet so he just avoided a killing blow from Prince Litu, who had charged up behind him. Stolen magic rushed to the crossing point of the stone circle, seeking its true owners in Avalon. The power passed through the glowing Round Table and into the ground beneath.

Oberon gave a hoarse cry and clutched his chest, trying to hold all that he had stolen to himself, a miser with a bag of spilled coins. Then the agony became too much—he crumpled and passed out, the connection with Rick broken. He fell on his face, twitching convulsively. His bronzed skin turned dull; white hair went grey.

'The king has fallen!' cried the nearest Fey. Leaderless now that Morgan too was down, Oberon's troops scattered. Some of the most disciplined stayed to put up a desperate defence but the majority could think only of escape back to Avalon. Rick staggered to his feet in time to see Linette and Tiago drive Prince Litu to his knees between them. Roxy shot down a last sycacopter soldier diving to retrieve the Fey King, then ran to Rick's side.

'Is Oberon dead?' she asked.

'I don't think so. Drained.'

'We'd better get him restrained then.' She blew a sharp whistle. 'Hey, Trix-E, got anything suitable for tying up a king?'

Trix-E and her parents hurried over. Frost-E produced a pair of suspiciously ordinary-looking handcuffs from a pocket. Some human police officer would be missing those.

'Thanks.' Rick kneeled and clicked Oberon's arms behind his back. 'That'll do until Titania finds a more permanent solution. Keep an eye on him, please, pixies.'

Having done what he could there, Rick turned his attention to Arthur. Merlin had joined Natalia and they were conversing in low voices. Peter stood with his multi-coloured beak touching Arthur's chest, willing him to get better.

'How bad is it?'

Natalia looked up, eyes brimming with tears. 'Very bad.'

Titania strode over to their position, taking in Morgan's body, Oberon in handcuffs and the injured Arthur all in one quick sweep of the battlefield.

Rick knelt beside Arthur. 'You need healing, sir. We'll have to take you to hospital.'

Arthur's eyes flickered open and went to Merlin. 'Been here . . . before.'

Merlin nodded. 'You certainly have, my friend. These are magical wounds, Rick: they won't heal here. He has to go to Avalon.'

'I offer him the attention of my best feysicians,' said Titania at once.

'As long as you don't shut me up on that wretched island again.' Arthur's eyelids slid closed. 'Been tricked once.'

Natalia took his hand. 'I'll go with you—make sure nothing happens that shouldn't.'

'Thank you—my lady.'

Titania gestured for her guard to make a stretcher for Arthur. 'Quickly now, every second is of the essence. There is much to do in Avalon to secure this victory.' She looked around the changelings gathered at Arthur's side. 'Who now commands in his place?' Her eyes went to Merlin.

The wizard looked taken aback. 'Me? You've got the wrong guy—I don't do military leadership, swords, fighting and that stuff. It's him.' Merlin pointed at Rick. 'He is Arthur's choice.'

'I leave you, Sir Elfric, to hold your position. I will send word soon by my children how we fare. I hope to see you again when we may have a chance to celebrate this victory.'

Feeling the eyes of all the changelings on him, Rick stood up a little straighter.

'Thank you, your majesty. The knights of the

Round Table stand ready to help, should you need us.'

'Then farewell for the present.' Titania led the way back through the gateway still held by Cerunnos. Natalia and Peter followed with Arthur's escort, then Oberon was carried off as a prisoner. Next, the remaining warriors passed through, taking with them the bodies of those Dark Folk on both sides who had died. In half an hour, the field of Stonehenge was empty but of the changelings, the pixies, Merlin and the Fey twins. There was a brief moment of shocked quiet then the pixies rolled into action.

'I know what we all need!' Frost-E quickly brewed some tea on a bonfire in the centre of the ring and danced around passing out cups to the exhausted warriors while his wife distributed chocolate. Trix-E and Tabitha unsaddled the horses and led them to a trough. After this short rest, Archer stood up and brushed the crumbs from his clothes. Cobweb tucked an extra chocolate bar in her pocket for later.

'Cobweb and I must help mother—there are still the dragons and any resistance to counter in Avalon. So I suppose this is goodbye for now,' said Archer, hugging Roxy, before shaking the others by the hand. 'It's been an honour fighting with you.'

'And you,' said Rick, stepping between the Fey and his friend in case Archer got it into his head to invite Roxy to go off with him.

'Rick, I'll be back soon. There's so much more I want you to show me. I want to go to a landfill next.' Cobweb slapped a kiss on his mouth before Rick could react.

'I'll . . . er . . . look forward to it.'

The twins passed through the doorway.

Well done, Cerunnos' voice whispered in Rick's mind for a last time. *You have the gratitude of all spirit beings for ending the polluted magic.* With the last glimpse of an antlered head, the portal winked out of existence.

Rick took a deep breath, knowing the changelings gathered around the circle expected him to show them what they should do next. Thanks to the protection of the Round Table, none had died but many were injured, Edgar the most seriously. Tabitha was sewing up his wounds with magical thread as he lay like a sacrifice on one of the flat stones.

'How is he?' Rick asked.

'He'll live,' said Tabitha. 'Saved my life and got that, the idiot.' She sniffed, holding back her tears. Clearly there were many more tales than his to tell.

It was just beginning to sink in: they'd done it. They'd defeated Oberon. The changelings were safe—for the moment. Rick picked up Arthur's shield, the Pen Draig back on its surface. He had already placed Aethel on a fallen stone, nestled in the folds of his jacket. She shivered in her living form, but her guardian had healed her wound. Too shocked to move, she let Rick pick her up and drape her gently round his neck.

'All right, legless. You're safe now,' he whispered.

Merlin chose that moment to drop the illusion he had been keeping over the area to hide the battle. Soon, the first coach party of the day would arrive and the tourists were going to wonder what they were all doing there. Never had a more tired and dirty bunch of humans gathered on this spot since it was first erected.

'My friends, I have no idea what Arthur had planned for us after the battle,' began Rick. 'But I know what I think we should do.'

'And what's that?' asked Linette, sitting once more in her chair, Gordon's head in her lap. Rick sincerely hoped it wasn't the last they would see of her unique horse.

'I think we should check in to a five-star hotel and celebrate. It's not every day you save the Earth is it?' The changelings cheered and laughed.

'If that's your first order as our leader,' said Roxy, 'I won't have trouble obeying.'

'Oh and I'm sure Pip Enterprises will pay, won't they, Merlin?' Linette asked cheekily.

Merlin grinned as he put the capsule of Round Table magic back in its bag and wrapped up the scrying glass. He gave Miz-Begotten a warning look as her fingers inched towards it. 'Yes, completely my treat. You did good—all of you. I've never been more proud in my life of any warriors I have served alongside.'

The young knights of the Round Table stood within the walls of Stonehenge for a moment savouring the praise. The newly risen sun bathed them in its gentle light. It felt so good to be alive and to be human.

'C'mon team,' said Tiago, breaking the spell. He picked up Bob. 'Let's go make some hotel's day.'

Chapter 24

ENGLAND was enjoying an Indian summer. With the October sun shining on the water, Rick dived in the pool at the Appletree Country Hotel near Glastonbury. Owned by Pip Enterprises, this mansion was one of Merlin's homes from home, built on the site where legend claimed he had once been trapped in a tree. It was beautifully landscaped but Merlin didn't allow any hawthorns in the garden. Too many bad memories, he claimed.

Rick cut through the water, completing three lengths before he came up for a breather. Bob and Gordon lay flat out in the sunshine doing what Tiago called their 'dead dog' impressions. Linette and Roxy were sunbathing side by side, gleaming with tanning lotion, black and golden-red hair shining. Three robins perched on Roxy's lounger, resting after their Avalonian adventure. Tiago was chatting with Merlin at one of the tables, sipping from a drink sprouting umbrellas and slices of fruit. Some of the more energetic changelings were playing a game of cricket on the lawn, Tabitha and Simon were in bat, facing bowler Ahmed. Edgar, still not completely recovered, cheered from the sidelines. Even Peony and Dewdrop were off-duty, relaxing in the paddock under an oak tree.

The only people missing were the pixies. They had gone shopping in Bristol. Rick thought it best not to ask what that meant for the personal belongings of other shoppers. Overjoyed by the opportunities for property circulation, the pixies seemed perfectly happy to stay on Earth for the long term and keep Roxy company.

Rick climbed out of the pool, wrapped a thick white towel round his waist and joined Merlin and Tiago at their table. Aethel slept curled round the umbrella in the centre, her little wings fluttering with every breath.

'Any news?' he asked.

Merlin nodded. 'Natalia sent word that Arthur is doing well in the hands of the feysicians. Early days yet so he's got a long way to go. The dragons still occupy Oberon's palace and are doing some redecorating of their own . . . '

'You mean tearing it apart,' said Rick.

'Exactly. So Titania has set up her headquarters at Dark Lore, the old capital.'

'I thought that was pretty much trashed,' said Roxy from her sun lounger.

'It did melt but she's got her architects rebuilding it—they've consulted me on the plans: it will be even more beautiful when it's finished.'

Rick grinned at Roxy, thinking how relaxed and happy she looked. He was waiting to ask her to go for a walk with him later. Just the two of them. 'So . . . er . . . what's Titania done with Oberon?'

Merlin raised a brow. 'I believe there's an island somewhere in the north with a new tenant.'

'Poor puffins.'

Merlin chuckled. 'I think Peter will probably ask them to make Oberon's life a misery after what he did to Arthur. But then, Mab has gone into exile with Oberon so I imagine they will be each other's punishment after a few weeks of living together with no luxuries—I couldn't devise a crueller prison if I tried. What else should I tell you? Ah yes. Cerunnos is brokering talks between the two sides— Fey and dragon—so for the moment Avalon is at peace. Natalia also said she would visit soon with the twins to check up on their favourite humans.'

Rick stretched and put his hands behind his head, well content with Merlin's answers. He stole a slice of pineapple off the side of Tiago's glass and popped it in his mouth.

'Pixie,' muttered Tiago.

Linette levered her sun lounger a few notches to be sitting upright. 'My parents are flying in tomorrow, Rick. They seem a bit confused but Merlin is sorting out their tangled careers.'

'Do you want to end up in San Francisco or Oxford?' Merlin passed her drink. 'Thanks to Natalia, your parents are now holding jobs in both places.'

'That depends on you guys. I want to be where you are.'

Merlin nodded in approval. 'And don't forget, you are my apprentice, Linette. Just because the battle is over, it doesn't mean you've lost your job.'

Rick knew that his holiday from responsibility was over. 'Where we end up depends on what happens to all of us changelings. There are a hundred of us to find homes.'

Roxy got up and moved to the seat next to him, taking a quick sip of his drink as she did so. 'The hotel can only just hold us all.' She took one of Tiago's drink umbrellas and put it in Rick's hair. He laughed and put a blue flower from a vase in hers. Pixie ways were catching.

'Ah, yeah, about finding homes.' Merlin cleared his throat. 'I've been thinking. I have some money. As you might know, my company is quite big.'

'Yes, only the largest technology firm in the world earning billions,' added Tiago in an undertone.

'Well, I thought that it would be possible to find foster parents for the younger ones among my employees. Those who wish to return to the countries they were taken from could go to people there—I do have offshoots in every major city. And by remaining in the Pip network you'd all be able to keep in touch with the infants until they are ready.'

'Ready for what?'

'To join our school. There's plenty more you have to learn to be fully fledged knights. You'll need the YKA.'

'Let me guess: the Young Knights Academy?' said Tiago. 'Cool—as long as you do everything the exact opposite of the Fey at Dark Lore.'

'Trust me, people—I wouldn't dream of repeating their mistakes. These last few weeks have taught me that I can't preserve the green power of Earth alone and more apprentices will be just what I need. Together we can train up the other changelings and prep the young knights in their mission for the future: save the humans from themselves.'

'That's great,' said Rick, the rightness of the idea striking him forcefully, 'and it's going to be tougher than fighting Oberon.' He reached for Roxy's hand under the table. After a slight hesitation, she took it and smiled shyly across at him. A huge inner smile stretched in his chest.

'Tough but all the more worth doing.' Merlin cooled his drink down with a tiny blast of frosting magic.

'What about Linette? Can she come to the academy too? She will want to be with her parents.' Rick looked over to Linette. 'Won't you?'

She swirled the ice cubes in her glass. 'Yes—but I also want to remain with you just as much.'

'That's no problem. We can establish the school wherever you are,' said Merlin. He tugged off a loose cotton thread on the sleeve of his washed-out favourite T-shirt. Linette still hadn't managed to persuade him he needed a makeover.

Tiago rubbed Linette's shoulder. 'So what's it to be? Oxford or San Francisco? You're the one with a life here already so it's your call.'

Linette grimaced. 'I hate making decisions. Let's toss a coin.'

'I'll do it.' Tiago dug a coin from his pocket, silver eyes glittering with mischief. 'Where's our home to be? Here goes: heads it's the UK, tails it's the US of A.'

Tiago tossed the coin high in the air. It spun, light flashing from its sides—heads, tails, heads, tails. The moment seemed to stretch but Rick realized it did not matter which face it landed on, for he already knew the answer. With their friends around them, they were all finally home.

JULIA GOLDING grew up on the edge of Epping Forest. After reading English at Cambridge, she joined the Foreign Office and served in Poland. Her work as a diplomat took her from the high point of town twinning in the Tatra Mountains to the low of inspecting the bottom of a Silesian coal mine. On leaving Poland, she joined Oxfam as a lobbyist on conflict issues, campaigning at the United Nations and with governments to lessen the impact of conflict on civilians living in war zones. Married with three children, Julia now lives in Oxford.

The
YOUNG KNIGHTS
Trilogy

Read them all?

Don't despair!

Turn the page to discover more

EPIC adventures by Julia Golding . . .

THE COMPANIONS QUARTET

BOOK 1

Mythical creatures still exist. You don't believe it?

*That's because for centuries they have been
protected by a hidden society.*

Now the society is in danger. Kullervo, a
powerful and evil force, is gathering an army of
creatures determined to destroy it, and then wipe
out humanity.

Connie has always been able to communicate
with animals, but does she also have the ability
to stop Kullervo and his allies, the Sirens? And if
she opens her mind to such dark forces, will she
be strong enough to resist their call?

THE COMPANIONS QUARTET

BOOK 2

*'How shall we kill the Universal?' asked
the chimera. 'Bite, burn, or venom?'*

Connie is the world's last Universal—she can
communicate with all creatures. This makes her
the one person who can keep peace between
humans and the mythical beings that are hidden
all around us. But the shapeshifter Kullervo
craves her power.

During the long hot summer, Kullervo prepares
for war. The serpent-like Chimera is just one
part of his frightening army. As Kullervo's hatred
blazes into life, Connie and her best friend Col
must stop him. But how?

THE COMPANIONS QUARTET

BOOK 3

Connie is a Universal—she can talk to animals and mythical creatures. But something dark is calling her, giving her dangerous power, and her best friend Col doesn't know what to do.

When her strange behaviour means Connie is rejected by the Society for the Protection of Mythical Creatures—the very group of people who are supposed to protect her—she hides in an abandoned tin mine where she is befriended by a blinded Minotaur.

But even deep underground she can't block out the voices in her head. Who is it, and where does it come from? And why does Connie feel so terrified by the power it gives her?

THE COMPANIONS QUARTET

BOOK 4

*Mallins Wood is under threat, and with it the home
of the last remaining gorgon—a mythical creature
that can kill with a look.*

Only a handful of people know that she still
exists. Col and his mother are among them, and
both are determined to save her, and the forest.

While Col tries to rally support among the locals,
his mum is hatching a more deadly plan. Egged
on by the evil shapeshifter Kullervo, she is ready
to sacrifice Col's best friend, Connie, to protect
the Gorgon. But first she needs Col to lure
Connie to the Gorgon's lair . . .

THE SHIP BETWEEN THE WORLDS

When David Jones finds himself aboard a pirate ship, he knows it must be a dream. Except that he's awake. And the 'dream' is more like a nightmare . . .

DRAGONFLY

Princess Tashi is appalled when she is ordered to marry Prince Ramil in order to unite their lands. And he's not too pleased either. They hate each other on sight . . .

Ambush, kidnap, war, peace, and rattling adventure form the backdrop to an epic tale of hatred and love.

THE GLASS SWALLOW

Living above her father's workshop, Rain secretly designs stained glass but when she is discovered she must go to the strange new land of Magharna.

Bandits roam the lonely roads and when Rain is ambushed she knows that she cannot win the fight. That is until a boy with a falcon saves her and an adventure of a lifetime begins . . .

WOLF CRY

Freydis's Viking father is bent on revenge after a raid on their homestead. Freydis must accompany him on his hunt.

The journey is fraught with danger. Friendships will be formed and loyalties tested every step of the way.